Breaking the Ice

What Reviewers Say About Kim Baldwin's Books

"Fast paced, with dazzling scenes that stir the heart of armchair travelers, *Thief of Always* grabs the reader on the first page and never lets go. (Kim) Baldwin and (Xenia) Alexiou are skilled at fleshing out their characters and in describing the settings…a rich, wonderful read that leaves the reader anxiously awaiting the next book in the series. " — *Just About Write*

"With each new book Kim Baldwin improves her craft and her storytelling. *Flight Risk*…has heated action and vibrant depictions that make the reader feel as though she was right in the middle of the story…fast moving with crisp dialogue, and effective use of the characters' thoughts and emotions… this reviewer could not put the book down. Baldwin outdid herself with *Flight Risk*…her best storytelling to date. I highly recommend this thrilling story." — *Independent Gay Writer*

"A hallmark of great writing is consummate characterization, and *Whitewater Rendezvous* does not disappoint…Captures the reader from the very first page…totally immerses and envelopes the reader in the Arctic experience. Superior chapter endings, stylishly and tightly written sentences, precise pacing, and exquisite narrative all coalesce to produce a novel of first-rate quality, both in concept and expression." — *Midwest Book Review*

"*Lethal Affairs* is an exciting read, which definitely puts its reader on the edge of their seat. We can only hope that it is the first in a long series of books." — *Just About Write*

"Nature's fury has nothing on the fire of desire and passion that burns in Kim Baldwin's *Force of Nature*! Filled with passion, plenty of laughs, and 'yeah, I know how that feels…' moments, *Force of Nature* is a book you simply can't put down. All we have to say is, where's the sequel?!" — Outlookpress.com

"'A riveting novel of suspense' seems to be a very overworked phrase. However, it is extremely apt when discussing… *Hunter's Pursuit*. Look for this excellent novel." — *Mega-Scene Magazine*

Hunter's Pursuit is "a…fierce first novel, an action-packed thriller pitting deadly professional killers against each other. Baldwin's fast-paced plot comes…leavened, as every intelligent adventure novel's excesses ought to be, with some lovin'." — Richard Labonte, Book Marks, *Q Syndicate*

"In a change of pace from her previous novels of suspense, Kim Baldwin has given her fans an intelligent romance, filled with delightful peeks at the lives of the rich and famous… the reader journeys into some of the hot dance clubs in Paris and Rome, and gets a front row seat to some very powerful sex scenes. Baldwin definitely proves that lust has gotten a bad rap. *Focus of Desire* is a great read, with humor, strong dialogue and heat." — *Just About Write*

By the Author

Hunter's Pursuit

Force of Nature

Whitewater Rendezvous

Flight Risk

Focus of Desire

With Xenia Alexiou

Lethal Affairs

Thief of Always

Breaking the Ice

by

Kim Baldwin

2009

BREAKING THE ICE

ISBN 10: 1-60282-087-2
ISBN 13:978-1-60282-087-6

This Trade Paperback Original Is Published By
Bold Strokes Books, Inc.
P.O. Box 249
Valley Falls, NY 12185

First Edition: August 2009

Credits
Editor: Shelley Thrasher
Production Design: Stacia Seaman
Cover Photo by Kim Baldwin
Cover Design by Sheri (graphicartist2020@hotmail.com)

Acknowledgments

Some years ago, I visited Alaska, dogsledding above the Arctic Circle for ten days in a challenging and unforgettable adventure of a lifetime. The awesome beauty of the Brooks Range inspired my first Alaska-based novel, *Whitewater Rendezvous*, but I felt compelled to revisit the state for a winter-themed story that could incorporate some of my own experiences. I have set Bryson Faulkner's cabin in the exact spot where my own trip culminated, and the photo used as the backdrop for the cover was taken there. It's my profound hope that this book inspires at least a few readers to join in the battle to preserve our greatest national treasure—the Alaskan wilderness—from the threat of oil drilling and other perils.

Breaking the Ice is also a very personal story in that I began the manuscript on the first anniversary of my mother's sudden death after a long battle with Alzheimer's. Revisiting some personal recollections and experiences in this novel proved cathartic in a way I could not have imagined.

My deep appreciation to all the women at Bold Strokes Books who contribute so much to making my books the best they can be. Radclyffe, for her leadership and vision. Senior consulting editor Jennifer Knight and editors Shelley Thrasher and Stacia Seaman, who inspire and challenge me to always improve my craft, and catch me when I fall short. Graphic artist Sheri, for another amazing cover. Connie Ward, BSB publicist and first-reader extraordinaire, and all of the other support staff who work behind the scenes to make each BSB book an exceptional read.

I'd also like to thank my dear friend and first-reader Jenny Harmon, for your invaluable feedback and insights. You help keep me on track and motivated during the writing of each manuscript more than you'll ever know.

Dick D'Archangel, thanks so much for generously providing expert guidance on everything I needed to know about small planes.

Marty, there are no words to tell you what your support and selflessness mean to me.

Xenia, you rock. 'Nuff said.

I am blessed to have a circle of close friends who provide unending encouragement and support. Linda, Felicity, Kat, Clau, and Es. Near and far, you are always close to my heart.

Thank you to my brother Tom, always willing to chauffer me to the airport.

And especially to all the readers who encourage me by buying my books, showing up for my personal appearances, and for taking the time to e-mail me. Thank you so much.

Dedication

For my Mother
I feel you watching over me
I miss you so very much

And my Father
With deep respect and gratitude
And always love

CHAPTER ONE

October 21, 9:30 a.m.
North of Bettles, Alaska

Bryson Faulkner jerked up the collar of her coat as she stepped off the porch of her cabin. She lingered there, basking in the amber light of the late-morning sunrise, surveying her surroundings for any hint of change. Beneath the rough-hewn table she'd lashed for cleaning fish and game, she spotted fresh wolf tracks in the mud, the animals no doubt lured there by the lingering scent of the sockeye salmon she'd had for dinner. There was no sign of the lurking predators now. Nothing stirred except the large raven that took off from a black spruce twenty feet away and zigzagged past her in an amazing display of aerial acrobatics to land on the porch railing.

The bird studied her with intelligent black eyes and let out a raucous croak that ruffled the shaggy ebony feathers of his throat.

"Mornin', Bandit." Even before she reached into her pocket he was in the air again, beating his wings slowly to hover a moment before lighting on her shoulder. She held up her hand and he gobbled the offered raisins, nuts, and sunflower seeds, careful to avoid pinching the callused skin of her palm with his stout bill.

As he ate, she looked past him to the white-capped mountains that surrounded her cabin. Mathews Dome, due north, was the most photogenic peak in her part of the endless Brooks Range. A rounded granite crest 4,600 feet high, it was set off from its neighbors by the Wild River, curving west, and Flat Creek, forking around its base to the east.

But she used an unnamed mountain three hundred feet higher to the northwest, a jagged and fiercely sharp pinnacle, as her weather gauge. The roiling slate gray nimbostratus clouds blowing past the top confirmed the news she'd just received on her satellite phone. A fierce storm was headed her way, fast.

The one-room cabin she'd built with her own hands was nestled in the taiga forest that lined the Wild River at its confluence with Flat Creek. The valley floor between the mountains was wide here, nearly a mile across. Built on a rise to shield it from the high water of spring breakup, the log structure had a matching outbuilding for her snowmachine and tools, an outhouse, and a small cache on high stilts to keep her winter supply of game and salmon out of reach of opportunistic wolves, grizzlies, and other predators of the far north.

She regretted not refueling the plane after her last hop, but she'd barely made it home before dusk. Though Bryson had memorized every boulder and stump that littered her makeshift airstrip, it was still suicidal to take off or land in the dark. The gravel bar was less than a hundred feet long. Any slight mistake and she'd end up in the swift, icy currents of the Wild River.

Once the river froze and she could land on skis, she'd have a longer, wider runway, but the daily window of opportunity to land at her homestead would be frustratingly narrow. The days were shortening fast. In another two months, at the winter solstice, daylight would last only two hours in her little piece of paradise above the Arctic Circle. Almost any job she might take would require her to remain overnight at the nearest improved and illuminated runway thirty miles away in Bettles.

She dropped the few remaining seeds on the ground, and as the raven hopped off her shoulder to go after them, she headed down the trail to her red Piper Super Cub. While the plane warmed up, she freed it from its lashings and carefully inspected the exterior for damage before beginning her preflight checklist. Though she needed to leave soon, she refused to be rushed through her meticulous and methodical preparations.

The high wings of the Super Cub allowed her to taxi close to uprooted trees and boulders as tall as she was, and the model was one of the best at handling impossibly short runways and uneven terrain. Like many other bush pilots, she'd had it specially outfitted for the punishment it endured on a daily basis, with long, heavy-duty struts, reinforced axles and springs, and a dual landing apparatus that allowed her to set down on skis or oversized tundra tires.

The trip to the Bettles airstrip took less than a half hour. Flying low, she followed the river south as it curved through steep canyons, the clearance to the cliff faces on either side of her wingtips a mere twenty feet or so. Though she knew nearly every mountain, boulder, and tree en route, she was always hyperalert when in the cockpit, because no matter how clear the sky above, the geography of the mountain ranges made the wind a constant and unpredictable threat to small aircraft.

The proprietor of the Den jogged out to say hello as she filled her wing tanks. The Den was the center of all socializing in Bettles, with a bar and restaurant on the ground floor and twenty rooms upstairs to accommodate the hunters, fishermen, hikers, photographers, and other adventure-seekers who used the village as a jumping-off point for forays into the bush. Most were headed to the nearby Gates of the Arctic National Park or Arctic National Wildlife Refuge, which together covered more than twenty-seven million acres.

"Hey, kiddo, what's shakin'?" Jerome Hudson was known by all as Grizz, and it was immediately obvious how he'd come by the nickname. A big brute of a man with massive shoulders, he'd had the unkempt silver-tipped brown beard and swept-back, shoulder-length hair for half his sixty-two years, and his dark eyes and slightly pointed incisors completed the resemblance to his wild ursine cousins. Since the death of Bryson's father, Grizz had taken it upon himself to look out for her. "Real ball-breaker coming in."

Bryson glanced once more to the northwest, to assess the thick wall of charcoal clouds streaming rapidly in their direction. "Yeah, I'm headed up past Gunsight Mountain to get that photographer. He's not equipped for a long-haul deep freeze."

Grizz followed her gaze. "Gonna be cuttin' it awful close to get there and back 'fore we're socked in."

"What else is new?" She unhooked the fuel hose and tightened the cap on the Piper's wing. "No worries, Grizz," she said, smiling at him reassuringly. "Probably won't be able to get home tonight, though, so save me a bed, huh?"

"Will do." He laid a beefy hand on her shoulder as she opened the door of the Cub. "Watch yourself up there."

"Always."

The photographer's objective was Dall sheep, which kept to the higher alpine elevations, so Bryson had dropped him off at the edge of a glacier three thousand feet up the side of an unnamed mountain. As she circled above it, she cranked down her skis and checked the glacier for the subtle color changes that pinpointed the hidden crevasses that dotted its surface. The ancient ice inside the crevasses was a deep blue that often shone through the thin, fragile snow bridges that covered them. The overcast sky was a blessing, for it helped her delineate the landscape and calculate her approach. The glare off the snow on a sunny day often made it impossible to adequately judge depth of field, let alone any crevasses or other hazards.

After three passes, she chose her spot, a four-hundred-foot-long expanse of solid white near a moraine at one side of the glacier. Landing uphill, she braced herself for the impact of her skis against the uneven ice beneath the snow and set the Piper down, reducing her speed to thirty-five miles an hour. When the plane had nearly stopped, she tweaked the throttle and turned the Cub around, readying for an immediate downhill departure.

A blast of icy air flash-cooled every exposed inch of flesh and insinuated itself deep into the open collar of her jacket as soon as she opened her door. Muttering a string of curses, she zipped up and pulled on a woolen cap and extra pair of gloves before leaning out to assess the snow depth. A fine powder completely covered her skis and half her oversized tires, so she strapped her snowshoes to her boots before she exited the plane.

The photographer was nowhere in sight, but Bryson wasn't worried. She'd seen his campsite from the air not far away, and the man had been instructed to hoof it back there, pack it up, and return immediately to their rendezvous point if he heard her plane approach before his scheduled pickup. Unless the wind was fierce and constant, the acoustics in the mountains were exceptional—you could hear the buzz of a small plane long before you could see it approaching.

While Bryson waited, she tramped out a runway with her snowshoes and inspected the exterior of the plane as thoroughly as she had just ninety minutes earlier. By the time the photographer appeared with his pack, she was done with her preflight checklist and had turned her attention to the rapidly deteriorating weather closing in on them.

Dark clouds obliterated all the highest peaks in every direction, the wind was a steady twenty-five miles an hour, and the temperature had dropped to a degree or two above freezing.

"I take it there's a problem?" her client shouted over the wind as he neared. A fiftysomething freelancer for *Big Game Hunter* magazine, the man wore a ski mask, thermal gloves, and brand-new Carhart insulated coveralls bulging from several layers beneath. He was so horribly out of shape he was gasping for air by the time he reached the Cub.

The plane was idling, and Bryson was standing by the open door to the cargo space behind the seats. "Big storm coming in." She gestured impatiently for his pack.

He frowned and stood his ground. "I'm not done. I need to—"

"No chance," she replied curtly and yanked the pack roughly from his shoulders. "Climb in, we gotta get moving." When he still hadn't moved by the time she'd stowed his gear, she fixed him with a glare and added, "*Now*, 'less you want to be stuck inside your tent freezing your ass off for a couple weeks."

Normally, she was nothing but polite with clients, most of whom were middle-aged businessmen from the lower forty-eight. She was used to the looks of apprehension that crossed their faces when they realized their bush pilot was a trim and taciturn five-foot-seven brunette who appeared ten years younger than her forty years, and not what they'd envisioned: some larger-than-life Harrison Ford look-alike who oozed machismo and bragged about his exploits in the air.

But most of her passengers refrained from anything more than the seemingly casual question about how long she'd been flying. This guy's grilling on the way up had bordered on rude and chauvinistic, and she'd had to force herself to rise above it and remain professional.

They were airborne in two minutes and only fifty feet from the surface of the glacier when they got their first hint of the turbulence to come. The tiny plane shook like it was caught in a high-speed Mixmaster, then dropped twenty feet without warning, the ground rushing up at them with alarming speed.

"What the…is this normal?" the photographer shouted from his seat behind hers. Bryson could picture his expression. Even the most arrogant, macho guys went lily-white at a time like this, but she didn't have time to confirm her suspicions in her mirror. She was too busy trying to keep the Cub in the air.

"We'll be fine, just hold tight. It'll be over before you know it." She fought the downdraft, pulling hard on the controls, but the plane plummeted another fifteen feet as she curved away from the glacier and over the steep, rocky face of the mountain. They were so close to it she could see the pale hint of a trail etched by decades of goat hooves.

"Fuck!" the client yelled, just before losing his breakfast in a splash of pink-speckled yellow against the right-side window.

"Not helping." Bryson gritted her teeth against the stench as her own stomach roiled, but she kept her focus on trying to regain control of the aircraft. The wind fought back with a vengeance, however, straining the muscles of her biceps. For every few feet of hard-won altitude she gained, the wind reclaimed half of it again, in bone-jarring lurches that threatened to shake the plane apart.

Finally they reached a bit of calmer air in a wide valley between two mountains, but the low, dense cloud cover kept her flying near the treetops, which did nothing to ease the unyielding grip her passenger maintained on the strap above his head. And the reprieve didn't last. Soon they were back in the Mixmaster, and thick, heavy sleet began to hammer the windshield.

It was now a race to get back before ice coated the wings and cowling, but the steady headwind limited Bryson's speed and forward progress. Among the myriad of matters demanding her attention she added one more: to constantly scout for places she could safely put down in a hurry, if it came to that.

Her radio crackled to life. "BTT to A2024B Piper. Bryson, you copy?" The voice, a raspy baritone, belonged to Mike "Skeeter" Sweeney, a fellow bush pilot who worked part-time manning the minuscule FAA station at the village airstrip.

"A2024B Piper," she replied, relaying the identification tag emblazoned in large black text on the side of the Cub. "'Sup, Skeeter? Kinda busy here."

"Grizz asked me to give you a shout. Really squirrelly here. Ceiling's down below two hundred feet, sustained winds thirty and better, and it's startin' to ice up like a sonofabitch."

A glance at her GPS told Bryson she still had eight miles between her and the airstrip. It didn't sound like much, but it was an eternity in conditions like this, so she kept checking the terrain below for suitable places to land. "Should be okay. Dicey, but seen worse."

"Roger that. I've got the strip lights up full, and I'll watch you on radar until you get in. Bettles out."

She spotted another narrow canyon ahead, so she gripped the controls and risked a quick glance in the mirror at her passenger. "'Nother roller coaster coming up. Barf bag's under your seat." She hoped the warning would prevent any further splatters on her windows. Visibility was tough enough already, without another dose of half-digested powdered eggs and Spam.

As the man fumbled for her stash of bags, she added, "If you keep from messing up my plane again, I'll give you a discount on future flights." It was an easy promise, because the greenish tinge on his face made it clear this was the last time he'd set foot in any kind of bush plane.

Just as she expected, the downdraft in the narrow canyon was fierce, but she'd gained as much altitude as possible before it hit them, so when the bottom dropped out again she was able to keep the Cub from plunging into the river below. More worrisome now were the cliffs on either side of her wingtips. The wind buffeted the plane from side to side with alarming unpredictability, twice putting them within arm's reach of the rocky façades.

She ignored the mumbled recitation of the Lord's Prayer from her passenger but took a few deep breaths herself when a subtle change in the whirr of the propeller told her the blades were accumulating a coat of ice.

It was bare-knuckle flying from then on, a steady battle against the wind and sleet, and those last few miles tested every bit of her considerable experience in the air. By the time she lined up for her approach to Bettles, the ceiling was only thirty feet, so she was grateful for her GPS and intimate knowledge of every mile of terrain in the surrounding area.

She cranked the skis back and peered anxiously through the haze of sleet for the airstrip, holding her breath. Skeeter had supplemented the dual strip of landing lights with four blazing fires in fifty-five-gallon drums, two on each end of the runway, and it was these she saw first.

As she made a mental note to buy him a beer, she descended the final few feet and made a perfect three-point landing. Her passenger exhaled loudly in relief, and she glanced in the mirror in time to see him making the sign of the cross.

"Thank you for flying with Thrillride Airlines," she said cheekily as the Cub rolled to a stop at the edge of the runway. "You can pick up your complimentary beverage at the Den, since our stewardess was too preoccupied to serve you during your flight." If the eclectic group of individuals who did what she did had anything in common, it had to be their readiness to daily stare death in the face with a sense of humor.

Still clutching his barf bag, the photographer staggered from the plane and headed directly to the roadhouse without a word, oblivious to his gear or the weather. Bryson chuckled. Grizz would get a few dollars from him tonight, at least the cost of several glasses of good Scotch.

CHAPTER TWO

October 21, morning
Atlanta, Georgia

"Karla? I know you're there. Come *on*, already, *please* pick up. I'm way past worry and halfway to panic."

During the brief silence, Karla pictured her best friend Stella pacing around the nurses' station with her cell phone. She was restless, the kind who rarely lit in one spot for more than five minutes, and Karla had given her good reason to be concerned. This call was the latest in a string of messages left since the funeral, none of which Karla had returned.

"Hon, I know you're hurting and don't want to see anyone right now. But this just isn't good. I'm coming by after work, and you'd damn well better open the door this time. At least let me take you out for a bite to eat or something. Love you."

Karla had no intention of allowing Stella in, for even in her fog of grief and confusion, she knew her friend would be shocked by the state of both her appearance and her apartment. She didn't have any energy to fend off well-meaning efforts to alleviate her downward spiral.

She'd lost so much weight that her pajamas hung loosely on her five-foot, four-inch frame, and dark circles under her eyes from too many sleepless nights marred her otherwise delicate features. Her collar-length, light brown hair was a shade darker than usual and plastered to her head, and at odd moments even she could detect the stench of her unwashed body.

Her two-bedroom apartment hadn't fared the turmoil any better. Dirty mugs, most half full of cold, stagnant coffee, littered the living room, some on tables and some on the floor. Here and there were a few plates of crusted foodstuffs, uneaten and unrecognizable. The heavy curtains, drawn tight, blocked the sun so well she barely registered day from night. Only the pale glow of a single floor lamp saved the room from cave-like darkness.

Scattered around where she sat cross-legged on the carpet beneath the lamp were a half-dozen photo albums and several boxes, large and small, their contents in such disarray it looked as though she'd been burglarized.

The boxes that held memories of her four years with Abby had consumed the first days of her current despair. It had been a month since her partner left, but the wound of Abby's betrayal was as open and raw as it had been the day she'd announced she was leaving Karla to follow her heart, having fallen in love with a coworker at her law firm.

Karla was still having a hard time wrapping her mind around the abrupt, unexpected ending of their calm domesticity. One day they were sitting down to dinner together as usual, chatting about what movie to go see, and the next, Abby was packing her bags. Since then she'd asked herself over and over if Abby's apparent happiness and devotion had been an illusion. Those boxes, full of ticket stubs and vacation souvenirs, small stuffed animals and other mementos, held no answers, no clues to how she could have been so wrong about their life together.

And then, two weeks ago, her mother died in her sleep, an apparent heart attack. Somehow, Karla had made it through the funeral, a walking zombie, feeling more alone and abandoned than ever before. She hadn't left her apartment since, or spoken to any of her well-meaning friends and coworkers. She'd opened her door just once, the day before, only because her visitor from the nursing home was there to drop off her mother's belongings. Fortunately her leave of absence from her job as an ER nurse at Grady Memorial Hospital was open-ended, because she couldn't fathom when she might have the strength to rejoin the living.

Karla hadn't summoned the courage to examine the contents of the delivery until now, but she finally pushed aside the boxes of her life with Abby for a new round of grieving. She didn't think she could cry any more, but the tears rarely stopped as she considered each item she withdrew from the cache of her mother's things.

The first box contained jewelry and the few scarves and clothes her mother had obsessively insisted on wearing after Alzheimer's claimed her once-impeccable fashion sense. In the end, she'd become so agitated if Karla tried to launder her favorite lavender blouse that Karla had searched the city's shopping malls without success for a duplicate.

The blouse was faded and nearly threadbare in places, but because her mother had worn little else in the months before her death, it was hard to picture her without it. Karla felt guilty for not burying her in it, opting instead for the new cream-colored dress she'd bought for her mother's fifty-seventh birthday. She clutched the blouse and held it to her face, inhaling deeply, seeking the familiar scent of patchouli, but the garment had obviously been washed. She felt as though she'd been robbed.

Sorting through the contents of the jewelry box consumed half the night. Her mother had saved the pearl necklace for special occasions: her college graduation, birthday dinners, weddings, holidays. All happy occasions that evoked fond memories. But her mother had worn the delicate tigereye necklace that matched her eyes so often it seemed almost a part of her, right up to the end. Karla stroked her thumb over the cool stone for more than an hour, lost in the past, sobbing until her sides ached. Then she tucked the necklace into her pocket, unable to let go of it.

After the jewelry she reminisced through a box containing a collection of bunny figurines and other keepsakes. The lopsided clay vase she'd made for Mother's Day in the fourth grade. Her old report cards and class photos. A lock of her baby hair. Several items she'd never seen before: another lock of hair, curly and red, which matched no one in the family. A colorful ashtray that looked to be a child's art project, when neither of her parents had ever smoked. Why had her mother saved these mementos?

Finally, about dawn, she began to sort through the final box, this one full of photos and documents: a copy of the will, insurance papers, bank-account statements, marriage and birth certificates, and her mother's long-expired passport. And beneath it all, she discovered a sealed envelope addressed in her mother's handwriting.

For Karla. In the event of my death.

Her mother had been unable to recognize words for at least two years, and it had been four or five since she'd been able to write legibly, so the missive clearly predated that. It had been so long since her mother had been able to communicate rationally—she hadn't even recognized her in the final months—that Karla felt as though God had gifted her with one final, bittersweet reunion. The three sheets of heavy bond paper transported her back to a time when her mother had still been the vibrant and intelligent woman of her youth.

My darling Karla,

I am watching you scurry about the kitchen as I write this, putting the final touches on the cake you are making for my forty-fourth birthday, pausing now and then over your lopsided creation to smile at me and apologize for your lack of culinary skills. But all I can think is that I am so proud of the woman you have become, so thoughtful and kind to all you meet. Your unwavering moral compass and commitment to helping those in need. And most of all, I admire your ability to rise to every challenge you have faced in life with optimism and determination.

You will need all of those qualities in the future. The inevitability of my decline seems certain, and if we are blessed to have many more years with each other, I have no doubt that you will make the right decisions for me when the time comes and ensure I have the best quality of life possible. I know it will be hard on you, my darling. I'm so sorry for that.

Take comfort in our many wonderful years together and view my passing as a blessing, for I will likely have long abandoned my body and already be looking out for you from Heaven, happily reunited at last with your father.

I know it will be much tougher on you than on me in the

years to come. I pray as you read this that you are able to remember me as I am now. And most of all, I hope you will seek to understand what I have to tell you and forgive me for not telling you until now.

You have a sister.

Karla stared at the words until they seemed to separate themselves from the others on the stationery, creating white space around them that wasn't really there, blurring the other words and becoming bolder, almost three-dimensional.

You have a sister.

How had her parents kept this from her? All her life she'd thought she was an only child, the progeny of two people who preached honor and truth and the importance of family. As a child, she'd wanted a sibling playmate so much she'd created an imaginary one, a little sister she called Emily. Her parents had patiently indulged her fantasy, tucking Emily in beside her at night and setting an extra place at the table for her at mealtimes, never hinting that a real Emily existed somewhere.

The sudden knowledge of their duplicity made her question everything she thought she knew of them and left her feeling more alone and adrift than ever.

She read the words a dozen times, then began to sob again, great wails of anguish that shattered the silence and seemed to echo off the walls. She couldn't read the rest for a long while.

Five years before I met and married your father, I became pregnant. I was only sixteen, still a child myself and naïve about such things, but I fancied myself in love with a boy at school named James O'Hara.

After talking with Jim's parents, mine sent me immediately to a home for unwed mothers to have the child and convinced me that it was best for both me and for the baby to give it up for adoption as soon as it was born. It was what girls did then, especially those from Catholic families. I knew from my brief glimpse of her that I'd had a daughter, born healthy and with curly red hair, like her father. Then the nuns took her away.

I regretted that decision many times and wondered what happened to my baby, but as the years passed, I came to accept that my parents' decision had been the right one.

When I met your father, I struggled for a long time over whether to tell him about the baby I'd had. I wanted to, but I worried that he would think less of me for what I did, and my parents urged me to keep my "youthful indiscretion," as they called it, a secret. Once I'd made the decision to do so, there seemed to be no going back. How could I tell him after a year of marriage? Or five? Or ten? Besides, I had no way of knowing what had happened to the baby, so I could think of no good reason to confess to your father what I'd done.

It was not until he was gone, and my mother deathly ill with cancer, that she told me she had known all along who raised my baby and where she was. She and my father gave my daughter to a couple they knew, Richard and Joan Van Rooy. The Van Rooys were unable to have children of their own, but desperately wanted one.

Unknown to my father, my mother asked only two things of this couple in return: that they move to another state but keep in touch over the years. They agreed and sent my mother photographs of the child growing up, pictures of her birthday parties and prom dates, vacations. She threw them away as soon as she received them, afraid that either my father or I would discover the evidence.

When she knew she was dying, she finally told me the truth.

Your sister's name is Maggie. She grew up in Alaska and married a man named Lars Rasmussen. They are living in an apartment in Fairbanks. As far as my mother knew, Maggie's adoptive parents never told her the truth about her parentage, so she, too, does not know that she has a sister.

I hope you can find her, so you can finally have the sister you always wanted. If you do, please tell Maggie I thought of her often and wished I'd had the chance to tell her I'm sorry, and that I love her.

All my love to you, my darling. Be strong.
Mom

So many secrets. So many lies.

Maggie Rasmussen. If she'd been born when her mother was sixteen, that meant she was forty or thereabouts, some four years older than Karla.

She wasn't alone. She still had family. Despite the lifelong deception, she felt as though someone had just thrown a life preserver into her churning sea of despair. What was this secret sister like? Would she welcome this news? And was she even still in Fairbanks? The letter was written thirteen years ago. Maggie Rasmussen could be anywhere by now.

Karla stood, still clutching the letter, and went to fire up her computer. You could track down almost anyone on the Internet these days. Couldn't you?

❖

October 21, evening
Bettles, Alaska

Despite the early winter snowstorm raging through interior Alaska, twenty-six of the twenty-seven residents of Bettles were happily enjoying dinner, drinks, and an evening's entertainment in the Den, provided by four of their own: Grizz on bass, his wife Ellie on piano, Bryson on drums, and Lars Rasmussen on alto sax.

The place was a typical Alaskan roadhouse, one large room with dark oak paneling and a wood floor dotted with peanut shucks. A stuffed grizzly bear greeted customers at the door, and the walls were decorated with mounted moose heads and caribou antlers, neon beer signs and dogsled paraphernalia. A bar ran along one side, booths ringed the walls, and a scattering of tables with mismatched chairs filled the rest.

The Bettles Band, as they called themselves, sat on a small raised platform in the back corner. Their performances were usually impromptu, dictated mostly by the weather and the number of tourists in town. If the sky was clear and clients ample, Bryson was usually flying and Lars was guiding some fisherman or hunter to their quarry.

But oftentimes when a whiteout or fog stranded the two of them in town, the call went out that the party was on. And tonight was jazz night, always a popular favorite.

Bryson and Lars were the only far-flung homesteaders present. It was too early in the season for snowmobiles or dogsleds, and the weather was too poor for boats, so those hardy souls who lived off in the bush somewhere were unable to make it in. But a handful of Athabascan Indians from the nearby native village of Evansville were here, along with a half-dozen Japanese tourists who'd come to the Arctic Circle hoping for a glimpse of the aurora borealis, or northern lights. The only other outsider in town, Bryson's photographer client, had spent a long while at the bar before he stumbled upstairs to his room hours earlier.

The band finished a rousing rendition of "All Of Me" to wild applause before pausing for a break. Bryson was stowing her drumsticks when Geneva De Luca, a waitress at the Den, appeared at her elbow.

"Heya, Bry. You guys are really cooking tonight." Geneva was a curvaceous brunette with flawless olive skin, smoky gray eyes, and full, pouty lips that invited kissing. Bryson had succumbed to them for three months before she decided it was best to keep their relationship platonic. Six months had elapsed since then, but Geneva never missed an opportunity to try to change Bryson's mind.

"Good easy crowd." Bryson got to her feet to stretch. "Not hard to please," she added with a smile.

Geneva laughed. "Neither am I, but that's beside the point, right?"

"Gen, we've talked about this, and—"

"Yeah, yeah. I know. Anyway, Ellie's getting better. She's in here all the time practicing."

"It shows," Bryson said. "Her repertoire's growing. Bet by spring breakup she'll be pretty damn good." All of the players got exponentially better during the long winter months when they often didn't have much else to do but practice. Ellie had only been playing for about a year. She'd taken up the piano when their last player, a wilderness guide, had packed it in for easier work in Yosemite.

"Pity there's so few outsiders in town, though." Geneva scanned the crowd before returning her gaze to Bryson. "I was kinda hoping we'd be full up and you'd have to stay with me tonight."

"Let it go," Bryson said, not unkindly. "You know that's not going to happen again."

Geneva let out an exaggerated sigh and pursed her lips in disappointment. "You can't blame a girl for trying. When I think back to that last time…"

The last time they were together, Geneva had surprised her with some new toys she'd purchased by mail order. Playing with them had been a lot of fun, until Geneva confessed that she was falling in love with her and wanted them to move in together.

Lars's return to the stage with two cold bottles of Black Fang saved Bryson from a detailed reminiscence of that particular evening. "Thought you looked like you needed saving," he said, once Geneva was out of earshot. "Though for the life of me I don't see why. Not like you two have a lot of other options at the moment."

"I get plenty of action, thank you very much." Bryson's outward appearance and glamorous occupation were an unbeatable combination. A high percentage of the town's female visitors, even straight ones, flirted with her shamelessly. And if a ready partner wasn't available locally, she simply got in her Cub and made the two-hour trip to Fairbanks, where she could arrange a quick rendezvous easily.

"Don't doubt that." Lars grinned. "Still, she's a sweet girl, and it seems a shame to turn down such pretty company."

"We have little in common, beyond…well, *that.* And while that may be plenty with someone I'll never see again, it's not enough. Besides, I'm not about to create hard feelings with one of the few women who live within a couple hundred miles." Though she was buddies with a lot of the men she came in contact with, she craved female company, even if for a drink or a movie. "I don't want to hurt her, and the spark I need just isn't there. Simple as that."

In her twenties, Bryson had dreamed of having more than a series of brief affairs, of finding that special someone who twisted her insides and made her walk on air the way they described true love in the books she read. The kind of supportive partnership her parents had shared: two souls united in building a future together.

But she needed the wild places, the truly wild places, as much as she needed air. When she looked out over her unspoiled mountains, she felt serene. Blissfully content and fully alive. And connected, somehow, to the primal and timeless nature of the universe itself.

Her four years in Fairbanks attending the University of Alaska drove home how ill-suited she was for an urban lifestyle. She'd loathed the feel of concrete and pavement beneath her feet, the smell of exhaust fumes, and waking up to a view of steel and brick and billboards.

No, she was different. She knew that. She didn't need most of the modern conveniences others relied on, except her MP3 player and a small, battery-operated DVD player. She had a generator, but rarely used it, heating her home and cooking on a woodstove, washing her clothes and her body in a big steel tub, and reading voraciously by the light of kerosene lanterns.

When tourists came to town, chatting about some hot new TV show or Internet gossip, she had no clue what they were talking about and didn't care to know. She had chosen an earlier, primitive way of life in one of the most inhospitable and ruthless environments on the planet, and she'd long ago accepted that she'd probably never find a woman willing to embrace it as she did. Someone who could share her dream and thrive here.

In her lonely moments, her close ties to her like-minded friends and neighbors comforted her. Of them, Lars and his wife Maggie were the closest she had to family.

"Got some nice caribou steaks from the Teekons for running them up to Anaktuvuk, and they need to be eaten," she told Lars. "When the weather clears, you two come over and I'll fire up the grill." Like most bush pilots, when Bryson wasn't booked with a tourist, she was filling whatever needs arose in her community. Her plane had served as hearse and ambulance, mail and supply transport.

She also frequently ferried the native peoples of Alaska, primarily Athabascan Indians and Nunamiut Eskimos, between the villages where they predominated. When she did, they usually paid her in moose meat, caribou, or salmon, and the arrangement worked out well. She had no refrigerator, only a thick metal box buried in the corner of her cabin and filled with straw, to keep food cool in the warmer months, so she had to eat perishables quickly. This way she had a steady supply of fresh game in addition to her stores of dried and canned food, and she rarely had to hunt. She did so only in extreme situations to survive, because it pained her to take the life of any animal.

"We'd like that," Lars said. "Maggie's getting a real bad case of cabin fever. Most days she's not up for going far, but she can probably tolerate the skiff to your place."

"Sorry I haven't been by more, but things are really slowing down now, so I'll drop over whenever I can."

"Do her good." He grinned. "But I'm warning you, she's a right ornery cuss at times these days."

Bryson had been sipping her beer. His words brought an image to mind that made her laugh so hard she choked. "You forget she chucked a ladle of stew at me for offering to help her wash her hair."

"You should see my clothes. Most of 'em are stained so bad I can't wear 'em around clients." He pulled back one side of his oversized flannel shirt to reveal a long ketchup stain running down the side of his T-shirt from chest to belt.

Bryson roared.

"What'd I miss?" Skeeter joined them with his own bottle when he saw them laughing, never one to miss sharing a good joke. Stocky but solid, he was recognizable at a distance by his bushy red beard and the black wool cap he wore year-round to cover a prominent bald spot. He'd gained his nickname shortly after he migrated to Alaska five years earlier, for complaining that the mosquitoes here were nearly as large as his four-seater Cessna 180.

"Just discussing Maggie's recent interest in flinging food," Lars replied, offering Skeeter a glimpse of the stain. "Good aim on that woman. I was at least ten feet away."

"Kinda resembles California," Skeeter observed, drawing another round of chuckles. When they subsided, he turned to Bryson. "Say, I'm grounded for a bit while I wait for a new prop. Any chance you're headed to Fairbanks when the weather clears?"

"Lemme see." Bryson reached into her back pocket and pulled out a growing "needs list" that contained the unavailable-locally items that the residents of Bettles wanted her to search for during her next trip south. She had added several items just this evening: a soccer ball, magnifying glass, microwave, down pillow, size 36C bra (black), four cartons of Virginia Slims menthol cigarettes, and two boxes of Frosted Flakes cereal. After she studied all the items on the list and calculated who had the money to actually pay her, she told Skeeter, "Guess there's enough here to cover my gas."

"Great. Add a couple dozen D batteries, a heavy iron skillet—big as you can find—and a couple gallons of OJ for me, would ya?"

"That fresh-squeezed stuff with the pulp, right?" Bryson penciled in the additions at the bottom of the paper.

"Yup. Bryson, I bet you and I know more about the people around here than most of their kinfolk do."

"Yeah. Fascinating stuff, too. Like I really needed to know that Dirty Dan has a bad case of hemorrhoids, and Pete has warts somewhere he wants to get rid of."

They all were laughing again as Grizz and Ellie made their way back to the stage for another set.

They launched into "Ain't Misbehavin'," which Ellie was still pretty rough at, but the crowd had had a few drinks by then, so they responded with the same raucous applause.

Geneva planted herself in Bryson's line of sight, and every time their eyes met, she licked her lips or winked flirtatiously. Bryson tried to ignore the come-ons, but she *was* human, and it had been a while. Damn, she wished Gen hadn't reminded her how much fun it had been breaking in all her new mail-order toys. Flying to Fairbanks pretty soon was sounding better and better. She had her own addition to the "needs list."

CHAPTER THREE

Atlanta, Georgia

"I'm not going away," Stella shouted through the door before Karla could rise to answer it. She'd forgotten entirely that her best friend had vowed to come by and was startled to realize it was after six p.m.

She'd spent most of the day searching online phone records for Rasmussens. Lars and Maggie were not among those listed in Fairbanks, but Whitepages.com had supplied her with a list of 148 individuals in the whole of Alaska that included their rough ages and even the names within their households. Her heart started to pound when she spotted an entry for a Lars Rasmussen living in Anchorage. He was over sixty, but she refused to give up hope. With shaking hands, she punched in the phone number. He wasn't the man she wanted; this one was a recent transplant to the state and his wife's name was Inga, not Maggie. He was sorry he couldn't help her, he said, but he'd never come across another Alaskan with his name.

Undeterred, she spent the next couple of hours calling every single Rasmussen, hoping for a relative. Those she reached couldn't help her. She left messages for the rest, asking them to call her back and reverse the charges. As she worked her way through the list, she began to clear away the debris of her depression, washing the dirty mugs and plates and packing up the boxes. She opened the curtains and let the sun in, and even took a long, hot shower and changed into jeans and a T-shirt. She paused at a mirror to look at herself before she opened the door to Stella. Her face was gaunt, and she'd never seen such dark circles around her eyes. Her hair had dried all willy-nilly, but at least she was clean and dressed. Her search for her sister had given her a purpose and a welcome distraction from her grief.

"If you don't open the damn door right this minute…" Stella's threat trailed away at the loud click of the deadbolt. She hadn't bothered to change from her whites, or even remove her hospital ID and name tag. Sometime in the last couple of weeks, she'd had her honey-blond hair cut, from shoulder-length to just below her ears. It suited her.

"You'll what? Pitch a tent out here? Call in reinforcements?" Karla tried to smile but knew it came off as forced and unconvincing. Stella was an expert at reading people, almost psychic, which made her an exceptional nurse. She could often determine what was going on with a patient even if they were too young or too ill to communicate effectively.

"I was about to say break a window, so I'm glad I don't have to." Stella frowned as she studied Karla with narrowed eyes, as though inspecting a bug under a microscope. "You look like shit. When's the last time you ate or got a full night's sleep?"

"Hello to you too, Little Mary Sunshine. You coming in or do you plan to stand there and insult me all night?" She stepped to the side, but Stella paused to hug her tight instead.

"Just because I love you, you know," Stella said into her ear without releasing her. "How you doing, hon?"

"I've been better." She eased away from the embrace and led Stella to the couch.

There, Stella glanced about the apartment, her gaze lingering on the boxes marked *Therese Edwards*. "Your mother's things?"

"I've been going through them." She took a deep breath and exhaled slowly. "Not easy. Especially when I got to the very bottom of the last box. Apparently I have a long-lost sister. My mother left a letter for me about it that she wrote years ago."

"Say *what*?"

"No shit, right? She had her when she was sixteen and gave her up for adoption. And I'm not the only one she kept in the dark about it. She never told my father either."

"Wow." Stella sat still for a moment. "That sure doesn't sound like your mom. I mean, she was such a…such a…" Karla's buddy since their days in nursing school together, Stella was one of the few people who knew her mother before she became ill.

"I know. Poster girl for 'honest as the day is long.'" A bitter laugh escaped her. "But she apparently got the ability to lie really well from *her* mother. My grandmother acted as though the adoption was the end of Mother's 'mistake.' But she kept track of the baby through the adoptive parents and never told my mother about it until right before she died. Goes to show you, I guess, that everybody, and I mean *everybody*, has secrets. It makes me feel like I didn't know either one of them."

"I bet it does. So...your grandmother kept track of your sister? Do you know where she is now?"

"Her name's Maggie Rasmussen. She was living in Fairbanks, Alaska, with a husband named Lars when my mother wrote the letter. But that was thirteen years ago." She glanced over at her computer. Her e-mail was on the screen, and she could see that she didn't have any new messages. "I've spent all day trying to track her down. No luck so far. Apparently she doesn't know anything about me, either, or even that she was adopted."

"What're you going to say to her if and when you reach her?"

"Hell, I don't know. I really haven't thought that far ahead."

Stella laid a hand on Karla's shoulder. "What can I do to help?"

"I wish I knew." She leaned her head back against the couch and closed her eyes, her sleep deprivation finally kicking in. "There's got to be a way to find them," she mused aloud. Then it hit her, and she sat up abruptly. "You don't happen to know anyone in law enforcement, do you? Maybe I can trace them through a driver's license or something."

"Sorry. Sure don't. But I'll ask around at the hospital. Someone's got to have a relative or friend who's connected." Stella squeezed her shoulder. "We'll find a way." When Karla frowned in disappointment, she added, "Hey, cops are in the ER all the time. If I have to, I'll pick out a cute, single one and throw myself at him. Anything for you."

Karla couldn't help but smile. "The supreme sacrifice, right?" Cops were definitely not Stella's type. She had a thing for bad boys, especially the tattooed, rough-hewn types who rode motorcycles.

Stella grinned. "Like I said, whatever it takes. I'm there for you. How about you let me take you out for a bite and we talk about this some more? Maybe we can come up with some ideas."

"I'd rather stay here and keep surfing." Karla glanced again at her computer. Still no new e-mails. "I'm checking out a bunch of Web sites that might give me something."

"In that case, I'll head home and change." Stella rose and reached for her purse. "I'll grab my laptop and come back and help you sort through them. Maybe get some Chinese takeout? You're starting to look like a skeleton."

"You worry too much." Karla followed her to the door. "But if you get some Mongolian beef, I might be coerced to have some."

"That's my girl." Stella hugged her close again. "We'll find her. Keep your spirits up, and I'll be right back."

After she left, Karla returned to her computer. Did both she and Maggie have their mother's eyes and oval face? Did she, too, have a dimple in her left cheek when she smiled? Did they sound the same? If they stood beside each other, could anyone tell they were sisters? And what would she say to her if and when she found Maggie? *"Hi there, you don't know me. But you're the only family I have left in the world, and I really need you right now."*

She braced herself for the possibility that Maggie Rasmussen could be living a very comfortable, happy life with plenty of family and friends and want nothing to do with her. And even if she did want to connect, would they have enough in common besides blood to bond them?

Don't think so far ahead, she told herself. She had to find Maggie first. She'd deal with the rest as it came. She knew she wouldn't rest until she did.

❖

Bettles, Alaska

Bryson Faulker stared out the large picture window of the Den, catching glimpses of red through the blowing snow—her Cub, parked at the edge of the airstrip. The blizzard had continued through the night, but the snow was light and powdery, and accumulation was minimal. The hazard was the wind, which whipped the four inches that had fallen into an absolute whiteout.

The door blew open and Skeeter appeared, shaking the snow from his parka and stomping his boots automatically before he crossed the room to sit on the padded bench opposite her.

"Any news?" she asked as he removed his coat and hung it on a hook at the end of the tall booth.

"Nothing's flying from here to Juneau. And the weather service has no idea when it'll let up. You're socked in for a day or two, at least." He pulled out a pack of Marlboros and lit one, then glanced around for Grizz or Ellie, but the two of them were alone at the moment. The music had continued late into the night and everyone else was sleeping in.

"Ellie's still in bed, and Grizz is in the kitchen," Bryson volunteered, getting to her feet with her coffee cup in hand. "I was about to pour myself another. Want one?"

"Read my mind."

She returned with two mugs and set one before Skeeter. "Any word on your prop?"

"Two, three weeks at least." He sucked on his cigarette and drummed his fingers noisily on the tabletop. "I'll go damn stir crazy if it's any longer."

She bit back a laugh. Bush pilots all got a bit antsy if they were grounded too long, but Skeeter was worse than most. Though he'd had a lot more mishaps than she'd had—including more than a dozen forced landings and three wrecks—they never affected his passion for flying. "What was it this time?"

"Nothing worth writing home about. Just the usual." Their frequent landings on gravel bars during the warmer months always kicked up stones into the propeller, and after some months the dents started to affect the plane's performance. With winter coming on, everything had to be in top working order. "Hear about Red Murdock?" he added, a glum expression darkening his features.

"No. What's up?"

"Had to ditch south of Barrow last night. Got a message out he was icing up. Nothing since. He was flying a guy and his sled dog to a vet in Fairbanks."

It could have been her just as easily, but she had learned not to dwell on the *what ifs* a long time ago. "When it clears enough to start looking for him, I'm in."

"Told the troopers that already. I'll ride along, if you don't mind."

"Sure thing." A second set of trained eyes was always welcome when you had to scour thousands of acres of wilderness, and that was especially true if they went looking for Murdock. He'd arrived in Alaska three years earlier in the same plane he'd used for crop-dusting in Iowa, a white de Havilland DHC-2 Beaver. With the new snowfall, he'd be almost impossible to spot from the air unless he built a fire or some other visible distress signal.

Bryson had chosen a red plane partially because of the frequent need to ditch, and Skeeter's was orange and gold. Anything to help your chances of survival.

Skeeter stubbed out his cigarette and almost immediately lit another. "Say, you seen Lars this morning?"

"Not yet. Why?"

"Got the damndest e-mail on the site this morning." Skeeter was one of the few locals who was well versed in computers, so he maintained the Web site for Arctic Independent Outfitters, a consortium of freelance bush pilots and wilderness guides based in Bettles. Bryson and Skeeter were two of four bush pilots listed on the site, and Lars was one of six guides.

"Weirdest thing. Just one line: 'Does Lars Rasmussen have a wife named Maggie?'" The long ash from his cigarette fell onto the table, but he ignored it. "Signed it 'Karla.' No last name, no phone number, nothing."

"Kind of strange."

He glanced around to make sure they were still alone. "Think Lars is having an affair?" he asked in a low voice.

"Lars?" The mere idea made her laugh. Not that women wouldn't take to Lars. He was tall and blond, with chiseled features and a body honed by hard work chopping wood and hiking miles upon miles with clients. Only the crow's feet around his eyes gave away that he was forty-two, not thirty-two. He was sweet and considerate, too, which was rare among Alaskan men. "Not a chance. He's devoted to Maggie."

"Well, you know 'em best."

"You answer the e-mail?"

"Yeah." Skeeter squirmed in his seat, as though he expected her to disapprove. "Wrote back that he did. But then I got to thinking about it and wondering if I maybe should've run it by Lars first."

"Don't see how it could do any harm." But something was

definitely *off* about the odd inquiry. What could possibly have been the motivation behind it? "Lars'll know."

Lars came through the doorway that led to the rooms upstairs and headed toward them, stifling a yawn. "What'll I know?"

Bryson got up to bring another mug and the coffeepot back to the table.

"Remember a client named Karla?" Skeeter asked as he slid over in the booth to make room.

"Karla?" Lars scratched at the pale stubble of beard on his cheek. "Can't recall. There might been one in that big bunch of women went kayaking. Why?"

Skeeter relayed the contents of the e-mail and his reply. "Thought it might be a former client, since she sent the note to the Web site."

Lars shrugged. "Could be. Just can't remember. We've had a lot of trips with women the last few months. Odd, though, her mentioning Maggie. Maybe it's somebody she knows, trying to track her down."

"I'll give you a holler if I hear back from her." Skeeter downed the last of his coffee, then shrugged into his parka. "Better get back. See if there's any news about Red."

Bryson and Lars watched him go, following his dark form as it disappeared into the whiteout beyond the glass.

"Red Murdock?" Lars's tone was as solemn as if they were at a funeral. He didn't say more, because he didn't need to. The mention of a pilot's name during a storm usually meant only one thing.

"He's a good flyer," Bryson replied. "And here long enough to know what to carry." Winter and summer, experienced bush pilots always carried survival gear: tent, sleeping bags, fuel, stove, food, and other emergency equipment. She'd had to rely on hers more times than she could count and had also, like many of her peers, learned how to make most simple repairs to her plane.

Lars leaned across the table and put his hand over hers. "I know you gotta be thinking about your pop."

Five years, and still the mention of his name brought tears to her eyes. "He died the way he lived. Least he didn't suffer." Some bush pilots survived their crashes only to die of starvation or exposure. Her father's plane had slammed into the side of a rocky cliff, the apparent victim of a williwaw—those violent arctic whirlwinds that arise out of nowhere and howl unseen through mountain passes toward the coast.

"You'll be heading out then, when it clears." Lars turned his attention back to the window while Bryson regained her composure, and she was grateful for his sensitivity.

"'Course. It'll be crowded up there. Always is." Her father was well known and well liked, and when his plane went missing, dozens of small planes from all over the state joined the search. It had still taken two weeks to locate the wreckage.

Lars patted her hand and then withdrew his. "Haven't forgotten those steaks you promised. So get back here fast, huh? Maggie's not getting any smaller."

"You both worry too much." Bryson rose and reached for her coat. She got antsy when a pilot went missing, so to pass the time, she'd head over and man the radio with Skeeter. Spread the word.

If her time came, and the odds were good that it would, she knew the others would do the same for her.

❖

Atlanta, Georgia

Karla tried her best to block out the noise from a tarring company that was fixing potholes in the parking lot of her apartment complex, but finally the din came too near for her to ignore. She held on to the dream as long as possible. She was nine again, busy peeking in the many closets of the old brick two-story in suburban Hapeville where she grew up.

The familiar routine never lost its magic. When she was a child, her parents never placed the present she wanted most for Christmas under the tree, but concealed it somewhere in the house or basement. She would rise before dawn to search for it, always in vain.

After breakfast, she'd open all her other gifts, knowing the true object of her desire wasn't there, and her parents would pretend for a while they couldn't find or couldn't afford that one precious thing. A pogo stick. A pair of hamsters. A guitar. Finally they yielded and gave her a clue where to find it, and she would go hunting, amazed at how cleverly they had hidden it.

They'd come through every single time except the year she was nine. The year she asked them to make Emily real, to give her a sister.

Her parents tried to prepare her, telling her in the weeks before Christmas that they couldn't deliver this present. What else did she want? But by that time, she'd gotten her heart's desire so reliably, the outcome was so predictable, that she was bitterly disappointed to find a brand-new bicycle under the tree instead of a sister.

Karla tried to cling to that netherworld halfway between sleep and awareness, though she knew she was dreaming. She wasn't really nine again, but the images were so vivid she was somehow certain that this time she would find the sister she longed for, hiding in one of the closets. She wouldn't resemble the Emily of her imaginings, but that didn't matter. Because this time she would be real.

Cursing the workers outside her apartment for chasing away her fantasy, she reluctantly pulled herself out of bed. Stella had stayed until after midnight, and Karla had remained at her computer for another three hours, sending e-mail after e-mail into cyberspace, until she finally couldn't fight off sleep any longer.

After a long, hot shower and a large mug of coffee, she booted up her computer and held her breath as she accessed her e-mail account.

She began to sort through the sixty-seven responses to her barrage of blanket inquiries. Most were as terse as her e-mail had been. *No, I'm sorry.* Or, *Afraid I'm not the Lars Rasmussen you're looking for. Don't know any Maggie.*

She opened the forty-ninth e-mail expecting more of the same. But there it was. She blinked hard to make sure she wasn't seeing things. *Yes. Lars has a wife named Maggie.*

Her heart pounded as she gripped the edge of the table and read the words over and over. It had seemed like such a long shot that she was dizzy with relief. *I found you, Maggie. Now what?*

She'd looked at so many Web sites the day before she couldn't immediately remember anything about the one that had finally hit pay dirt, so she went back and scoured it.

This Lars Rasmussen was a wilderness guide in Bettles, Alaska.

She typed the location into Google maps and got her first indication of just how far away her sister was. Just shy of forty-five hundred miles. Europe was closer.

For the next hour, she read everything she could find online about Bettles. "Began as a trading post during the 1898 gold rush. Smallest incorporated city in Alaska. Classified as an isolated village center."

The only school had been closed due to low enrollment. Not surprising, she thought, since the 2000 census gave the population as a mere forty-three people. Apparently her sister could not have chosen a more remote place to live. No roads led to it, except in the dead of winter, when lakes and rivers, marshland, and spongy tundra were frozen over and a solid pathway could be plowed over them to connect the village to the paved Dalton Highway.

"Ranks second on a national list of cities with the largest annual temperature variation, with summer highs in the eighties and nineties, and long periods of minus forty degrees in winter. The lowest temperature ever recorded was minus eighty-two."

Born and raised in the South, Karla despised the cold. Give her a sunny beach and temperatures above eighty, and she was content. On those rare occasions when Georgia got a dusting of snow or an ice storm, she saw no beauty in it, only a headache for getting to work. "Average annual total snowfall: 82.4 inches." In other words, she lived in Siberia. They couldn't be more different.

Why would anyone choose such a place? She kept reading. Okay, so it was apparently a great area for seeing the northern lights. And a lot of people went there to visit the Brooks Range and the massive national parks it contained. She was definitely not into camping out. Doing so in Georgia meant black flies, fire ants, copperheads, and water moccasins. And she liked her creature comforts, not sleeping on rocks. But some people enjoyed that sort of thing for vacations. A week or two maybe, but to live there?

The photographs she called up of the area gave her some insight. Majestic peaks stretching forever. Mountain valleys so crowded with wildflowers they looked like paintings. Herds of migrating caribou, thousands upon thousands of animals. Awesome curtains of red, green, blue, and yellow stretching across the night sky.

People who had traveled there extolled it with superlatives. Unparalleled beauty. Unforgettable views. Unbelievable scenery. Breathtaking. Magnificent. The trip of a lifetime.

The ringing of her phone jarred her back to her civilized apartment.

"Any luck yet?" Stella inquired.

"Yeah. She lives in Bettles, Alaska. A little village in the middle of nowhere. And I mean *really* in the middle of nowhere. Above the Arctic Circle."

"No shit. Long way away. Who can possibly want to live at the North Pole?"

"Who knows? Someone with thicker blood than mine, that's for sure. Shows how different we are."

"Have you talked to her?"

"No. Not yet. I just got an answer to my e-mail that the Lars there has a wife named Maggie. He's a guide for a wilderness outfitter."

"So what's next?" Stella asked. "What are you going to do?"

What should I do? Karla turned in her chair and stared at the boxes of her mother's things. There was only one thing *to* do. Her mother had set her on an irrevocable path of discovery. Cold or no cold, half a world away or not. A phone call would never be nearly enough.

"I'm going to buy a plane ticket."

CHAPTER FOUR

October 25, 5:50 p.m.
Over Mount McKinley, Alaska

Karla stared down in wonder at the nation's highest peak, the mountain that natives called Denali, the Great One, shining reddish-gold in the alpenglow of the setting sun.

Those superlatives she'd read about Alaska were no exaggeration. She'd kept her face glued to the window ever since they took off from Seattle. The landscape was surreal in its immense, endless beauty. Stark and forbidding, devoid of any sign of human habitation. But somehow it was serene and peaceful. A world untouched and unscathed by war, pollution, and urban crowding.

When the view outside the plane grew black, she thought about her sister and the still unresolved questions about what she should say to Maggie when they met.

In the three days it had taken Karla to make arrangements to leave, she'd thought of little else. She had battled with herself over whether to contact the Rasmussens first, to prepare them for her arrival. It would certainly be polite and prudent to do so, and under any other circumstances she certainly would have.

But the fear that Maggie might tell her not to come overrode her usual sense of decorum. Because she was arriving unexpectedly, Maggie might reject her totally or welcome her warmly and invite her to stay for a while.

So she'd paid her bills in advance, arranged for Stella to water her plants, talked to her supervisor at the hospital, and gone shopping.

She'd had to go to REI, a specialty store, to find clothes warm enough for her adventure. This time of year, the temperature in Bettles could drop well below freezing at night, so for the trip up, she chose silk long underwear beneath jeans and a long-sleeved T-shirt, fleece pullover, and a new down-filled jacket. The lined Sierra hiking boots were too warm for the plane, so she had tucked them beneath the seat in front of her. In the overhead bin were her new ski gloves and fleece-lined bomber's cap, which looked ridiculous on her but was the warmest thing in the store. Her new outfits had cost more than a week's salary.

The pilot announced they were beginning their descent into Fairbanks and apologized for the delay. Earlier weather problems had backed up flights in a chain reaction, so she'd already missed her connection to Bettles.

If she couldn't find another one this evening, she'd have to overnight in Fairbanks, which she dreaded. It had been hard enough to wait three days to leave. With her mother and Abby both so abruptly gone from her life, she had only her sister left to cling to. And though normally not the superstitious type, Karla couldn't shake a growing unease that pushed her to get to Bettles as fast as possible. Bad things came in threes, and the fear that something might happen to Maggie before they had a chance to meet nagged her. She was being irrational but couldn't dispel the prevailing sense of urgency about this trip. As soon as they landed, she'd find another way to close the final miles.

There just had to be another flight out tonight.

❖

October 25, 7 p.m.
Fairbanks, Alaska

Bryson had to make four trips between the van and Cub to load all the bags and boxes from her massive shopping expedition. The van belonged to Grizz and was permanently parked at the small hanger that Arctic Independent Outfitters leased at the airport. Fortunately most of the items on her list were small, so everything fit into the back of the plane with her survival gear. Even the passenger seat was packed with goods, and the added weight made her glad she had a long runway both in Fairbanks and Bettles.

She had spent hours accumulating the wide diversity of objects and hated to disappoint any of her friends or have them spend a dollar more than necessary. She hit Wal-Mart, Home Depot, and Sam's Club, as well as Fred Meyer for food and one small specialty store, Cold Spot Feeds, for dogsled supplies.

When everything was ready, she locked the van and headed into the terminal to file her flight plan and check out the latest weather conditions, anxious to get home before another storm blew in. She was ready to kill for a good night's sleep. She'd been in the air except for brief refueling stops for nineteen of the previous twenty-four hours, searching for Red Murdock's plane. As soon as she got word he'd been found—his plane a mess, but he and his passenger unharmed—she'd diverted immediately to Fairbanks.

The weather forecast checked out fine, with some low-level turbulence reported just north of the airport, but no sleet or snow yet. Earlier storms, however, had backed up commercial flights so much it would be forty minutes before she could get clearance for takeoff.

She grabbed a cup of coffee and headed over to the Bettles Air gate to see who was working tonight. The small firm handled ticketing and check-in for Arctic Independent Outfitters in addition to their own clients. Sue Spires was manning the counter.

Though Bryson didn't have the energy or time to hook up with the curvaceous blonde this evening, she did have a few minutes to set up a date in the not-too-distant future. If only the customer Sue was waiting on would finish her business and give her the opportunity.

She stood to the side at a distance and studied them. The last flight to Bettles had left twenty minutes earlier, and evidently the customer was supposed to have been on it. She was alone, and her frustration was evident. She frowned and fidgeted, gesturing frequently with her hands. She was obviously anxious to leave and determined to find a way out before the next scheduled flight. She glanced up frequently at the departures board, as though she hoped another alternative would magically appear there.

Bryson couldn't recall ever seeing the woman before in Bettles, and she'd have noticed her. With her shapely but slender body, she was close to Bryson's age, perhaps a few years younger. And a couple of inches shorter, probably five-four or five-five. Her light brown hair with blond highlights featured soft waves that ended at her shoulders.

It framed an oval face with flawless skin and delicate features: high cheekbones and a small, slightly upturned nose. But her beautiful hazel eyes looked haunted, and her expertly applied makeup couldn't hide the dark circles beneath them.

Sue was being her usual patient self, listening intently and smiling in empathy as she typed away at her computer. It was a common scene these days, but this time the customer apparently wouldn't take no for an answer, even when Sue stopped typing, shrugged, and shook her head helplessly.

It was a shame, she thought, that so many beautiful women were so completely self-absorbed they acted like the world revolved around them. What could possibly be so important in Bettles that a few hours made that much difference?

But the woman continued to harass Sue, leaning over the counter on her elbows as she talked to crane at the computer screen, as though she wanted to see for herself if there was any way possible for her to get to Bettles tonight.

Come on, already. Let's go. Move on. Give it up. Bryson chanted the words to herself over and over like a mantra, hoping to somehow psychically implant the suggestion in the cute but irritatingly persistent customer who was monopolizing Sue's attention. If Bryson lingered much longer, she would miss her takeoff slot. She stepped a little closer, near enough to overhear snatches of their conversation.

"Check again. There just has to be another way there. Something you haven't thought of." The woman sounded frantic. "You can't have checked every single small carrier."

"I'm sorry, Miss Edwards." Sue was trying her best to remain congenial, but Bryson could hear the irritation in her clipped tone. "As I've said, the flight you missed is the only evening one out. The very earliest you can leave is on Wright Air's ten a.m. departure. I show one open seat on that flight."

"What about a charter?" the woman asked. "How much are those? I saw all sorts of brochures for them near the restrooms."

"A last-minute solo charter at night would be quite expensive," Sue replied. "Probably in the neighborhood of nine hundred dollars or more to Bettles, I would expect."

Considering that was roughly five times what the woman had probably paid for her original ticket, Bryson wasn't too surprised to see shock and dismay cross her face. "Nine hundred dollars? That's outrageous. Who would pay that for a two-hour flight?"

When Sue didn't answer, it seemed for an instant that it was finally sinking in that the woman wasn't going anywhere tonight. Her shoulders hunched in disappointment, and she seemed almost ready to cry. But the change was short-lived. She took off her new-looking coat and hat and laid them on the counter, preparing for a long entrenchment. It was clear she didn't plan to leave until she got what she'd come for.

"Try again," she commanded. "Make some calls, don't just rely on the computer. Maybe if you actually *talk* to somebody at these other carriers, you can find somebody willing to get me there tonight."

Bryson glanced at her watch. Her slot was in fifteen minutes. She couldn't hang around much longer. Ordinarily, she'd never think of interrupting Sue when she was with a customer. But what she had to say would only take a minute—*Are you free tomorrow night?* And it looked liked Sue could use some rescuing. Maybe a brief interruption would push the dogged customer on her merry way.

She stepped out from behind the column where she'd been watching them and moved into Sue's line of sight. The gate attendant's face lit up when their eyes met.

"Bryson! Hi." She waved Bryson forward as the customer turned to look, scowling at the intrusion. "How're you doing? I was—"

"*Excuse* me," the stranger interrupted angrily. "I was here first, and you're not done helping me."

"That's exactly what I'm *trying* to do," Sue replied through gritted teeth. Her eyes beseeched Bryson for help. "Please tell me you're heading back home tonight and that you've got room for a passenger."

A flicker of hope registered in the stranger's eyes. This close to her, Bryson could see tiny specks of gold in the hazel. The scowl on her face faded. "Wonderful!" she said, as though the decision was a fait accompli.

Crap. This wasn't in her game plan at all. No way was she taking Miss Gripe-a-lot in her plane. "Sorry, no can do. Full up."

"You have to. I'm desperate! I have to get to Bettles tonight." The woman took a step forward and grabbed Bryson's leather coat at the elbow. "Let me talk to your passengers. Maybe I can get someone to swap with me, take the morning flight."

Bryson shook her head. "Not possible. There's no way—"

"How do you know if you don't let me try?" The woman's demeanor changed again. In a flash she'd gone from angry, to hopeful, to frantic, and now angry was back for a return engagement. "Just give me five minutes with them. What the hell harm can it do?"

Bryson extricated her elbow from the woman's manic grip. "You don't understand. I'm flying supplies, not passengers, and I have a very full plane. I mean packed-tight full. And I have to be leaving, or I'll miss my takeoff slot." She started to wave good-bye to Sue, but the stranger grabbed at her elbow again.

"Supplies?" she said incredulously. "Well, surely there's no problem leaving a few *things* behind for the time being so I can go? I'll pay extra for your inconvenience."

The nerve of this woman. To presume that she couldn't be carrying anything more important than this impatient princess with a big wallet. Okay, so her baggage was mostly stuff like wart remover and toys, not critical medical life-support equipment. But the princess here didn't know that. And the intended recipients certainly considered her cargo precious freight. Hell, they were all probably at this very moment celebrating its imminent arrival. "Like I said, I'm sorry. But no can do."

"It's not that you can't." The woman let her go and slumped against Sue's desk with a resigned look of disgust on her face. "It's that you won't. Don't you have an ounce of humanity in you? Where's this infamous Alaskan hospitality I've read so much about?"

Bryson bit her lip, determined to remain polite and professional, since this woman was a client of Sue's. "I've got a lot of people—friends, mostly—looking forward to what's in my plane. Half the town will be waiting for me to land, and I don't want to disappoint them. The weather might keep me from getting back here any time soon to pick up what I'd have to leave behind." She was about to add a final, firm *NO* when Sue came around from behind her counter and hustled Bryson off to one side.

"Bryson, *please*," she begged in a whisper. "She won't let up. You don't want me stuck here all night, do you? Do me this favor, and I promise I'll make it up to you."

"I'd hardly take up any room," the stranger said. "And this is all the luggage I have." She gestured toward the REI duffel bag at her feet. The bag was brand-new, Bryson noted, just like the woman's clothing.

Her boots hadn't been out of their box long, and the down jacket draped over the counter was so pristine and shiny she half expected to find the price tag still attached. Obviously this woman came from a much warmer climate, but at least she had the common sense to dress appropriately for where she was going.

And the mysterious Miss Edwards got a few more points for not being the type of woman who traveled with a half-dozen pieces of enormous, hard-backed luggage. Clients hated being told they'd have to leave most of their belongings behind because they wouldn't fit in the Cub. She half turned to Sue. "You owe me so big-time for this," she said in a low voice.

"I look forward to you collecting." Sue gave her a quick wink of promise. "You're the best, Bryson. Thanks."

"I'm just too tired to argue any more." Forcing herself to smile, Bryson turned toward the stranger. "Okay. If you're coming, grab your bag and follow me." She headed toward the access door nearest the hangar with the client on her heels.

"We haven't discussed payment." Miss Edwards dug into the pocket of her jeans and pulled out the boarding pass for the flight she'd missed. The name printed along the top was "Karla" Edwards. "I didn't get a chance to get a refund on this."

"You can do that in the morning in Bettles." Bryson pushed the door open and they stepped out into the night. The temperature was around twenty-five, she guessed.

The sound of a duffel bag hitting the pavement made her pause and look around. Her client scrambled to get her down jacket on, then a pair of enormous ski gloves, and finally, a fleece-lined bomber's hat two sizes too large.

Bryson bit the inside of her cheek to keep from laughing.

"So how much are you charging me?" Karla Edwards asked suspiciously as they resumed their trek to the hangar.

"I'm okay with whatever you get for your ticket. I won't charge you extra because you'll be cramped all the way. I want to take out as little cargo as possible."

"That's very generous of you," the woman said. "The gate attendant told me you guys usually charge an arm and a leg for a night charter flight."

The accusatory tone made Bryson bristle. *Quit while you're ahead, honey. We're not off the ground yet. I can still change my mind.* "Some pilots charge a higher rate at night, yes," she admitted. "It's more dangerous to fly then, especially some routes. And they want an extra incentive to work overtime, when they'd rather be at home with their families. That so wrong?"

"No. I guess not. Why aren't you charging me more, then? You certainly could, you've got me over a barrel."

"This wasn't my idea," Bryson reminded her.

"Oh, right." The woman went silent as they crossed the tarmac to the hangar. "You look awful young to be a pilot," she said as they reached it. "You are qualified to carry passengers, aren't you?"

"I've had my license twenty-three years." She rolled the door open and flipped on the lights. "Been flying in Alaska all that time, in every kind of weather you can imagine." The words didn't convey the reassurance they normally did, because her client's response was not what she expected.

"Oh. My. *God*."

Bryson whirled to face her. Miss Karla Edwards was staring in horror at the Cub.

"We're going up in *that* little thing?"

CHAPTER FIVE

"That looks like a stiff breeze would blow it right out of the sky." Karla had certainly seen such tiny planes before, though never up close. Only in films: chasing after Cary Grant in *North by Northwest*, crashing in *The Edge*, *Six Days Seven Nights*, and *Hey, I'm Alive!* Falling into the ocean in dozens of old war movies. TV news broadcasts always seemed to show them in pieces, after slamming into homes or plowing into fields. They seemed to be such fragile things.

Lots of celebrities had died in them. Buddy Holly. John Denver. Patsy Cline. JFK Jr. She had an aptitude for such trivia. It came in handy at bar contests and radio call-in shows, but she wished to God she could purge it from her mind right now.

"I'm well qualified," her pilot reiterated with confidence. "And this is an exceptional plane for bush flying. Super Cubs are very maneuverable, and I can land most anywhere."

"What have I gotten myself into?" Karla spoke aloud, though she didn't mean to. Her feet refused to move any nearer to the plane.

"Hey, no skin off my back if you don't want to go. You can always wait for the Wright Air flight tomorrow," the pilot said. "It's a nine-seater."

Peachy. So it was a few feet longer. It would still be a wretchedly tiny thing compared to any plane she'd ever flown in. Better to get this over and done with as fast as possible. "No, I'll go with you."

"Suit yourself." The pilot glanced at her watch, then opened the passenger door of the plane and the cargo hatch behind it. "Gotta hustle to make my takeoff slot. Could use your help."

"All right." She forced herself forward and set her duffel bag near the pilot's feet. The moment she'd decided to go, her heart began to beat furiously and she felt a bit woozy. She took a few deep breaths to try to calm her nerves.

The pilot handed her a set of keys and gestured toward a beat-up van parked in the hangar. "Unlock the rear door, would ya? Then you can take whatever's on your seat there and move it over, while I make room back here for your bag. Take out only what you need to get seated."

"Okay." The plane looked even smaller from the inside, especially since it was absolutely jammed from floor to roof with boxes and bags. Three large bags were seat-belted to the passenger seat. As she carried them to the van, she glanced inside one. Orange juice. Cereal. Oreos. In another, bras and a large down pillow. Vital supplies indeed, she thought. Millions would suffer a terrible fate if this shipment didn't get to Bettles tonight. She gazed surreptitiously at the dark-haired woman she was about to entrust her life to. *You just didn't want to take me. You couldn't be bothered. What an ass.* Pity, too, because the woman was attractive. She had on a thick leather coat, so it was hard to gauge the physique of her upper body, but her jeans were molded tight to her legs. Her thighs and calves were smooth and firm, and when she leaned into the cargo area to stow her bag, Karla noticed her well-toned ass. It was hard to determine the woman's age, but she'd have guessed thirty or so at most, which was impossible if she'd had her license for twenty-three years.

She sure didn't look much older than thirty, though—no trace of crow's feet around her dark brown eyes, no lines around the full, lush lips. Her jawline was rounded, but firm. Her long, dark hair was pulled back in a ponytail, and with the ball cap she wore, emblazoned with the slogan I Can Take You There, she wouldn't have looked out of place on a college softball team. She seemed youthful and exuberant, but something about the way the pilot carried herself, a look in her eyes, made her seem mature. She might not be the nicest person on the planet, but she conveyed a self-confidence that helped alleviate the unease in Karla's stomach.

She walked back to the plane to transfer two boxes that were taking up the floor space in front of the passenger seat. One was marked Sorel Mounty II Boots, Men's, size 12. The other contained drugstore supplies: hemorrhoid cream, wart remover, antifungal cream, hair dye to remove the gray, laxatives. *Charming friends you have.* She glanced over at the pilot. *Big-footed friends, with hemorrhoids, athlete's foot, and constipation. And let's not forget the warts.* She couldn't help giggling at the visual. A little more of her anxiety faded.

The pilot paused and turned to her, confusion in her tone. "Did I miss something?"

Her cheeks warmed. "No. I just had a funny thought."

This was the first time she'd laughed in weeks. And just as quickly as the brief euphoria came, it evaporated, pushed aside by grief and uncertainty. This emotional roller coaster was exhausting, but she had no control whatsoever of her feelings from one minute to the next.

What the hell was she doing? Flying halfway around the world to surprise Maggie wasn't like her at all. Her impetuous decision to fly to Alaska hadn't stemmed her feelings of isolation. If anything, it had amplified them, for she'd left all that was familiar—friends, home, job.

Yet again, Karla considered the irrationality of this trip. From the moment she opened the letter, the idea of chasing down her secret sibling had possessed her. She felt almost out of control, and now that she was here she understood her urge more clearly. In a mere matter of days, all that was truly important to her had been stripped away—her sense of family and belonging, her happiness, her plans for the future. She was hollow, with nothing left to lose. Her vision swam, and she gripped the edge of the door.

"You all right?" The voice came from beside her as a steadying hand grasped her elbow.

"I'm fine." She shook off the hand. She'd had it with people wanting to help. This was something she had to get through on her own. "Just more tired than I realized."

"Whatever you say." The pilot sounded a little hurt as she buckled Karla firmly into her seat. "You can sleep on the way if you like."

Fat chance. Tired or not, once she was in the plane, staring past the pilot's seat at the controls, the full force of the risk she was taking on a mere *chance* her sister might welcome her squeezed the breath out of her. As the pilot slowly circled the exterior of the plane, inspecting the wings, the cowling, the tires, and the fuselage, Karla fought the urge to bolt.

The pilot towed the plane outside and locked up the hangar door.

Then she climbed into the seat in front and half turned to Karla. "I'm required to do the in-the-event-of-emergency spiel that most people have memorized," she said. "But it is a little different, being it's just you and me in here, and Alaska is a more unforgiving environment than most." Her tone implied that the speech was only a formality, but Karla hung on every word.

"You may feel turbulence more than you're used to in a big plane. There's some rough air just north of here, but nothing I haven't encountered a thousand times before and nothing the Cub can't handle. We won't be flying high enough to need oxygen for any reason." The pilot's voice remained matter-of-fact. "In the unlikely event we have to ditch, your seat cushion can be used as a floatation device. There's a fire extinguisher strapped beneath my seat and a first-aid kit in the back. Pry bar is there." She pointed to a small iron bar clamped to the side of the pilot's seat. "And there's a red duffel in the back with survival gear in it. Tent, sleeping bag, stove, food, water, and a gun."

Survival gear? A gun? That hammering in her chest returned with a vengeance.

"Clear on all that?" the pilot asked.

She nodded, afraid her voice would betray her rising panic.

"Then we're good to go. The name's Bryson, by the way, Bryson Faulkner," she said as she buckled herself in and put on her headset. "Let me know if you have any questions."

She started the engine and the propeller began to spin. It sounded alarmingly loud, but the pilot gave no indication that anything was amiss.

The Cub began to move, and Bryson spoke to the control tower as they taxied into position behind another small plane. Then they were on their way, lifting off after an amazingly short roll down the runway, and the lights of Fairbanks faded from view. Within minutes, there was nothing but black beneath them.

Karla had seen enough of Alaska from the window of a plane, however, to be able to picture the landscape they were flying over. White-capped mountains stretching in every direction to the horizon. Wild rivers. Endless desolation.

The plane hit a pocket of rough air, but it wasn't too bad. Bumpy, like riding the Mind Bender roller coaster at Six Flags Over Georgia. And Bryson had warned her, so Karla was able to ride it out without becoming too alarmed. Then the plane dropped abruptly, ten feet or more, and her stomach lurched.

"I'm cold," she said, bunching her fingers around the tigereye necklace in her pocket. "Can't you turn up the heat any more?"

"Yeah, sure." The pilot turned a knob on the control panel but Karla couldn't feel any measurable difference. She craned her head, trying to spot where the heat was coming from, and saw Bryson yawn and rub her eyes. Not a minute or two later, she yawned again.

"Are you sure you're all right to fly? You look like you're about to fall asleep."

She sat up a little straighter and blinked several times. "I'm fine."

Karla's unease grew when she soon yawned again. Maybe if she got Bryson to talk, she would stay awake. Karla could also perhaps forget that she was careening over a vast winter wilderness in a flying sardine can with a sleepy pilot. "Don't get me wrong, the scenery is nice and everything, but why does anyone want to live here?"

"Sure not for everyone," Bryson replied. "Most people can't live without their big-screen TVs and cell phones, never mind having to do without things like refrigerators and electric lights, if you live in the bush like I do. Heck, it's hard sometimes even getting the basics, like Band-Aids and aluminum foil. Especially during fall freeze-up and spring breakup. Everything stops for weeks, or weather can keep you homebound for really long stretches and you gotta rely on what you have on hand. You learn to improvise."

"So you don't live in Bettles?" From what Karla had read, the village itself was isolated enough. What did living in the bush mean?

"Got a cabin thirty miles from there, in the mountains," Bryson said. "Well, thirty miles by air. By boat, it's almost double."

"So you really do spend a lot of time in this plane."

"Yup. Ferrying clients, mostly. And a couple times a month, I run supplies for the village. During the warm months, anyway. Once everything freezes, they plow a temporary road that links up to the main highway, and semis haul in everything, including all the big, heavy stuff planes can't handle. Lot cheaper to get stuff that way, so that's when everybody stocks up for the whole year."

"I read online there are only forty-something people in the village."

"Got to be from the 2000 census. Just twenty-seven now. Once the school closed, we lost some families. And a couple of cheechakos moved on."

"Cheechakos?" It sounded like a breakfast cereal.

"Newcomers. Outsiders who come here loving the idea of Alaska and *think* they want to live here, till they find out how tough it is. You spend a couple of hard winters here, you're a sourdough. Term started during the gold rush, 'cause prospectors used to survive on the stuff. Think we have it tough today, you should see the way they had to live."

"So that brings me back to my original question." The plane abruptly fell several feet again, and Karla gripped the edges of her seat. She didn't continue until the plane had evened out. "You said you've been flying in Alaska more than twenty years. Why does anyone choose to live here? Why did you?" Maybe she could get some insights into the kind of person her sister was.

"As many reasons as there are mountains, why people live here." Bryson recalled the many discussions she and her friends had had in the Den on that very topic. Some locals were secretive about why they'd come, which provided ample fodder for lengthy speculations over a few beers. On the run from the law. Antisocial. Unabomber. Illegal alien.

Most folks, though, were pretty forthcoming about what drew them to Alaska. Grizz and Ellie were eternal flower children, homesteaders who came to live off the land and start a commune that never really materialized. Instead they founded a roadhouse as a way to draw the community together, which it had accomplished in spades. Their past showed in the peace-symbol T-shirt that Grizz wore a lot, fashionable again with a new generation, and in the preponderance of classic tunes from the sixties and seventies that made up the bulk of the 120 selections in the jukebox, a 1954 Rock-Ola 1438 Comet that Ellie found online in a Seattle antique shop.

Skeeter had been a commercial pilot with a major airline, and his routes often took him over Alaska. Seeing it from above had made him determined to experience it up close in a small plane, and when he had a taste of it during a month-long vacation, he was hooked. He quit his job and found a plane of his own, settling in Bettles to join the freelance cooperative after a month of tagging along with Bryson, Red Murdock, and half a dozen other veterans of Arctic Circle flying. Skeeter made the transition pretty easy, especially since he'd been based in Minneapolis and had seen his share of bad storms and bitter temperatures. He loved the scenery and independence of his new job, along with the fact he could chain-smoke if he wanted to and stop shaving every goddamn day.

Lars and Maggie had met in the Gates of the Arctic National Park when they were just out of their teens. Maggie was backpacking, doing field studies for her courses at the University of Alaska, and Lars had decided to spend his spring break from Michigan State on a solo fly-fishing adventure in the bush. Both were immediately smitten. When Lars's charter pilot, Bryson's father, returned to pick him up eight days later, Maggie went with him.

They married and lived in Fairbanks long enough to get their degrees—Lars in ecology, conservation biology, and environmental science, and Maggie in wildlife biology and plant biology—then settled north, near where they'd met, to work and raise a family.

"Most folks, I guess, are just the rugged-individual type," Bryson explained. "They move here for the chance to live simply—off the land, by their wits. Testing themselves against the worst nature can offer. A few are running away from something or someone, and don't want to be found. Or they want to get as far as possible from stupid laws and regulations that restrict how they can live. For me, Alaska is in my blood. I was born here."

She didn't ordinarily volunteer a lot of personal information to her clients, but the chitchat was helping her fight her fatigue. "Lived in Fairbanks for a while, and even that was too much big-city for me. Can't fathom being anywhere else. Have to be able to breathe fresh air, see the stars, hear the wolves howl at night. Wake up to a view that always stuns me."

"But you sure have to sacrifice a lot to get all that, don't you? You really don't have a refrigerator?"

"That's just what I mean. People like you who've never known any difference think those are such big necessities, but they're not, really. You get back so much more here than you ever have to give up. I've pretty much always done without such things, so I don't miss 'em. I live a very comfortable life." She rarely wanted to explain or justify her choices, but this stranger had put her on the defensive. "Hear my clients talk about how a simple power outage for a day or two makes 'em crazy, worrying about pipes freezing and doing without their Internet. Free yourself from all of that, you live a lot less stressful life."

"You definitely have different priorities than most of us."

"Won't argue that. One of my favorite quotes is from the Greek philosopher Epicurus. *If you live according to nature, you will never be poor; but if according to opinions, you will never be rich. Nature demands little, opinion a great deal.*"

"No offense," her passenger said, "but you don't strike me as a philosophy student."

Bryson wondered, not for the first time, why so many outsiders perceived Alaskans as ignorant hicks. "Reading is a popular pastime up here. And you get lots and lots of time to think and reflect."

"Precisely what I don't need," Karla Edwards mumbled.

The answer didn't strike Bryson as odd or unusual. Many people who were constantly on the go were afraid of taking a long hard look at their lives and the choices they made. Some of the people she and Lars met had their first chance to do so during their trips to Alaska, and they weren't always happy about what they discovered about themselves.

"Lot of benefits to living here," she said. "Hardships draw people together. Neighbors and friends become your extended family, 'cause you have to rely on each other. Can't tell you how many clients I talk to who live in big cities, never even met the people living next door."

Her passenger was silent for a long time. "That's true of me. I live in an apartment building in Atlanta, and I don't know the name of anyone on my floor, even though I've lived there six years. I nod or wave sometimes at familiar faces as I come and go, but that's about it. When news reports of local shootings, break-ins, and people stealing your identity constantly bombard you, you become leery of inviting strangers into your home. Afraid of people knowing too much about you."

"That's just what I mean. Here, you got bush hospitality. Most people in the wild never lock their door when they're away, 'cause you never know when someone might get lost, or hurt. Your home might be their only chance to survive. Gotta trust they won't take advantage of that." Bryson thought back to the time she and her father needed to enter a stranger's unoccupied cabin because they'd had to ditch the plane in a sudden blizzard, when the wind chill was thirty below zero.

They'd left behind some money for the firewood and food they'd used, and a note thanking the owners for keeping to the tradition of providing an open, well-stocked shelter for those in need.

"I can't imagine being that trusting," Karla said. "Then again, I can't imagine living so far out in the wilderness that such a thing could be necessary. How do you deal with the isolation? Don't you get lonely?"

"Sure. Doesn't everyone, regardless of their geography? Do your location and luxuries mean you never get lonely?"

There was a very long pause before she got an answer. And Karla's voice, when she finally spoke, was melancholic. "No. They don't."

Bryson had obviously hit a nerve. "Didn't mean to pry."

"You're not. Besides, I asked you first."

"But *I* didn't have to *think* before I answered."

Another long silence followed. Bryson glanced in the mirror, but it was too dark to see Karla's expression. The dim light from the control panel only let her see that she was staring out the window into the darkness. "You can't run from it, you know," she said. "It'll follow you wherever, even up here."

"I'm not running from anything," Karla shot back angrily.

For a while there, she'd been almost pleasant, but the reprieve was short. The petulant child from the airport was back. "If you say so," Bryson replied. "Then why are you here?"

"Not that it's any of your business, but I guess you could say I'm on a voyage of self-discovery."

If you ask me, you're already a little too self-absorbed. Bryson spotted the welcome lights of Bettles in the distance. "What makes you think you'll find yourself here?"

"I'm not sure," Karla said. "But a part of me believes that whatever I'm looking for is here."

Chapter Six

"You'll soon find out. That's the village up ahead." Bryson wasn't sure whether it was her fatigue or the company, but the trip up had seemed to take an eternity. She'd had more than enough of her difficult passenger. Sue was due to pay up in spades, and soon. Bryson hit the transmit button on her radio. "A2024B Piper to BTT."

"BTT to A2024B Piper. Where ya been, Bryson? Everybody's waiting for you." The voice wasn't the raspy baritone she expected.

"Got held up. Where's Skeeter? Why're you manning the radio?"

"You're the only traffic left tonight. Skeeter ate somethin' baaad. *Way* bad. He's been in the can the last hour."

"Coming in on final approach. Pass the word, will you, Lars. I don't have everything. Only about half."

"You better have a good reason ready." The reply was lighthearted, but Bryson knew Lars well enough to catch the undercurrent of concern in his voice.

The warning wasn't necessary. Bryson was already doing a mental checklist of who was expecting something, which included most of Bettles, a few Evansville natives, and a handful of bush residents. She focused on the ones who might react poorly to the news they'd been waiting for her in vain.

Everyone was cautious around Dirty Dan, because even though he seemed harmless, no one knew anything much about him, and there were plenty of crazies in Alaska. Crazies who holed up there because society had shunned them elsewhere, and people who cracked from the strain of cabin fever. Both types could be unpredictable. There were also the chronic alcoholics who occasionally got mean when they were soused, and more than a few of those were around.

Bryson glanced at the illuminated dial on her watch. It was almost nine thirty. She might have been back as early as four or five, if she hadn't had to make so many shopping stops only to get further sidetracked by her unexpected passenger. The folks waiting for their orders had probably started gathering at the Den around three—such supply trips were a highlight of the week, or month. So everyone had certainly had ample time to get loaded while they all sat around waiting for her.

The double strip of lights ahead was set on low, which was all she ever needed on a clear night like this. But she was so bleary-eyed she clicked her mic seven times, which automatically triggered the lights to brighten to full. As she did, Bryson heard a sharp intake of breath from the woman behind her.

"You said…Lars? God. I just realized. Bryson Faulkner. You're on the Web site, too, aren't you? Arctic Independent Outfitters?"

"That's me. You know Lars?" They were dropping fast, the ride smooth as silk as they descended. They'd be wheels down in another two minutes.

"Lars Rasmussen?" It came out as a squeak.

"Yeah." *What the heck is going on?*

"I can't do this! I can't." Her passenger's voice shook. She was clearly in a state of panic. "I'm not ready. I thought I was, but I'm not. This is crazy. Just crazy. I'm not ready." She was talking to herself more than Bryson, a kind of reverse pep talk, but Bryson couldn't ignore it. "We can't land. Pull up!" the woman ordered.

"Spare me the drama-queen routine, huh? First you can't wait to get here, and now you—"

"Take me back to Fairbanks. Right now."

"Are you nuts?" They were thirty feet up and closing in fast on the runway.

"I can't face them. I'm not ready." The woman's tone was desperate.

Bryson could make out the lights of a handful of cars and ATVs at the end of the runway, near the Den. And in the glow of them, at least a couple dozen dark silhouettes of gathered townspeople.

Suppressing a sigh, she pulled back on the controls, gave the Cub some gas, and began to lift away from the ground just as they reached the first lights of the runway. She wouldn't be winning any popularity contests tonight. "Who are you afraid of facing? Lars?" she asked as they passed over the crowd. She could pick out a few of her friends by their shape and clothes, but it was too dark to read their expressions.

"Is *she* there, too?"

A hand reached up and grip Bryson's elbow.

"Maggie? Is she there?"

It all came to her, then. It would have sooner, if she hadn't been so exhausted. *The e-mail.* "Are you *that* Karla?"

The woman gasped. "How could you possibly know that?"

"You sent an e-mail to the Web site, right? Asking whether Lars had a wife named Maggie?"

"Jesus. I never thought…I mean, it was just a quick line. How did you find out about it?"

Bryson started circling the village, a wide loop that would give them time to sort this out and figure out what to do. "Just came up, is all. Skeeter—he does the Web site—mentioned it to Lars and me because it was kind of unusual. Anything a little mysterious around here tends to get talked over."

"So Lars knows, too?"

"Well, he wondered who you were and why you were asking about him and Maggie, yeah. Didn't recall ever meeting a Karla before."

"We haven't met." Her client's breathing was so loud and fast Bryson was afraid she might hyperventilate. "I came here to see them. Kind of on impulse. And I know it probably sounds crazy, but I'm just not ready to face them yet."

Lars's voice came over her headset. "Hey, Bryson, what's going on? Problems?"

"Give me a couple minutes, Lars," she replied. "Nothing wrong, just checking something." She switched off her mic. "We have to set down," she told Karla. "I don't have enough fuel to get back to Fairbanks, and there's a whole lotta people down there camped out waiting for me. If it matters, I don't think Maggie's there. Only Lars."

Karla was silent for a minute or two. "I have to ask you a favor. Can you…can we…not tell Lars who I am?"

"You're not giving me a lot to work with here. Lars and Maggie are good friends," she said. "I won't lie to him, especially if this is about something that'll upset them. Frankly, lady, you're acting a bit unhinged."

"I don't know how they'll react to what I have to tell them," Karla volunteered. "I'm hoping they'll think it's good news. Mostly, anyway. But I need some time to think about what I'm going to say. I can't explain any better than that. I'm just asking you to respect my privacy and not say anything to anyone."

"All right. But you better not make me regret giving you a lift here." Bryson hit her mic button. "Coming in, Lars. See you in a few."

"Roger that, Bryson."

She lined up the Cub for another approach and descended toward the runway. The crowd gathered at the end had increased significantly during their circling.

"Where can I stay?" Karla asked as the wheels touched down.

"Only one place in town, the Den. Right there." She had both hands busy with the controls, so she tilted her head in the direction of the roadhouse. "Should warn you, gonna be some curiosity about you. Especially since a lot of people won't be getting the supplies they're expecting." The Cub rolled to a stop twenty feet from the gathered crowd. Immediately the townspeople began to converge on the plane.

"Don't worry about it. I'm not your concern now," Karla said.

The declaration was welcome news, but Bryson refrained from saying so.

Lars and Geneva were at the head of the pack. They reached her door just as she opened it.

"A*ha*. Now I see why you got held up." Lars grinned as he looked past her approvingly to Karla, who was unbuckling herself.

"Who's she?" Geneva asked with much less enthusiasm.

"Missed her flight, so I let her hitch along." Bryson climbed out of the Cub and started around to the other side, but a burly six-three pipeline worker named Hank stepped in front of her, blocking her path. He reeked of whiskey.

"Lars says you didn't get evythin'." He slurred his words. "Better have that damn ax I been waitin' for all day."

"And my ointment," said the hulk's shadow, a twitchy ferret of a man named Jerry who'd obviously consumed nearly as much alcohol as his chum. The two shared a cabin several miles outside the village.

"Fucking rash is driving me nuts." He scratched a greasy hand across his chest as if to illustrate the extent of his misery.

"Got everything on the list, just had to leave a few things behind till I can make it back there. Maybe in the morning." Bryson stepped deftly around both of them as they started to protest and reached the passenger door just as Karla emerged.

"You got my cigarettes?" a woman shouted, and Bryson winced. The cigarettes, she knew, had been in the bag that had been on the passenger seat. Those had definitely been left behind.

"Sammy's waiting up for his soccer ball," another voice hollered.

"*She* the reason you didn't get evythin'?" Hank had trailed her, and he and his drunken ferret-shadow were now staring at Karla, Hank with disgust and Jerry with a leer.

And more trouble was brewing. Bryson caught a glimpse of Dirty Dan, pushing angrily through the crowd toward them.

"Hold on, everybody. Chill." She held up her hands. "I promise, what I don't have with me, I'll pick up tomorrow if the weather holds. Now, if I can get some hands to help haul this stuff into the Den, we'll sort out what's here and what's not, *yet*."

Karla looked a bit shell-shocked to be the center of attention. She shrank against the door of the Cub. Bryson glanced around for Lars as she opened the cargo hatch and was relieved to find him positioned directly behind Dirty Dan, who had pulled up short to study Karla with narrowed eyes and an annoyed frown.

She took out the nearest box and thrust it toward Hank. "Make yourself useful." He shouldered it without further complaint, and his companion accepted the sack of groceries that was next out of the plane. Others stepped forward to help unload, and soon most of the crowd had dispersed, all headed back to the Den. Geneva stood off to one side, and Dirty Dan also remained, still eyeing Karla suspiciously, with Lars behind him.

Karla, withering under the glare of attention, had inched ever closer to Bryson's back during the unloading, so that by the time it was done, she was standing so near that Bryson almost knocked her down when she turned around.

Her elbow impacted Karla's side, and Karla, startled, jumped back, off balance. But Bryson's fatigue had faded entirely under the threat of trouble and her curiosity about Karla Edwards, and her senses were on hyperalert. She grabbed for Karla as she fell back and managed to wrap one arm around her waist. She caught her, though the momentum carried her forward and she landed hard on one knee.

Bryson grimaced in pain and muttered a curse under her breath. The woman in her arms scrambled to regain her feet as Lars shot forward. "Hey! You okay?" he asked, putting an arm around Bryson's shoulder.

"Fine," she said through clenched teeth.

"That sounded painful." Karla stooped next to her. "You sure you're all right?"

"Said I'm fine." Would this nightmare of an evening never end? Bryson struggled to her feet, wincing as new pain shot through her knee. That would leave a bruise. Forcing a smile, she gave Lars a subtle indication with her eyes to keep alert to Dirty Dan and got a small nod of acknowledgment in return. She reached into the hold for her daypack and slung it over one shoulder, then extricated Karla's duffel.

"I'll take that," Lars offered, stepping forward.

"I can—" Karla started to reach for it herself but Lars waved her off.

"No. Let me. I'm happy to." Lars took the duffel in his left hand and offered his right to Karla. "I'm Lars. Welcome to Bettles. You staying with us long?"

Karla's heart was thundering as she reached for her brother-in-law's hand. "It's nice to meet you, Lars. Thank you. I'll be around a while." She hoped so, anyway, but that all depended on Maggie.

Her first impression of him couldn't have been better, a stark contrast to Bryson's aloof demeanor. His welcoming kindness was genuine; she could see it in his sweet smile and feel it in the firm grasp of their hands. And Lars was a strapping, handsome man. Six feet tall. Blond. With a square jaw, high cheekbones, and clear blue eyes.

They all headed into the roadhouse, where a chaos of activity greeted them. Only a few patrons were seated at the bar and scattered tables. Most of the sizeable crowd was gathered anxiously around the boxes and bags from the plane, which were now piled in the corner on a small raised platform stage. A stocky man with a bushy red beard and black wool cap was doing his best to dissuade anyone from rummaging through the contents, but the irate voices of the drunks in the crowd indicated a few tempers were beginning to boil.

Bryson headed purposefully toward the melee, and Lars followed suit, pausing just long enough to deposit Karla's duffel at her feet.

Karla grabbed the bag and took a seat at the end of the bar, grateful to have the attention of the town shifted elsewhere so she could take a moment to breathe and think about what she was going to do.

"Settle down, folks." Bryson's voice rang out over the crowd as she pushed her way through to the stage. "Got my list right here." She doled out the supplies, with Lars flanking her on one side and the red-bearded man on the other.

"Hey, there. Welcome to the Den. What can I get ya?" The bartender smiling at Karla epitomized her image of the typical Alaskan roughneck. Big and broad-shouldered, with a silver-tipped beard and hair that hadn't seen clippers in a decade or more.

"Mmm. White wine?"

"You got it." He set a well-polished wineglass in front of her and filled it to the rim with Chardonnay. "If you're hungry," he added, tapping one of the menus tucked between the salt-and-pepper shakers and napkin holder to her left, "kitchen's open until midnight."

"Thanks." As the bartender retreated to his other customers, she downed a long sip of her wine. The place reminded her of the Brick in *Northern Exposure*, with its taxidermy décor and quirky Arctic accents. A broken dogsled hung from the ceiling, along with ancient gold-mining paraphernalia: pans and picks and broken shovels. The neon beer signs behind the bar advertised local brews she'd never heard of, with colorful names like Forty-Niner Amber, Solstice Gold, and Caribou Kilt.

The bartender delivered a large bowl of stew to a patron two stools down, and the savory aroma reminded her it'd been hours since she'd eaten anything. She reached for the menu, which was as eclectic as the bar. Reindeer stew. Caribou steaks. King crab. Smoked salmon tacos. And for dessert, wild berry crisp with home-churned vanilla-bean ice cream.

"Go for the stew," Bryson suggested as she claimed the seat to her right. "Specialty of the house."

Karla looked past her and saw that the mob of townspeople had dispersed back to their tables and booths, some smiling over their purchases, a few glaring unhappily at Bryson's back.

"I didn't realize what a problem it'd create for you to have to leave so much behind to get me here," she said. "Looks like a lot of your friends are pretty upset."

"They'll get over it. Hopefully I can make a quick run down at first light and be back with the rest before they sleep off their hangovers." Bryson hailed the bartender, and he hurried toward them with a smile.

"Handled that like a pro," he told Bryson as he popped the top off a bottle of Black Fang beer and set it in front of her. "How'd you defuse ol' Dan?"

Karla followed Bryson's eyes to the other end of the bar, where the man who'd been staring at them out by the plane was buttoning up his filthy overcoat and preparing to leave.

"Told him I'd do his next delivery freebie."

"Pretty hefty price tag."

"Not so much." Bryson glanced her way. "Take it you two've met. You get a room?"

"No, not yet," she replied, looking uncertainly toward the bartender. "You're the proprietor?"

"Grizz." He folded both large hands around hers in a warm, extended greeting. "Sorry to say, though, we're full up tonight." He looked to Bryson. "Lars snagged the last couple of rooms for you two when he realized you wouldn't be able to make it home before dark."

Oh crap. "I should've called ahead. Any suggestions?" She glanced from one to the other.

"I've got a solution." One of the waitresses materialized on the other side of Bryson, the curvaceous brunette who'd lingered by the Cub and followed them inside. "Bryson can bunk with me. That frees up a room."

Bryson took a long swig from her beer and seemed to consider the suggestion. She turned away from Karla to face the waitress. "No ulterior motives, right, Gen?"

"That's entirely up to you," the woman answered. She was smiling at the pilot with a look full of mischief and promise. For some reason Karla didn't expect to find lesbians so far out in the boonies, and she was so absorbed with other matters that it hadn't crossed her mind that her hunky pilot and she might have that in common. Though perhaps it should have. That gate clerk back in Fairbanks had given Bryson a similar come-on smile.

On the surface, anyway, she could understand their interest in Bryson Faulkner. She was easy on the eyes, with her natural beauty and athletic build. And Karla imagined some women might be attracted to her adventurous lifestyle as a pilot. But give Karla kind and sweet over daring and detached any day.

However, this revelation might be a positive development in terms of the reception she might get from the Rasmussens. If they were close to Bryson, they obviously had no issue with her being gay. At least Karla apparently didn't have to worry about that.

"All right, then," Bryson told the bartender. "She can have my room."

"I don't want to put you out..." Karla began, but in truth she was grateful for the opportunity to crash for a while. And she didn't imagine Bryson would feel too inconvenienced, considering the enticing alternative.

"Oh, she'll be comfortable, don't you worry," the waitress interjected. "Not like we haven't done it plenty of times before, right, Bryson?"

Bryson turned to meet Karla's eyes. "We're old friends. It's fine."

"Thanks." Addressing the bartender, she said, "I'm pretty beat. If someone can show me to my room now, I'd be very grateful. And maybe I can get a bottled water and a bowl of your reindeer stew sent up?"

"Done." Grizz wiped his hands on a bar towel and snagged a key from a rack behind the cash register. "Right this way," he said, rounding the bar and stooping to retrieve her duffel bag.

She followed him toward the door that led upstairs, then paused to glance around the bar. Lars had disappeared somewhere. It was just as well, because the time had come for her to figure out what the heck she was going to say to them.

The room was comfortable, if modestly furnished. A queen-sized bed, small dresser, and twin nightstands with matching lamps. Two padded chairs flanking a small round table faced the one large window. The truly eye-catching feature was the array of photographs on the walls—spectacular blowups of the northern lights. "Bathroom's down the hall at the end. You'll find fresh towels in the cabinet there. You here just the one night?" Grizz asked as he set her duffel bag on the bed.

Good question. "Um. Not sure. I'll probably be here at least a couple of nights, maybe more. Are you booked up?"

He laughed. "Naw. Tonight's an exception, because so many backcountry folks came in to meet the plane. This time of year, we almost always have a fair amount of rooms free."

"Great. Can I kind of play it by ear, then? Let you know?"

"Sure. Come find me tomorrow, and we'll get your credit-card info and all that done." He started toward the door, but stopped with his hand on the knob. "Anything else I can get you?"

"Just the food, thanks."

"Coming right up. Enjoy your stay with us."

He left her alone, and she unpacked her bag. At the bottom was a copy of the letter her mother had written, along with a small photo album. She sat on the edge of the bed and studied the pictures of her mother, arranged chronologically from when she was just a girl in pigtails to the last one taken just before her death.

She paused when she came to an Easter snapshot that could have been a Norman Rockwell painting of the idealized American family. She and her parents were about to dig in to a feast of ham and all the trimmings, the table set with their finest china and linens. Her father sat at the head of the table, still in his navy suit from church. Her mother wore a pale yellow dress, and Karla sat opposite, in pink, her basket of candy eggs and chocolate rabbits on the floor beside her chair. Her father had bought a tripod so they could capture every holiday together, and there were dozens of similar photos in a box at home.

But though she'd looked at this picture countless times, Karla only now noticed that the smile on her mother's face seemed forced, and the look in her eyes was melancholic. Had she been thinking about the child she'd given away, wondering what her daughter's life was like, imagining how she might be spending the holiday? Surely on occasions like this, her mother must have had some regrets about her decision. Karla was eleven in the picture, so Maggie would have been fifteen or so, already in high school.

The photo allowed Karla a glimpse of the anguish her mother endured. She'd never fully realized how difficult it must have been to keep that terrible secret. *I miss you so damn much, Mom. I wish you could have told me.*

She felt ashamed that she'd focused entirely on her own feelings of betrayal when she learned about Maggie. She had to respect her mother's decision; she'd done what she thought best for her firstborn child and had suffered the consequences of her actions. Maybe her sister would somehow remind her of the woman that gave birth to them both. *Do you look like her, Maggie? Will I see her in your eyes?*

Two sharp raps brought her out of her reverie. When she opened the door, Bryson stood on the other side, holding a tray with her stew, water, and a basket of fresh rolls.

"Didn't expect to see you again," she said, stepping aside.

"I was headed up here anyway, and Grizz asked." Bryson set the tray on the table by the window and turned to go.

"Hey, you mind hanging around for a couple of minutes?"

Bryson's eyes narrowed suspiciously. "What for?"

"You said you were friends with Lars and Maggie, right? Would you mind answering a few questions for me?"

"I guess not."

Karla took one of the chairs, and Bryson the other. "Would it bother you if I eat while we talk? I'm starving." Not waiting for anything more communicative than Bryson's shrug, she reached for one of the rolls and dipped it into the thick gravy. The rich, savory stew, filled with chunks of lean meat, quelled the ache in her stomach. "What's Maggie like?" she asked between bites.

"Maggie? Independent. Strong-willed. Bright. Funny." Bryson smiled at some memory, but didn't offer details. "Protective of people she cares about. Just about fearless—she's had a couple of pretty close encounters with wolves and grizzlies and always kept her cool."

Wolves and grizzlies? The huge stuffed bear at the entrance to the Den was intimidating enough. She couldn't imagine coming face to face with one in the wild.

"Maggie can be kind of particular," Bryson continued, still staring out into the night. "Wants everything in its place." She grinned to herself. "But not so much, these days."

"Why? What's different 'these days'?"

"Don't think I should answer that. Maggie and Lars are like family to me, and I don't feel right volunteering a lot of private information about them. Especially since I don't know why you're here, why you want to know all this in the first place."

Bryson probably wouldn't answer most of her other questions, either, but she had to try. "Okay, I can respect that. Can you at least tell me how to get to their place?"

"I'll tell you this much. This time of year, only two options. Boat and plane. By skiff, it's a good two or three hours or more. And that's not a trip you'd ever try to make alone, unless you really know the territory. Lars usually gets here and back hitching a ride with me. I live a few miles downstream of them, and he boats from there, which is an easy trip."

"In other words, I can't exactly just drop in on them and say hello."

"No. Not so much." Bryson tried unsuccessfully to stifle a yawn.

"I'll let you go get some sleep. I guess you can't really answer my questions, anyway. But I appreciate you staying."

Bryson got to her feet. "No problem. Can I offer you some advice?"

"Sure."

"Lars is stuck here until I get back from Fairbanks tomorrow, probably some time in the early afternoon. He should be easy to find, either downstairs or hanging out with Skeeter in the FAA hut at the edge of the airstrip. Be a good time to talk to him."

She followed Bryson to the door. "Thanks. I'll do that."

Bryson met her eyes. "Good luck. Hope you find whatever you came here for."

CHAPTER SEVEN

Karla woke to the faint sound of an engine, a steady but choppy cadence that took several seconds to recognize as Bryson's plane. The room was dark, but she could dimly make out the silhouette of the chairs and table. She threw back the covers and shivered; it was several degrees cooler in the room than the seventy degrees she set her thermostat at home. Her thin flannel pajamas were inadequate and she hadn't packed a robe, so she put on her down jacket and an extra pair of socks, and went to the window.

Dawn hadn't broken yet, but it wasn't far off. A thin line of faint gold light illuminated the eastern horizon, to her left. Far below were the runway lights, stretching nearly parallel to the horizon. A white aircraft, slightly bigger than Bryson's and with a painted tail logo that read *Bettles Air*, was parked on the first half of the airstrip beneath an overhead light.

Bryson's red Super Cub sat at the beginning of the strip, poised for takeoff, its propeller a faint gray blur. Its large tires began to turn, and the plane gained the sky seconds later, not yet sixty feet down the runway.

A life that entailed facing down the weather and deadly terrain of Alaska every day, year round, in such a fragile aircraft was unimaginable. Like a sparrow trying to navigate the perimeter of a hurricane. Bryson Faulkner was certainly a braver woman than she was. Or more foolhardy. She headed toward the door, desperate to pee, and was shocked to discover it was already nine forty-five. Back home it was already full light out by eight, when she left for work.

A male singing loudly off-key already occupied the bathroom at the end of the hall, so she retreated to her room cursing under her breath. The first time in ages she was able to sleep like a rock would be the morning she didn't have a private bathroom.

Her annoyance faded instantly when she opened her door. The scene outside the window stunned her. The rising sun cast a vivid pink light across the mountains that filled the glass, highlighting their sheer facades and snow-peaked tips, and painting the shadows at the base of each one an ethereal shade of blue, almost turquoise. The sunrise looked like a watercolor painting. She walked slowly forward until her face was inches from the pane. The mountain range, some ten or fifteen miles distant, defined the northern horizon, extending as far as she could see in either direction.

Karla held her breath briefly. The light had a magical quality, a photographer's dream. She rummaged through the dresser drawers for her pocket digital camera and took a few shots, knowing they would never capture this splendor.

Bryson's words came back to her. "Have to be able to breathe fresh air, see the stars, hear the wolves howl at night. Wake up to a view that always stuns me."

She was beginning to understand at least some of Bryson's reasons for choosing to live in Alaska. What were Maggie's?

It was time to tell the Rasmussens who she was and why she was here, but how to begin? After she learned that Maggie existed, she was able to keep her grief tolerable by preoccupying herself with planning, organizing, and researching. Tying up all the loose ends so she could travel halfway around the world, return date undetermined.

But she was *here* now, and the challenge ahead was suddenly all too *real*. Imminent. Ominous. Ordinarily, she planned life in detail to minimize surprises.

This time, though, she hadn't allowed herself time to consider exactly what she would do and say. Perhaps if she'd thought about it too carefully, she wouldn't have come. It was completely out of character for her to just drop in unannounced on anyone—even a good friend, let alone a long-lost sibling—armed with a bombshell.

But she couldn't stand to be rejected and abandoned again. If she'd told Maggie she was coming, she'd have had to say why. And if

Maggie didn't like the idea, she could simply cut her off, then and there, without explanation.

She had to do it in person.

As if answering her resolve, Lars came out of a small building at the edge of the runway, near where the planes parked. He was headed toward the Den.

Karla gathered a change of clothes and returned to the bathroom. If Mister Off-key wasn't out of there yet, maybe she could persuade him to hurry. She didn't want to waste this opportunity to talk to her brother-in-law.

❖

Karla found Lars sipping coffee in a booth, alone. She'd showered and spent several minutes putting on makeup and styling her hair, as she usually did, at least on her working days, and she especially wanted to make the best impression possible today. However, the majority of the women in the Den, Bryson included, apparently didn't bother with cosmetics and curling irons.

Gathering her courage, she crossed to the booth and waited for Lars to look up. "Do you mind if I join you?"

"Sure thing." He smiled and extended his arm toward the seat opposite. "Want some coffee?"

"Desperate for some."

"Oh! Desperate, eh? Calls for extreme measures, then." He winked and slid out of the booth, ran comically across the wood-planked floor, to the applause and laughter of the Den's half dozen other patrons, and back behind the bar, where he poured a mug full from a fresh pot. Snatching a couple of creams from a basket, he hustled back over to the booth, holding the mug well in front of him in case it spilled.

"What service. I'll have to leave a big tip." She brought it to her lips to take a long sip and realized her hands were trembling.

Lars noticed, too, and frowned. "Are you okay?"

"Nervous."

"Nervous?" His forehead creased in confusion. "About what?"

She glanced around to make sure they wouldn't be overheard. "Lars, I came here to see you and Maggie. My name is Karla Edwards."

"Karla? The Karla from the e-mail?"

She nodded.

He leaned back in his seat, his face registering confusion and curiosity. "Okay. What's this about?"

"I should've probably given you both some notice I was coming. I really didn't mean to blindside you, but…" Her heart was drumming so loud in her ears her voice sounded oddly muted.

"What is it? Is something wrong?" She could see in his expression that her evasiveness alarmed him.

"No. I mean, hopefully you'll both like my news, though there's part of it I know you won't want to hear. God, this is difficult." She wrapped her hands tight around her mug to keep them from shaking.

"Please." He leaned forward and met her eyes. "Just tell me."

She took a deep breath and let it out. "Maggie is my sister."

Lars let the news sink in. "I don't understand. Maggie's an only child. How is that possible?"

"Maggie was adopted. I gather she doesn't know that?"

"Adopted? Are you sure?"

She nodded. "Our mother had to give her up when she was a baby. The Van Rooys were family friends. They moved here with Maggie right after the adoption."

"Maggie doesn't know anything about this. I think she always wanted a brother or sister, but to find out her parents lied to her, that's not gonna sit easy with her." He studied Karla's face as if to find some trace of his wife in her features. "How do you know all this?"

"My mother…*our* mother, died three weeks ago." Tears sprang to her eyes, and she wiped them away.

"I'm sorry for your loss," Lars said. "I know how awful it is to lose a parent. Both of mine are gone."

"Still kind of raw. It was sudden. A heart attack." She steeled herself to tell him the rest. "She'd been sick for a long time with Alzheimer's."

"Oh, that's gotta be the worst. Can't say I know much about it, but it sure has to be tough on the person who has it and their families."

"Tough doesn't begin to describe it." Karla remembered the many phases her mother had gone through. Denial. Anger. Frustration. "Those who have it are aware they'll lose their memories and their ability to function a little more every day and there's not a damn thing they can do to stop it. The disease shatters their dreams for the future. And, most painful of all, they know their loved ones will have to watch them and most likely put their own plans on hold to deal with all of it."

"I can't imagine." Lars seemed sympathetic. "But I don't understand something, Karla. If your mother was bad off for a long time, like you said, how did she tell you all this stuff about my wife?"

"Mom never actually *told* me anything about Maggie. But she left a letter that she wrote many years ago, before she got sick, explaining everything. I found it among her things last week."

"So that explains the e-mail."

"Yes. The last Mom knew, you and Maggie were in Fairbanks. I did searches on the Internet to find you. You're the only family I have left now." Karla was so nervous about Lars's reaction she had been ripping her napkin into little pieces beside her mug. She glanced at her unconscious evidence of her state of mind. "And once I *did* find you, I decided on impulse to come out here and tell you all this in person."

Lars took both of her hands in his, smiling at her small pile of shredded paper. "I have a new sister-in-law, it seems. Let me be the first, then, to welcome you to the family."

She wanted to relax under the sincere gesture, but she had to tell him everything. "Lars, how much do you know about Alzheimer's?"

His smile faded. The look on her face must have told him that he'd missed something important, and she could almost see the wheels turning as he tried to figure out what it was. "I don't..." Then he apparently realized what she meant. "Shit. Alzheimer's. It's hereditary, isn't it?"

"They don't know for sure about most cases. But a rare type, called Familial Alzheimer's, or early-onset, is conclusively hereditary. The doctors weren't sure, but they think that's what my mother had." Karla had accepted this news long ago, but was sensitive to the impact it would have on Lars. She couldn't sugarcoat it. "If they're right, Maggie and I both have a fifty-fifty chance of getting it too. My mother started showing symptoms when she was in her early forties."

He exhaled loudly and ran his hand through his hair. "Jesus."

"I'm sorry, Lars." Working at the hospital she had to be able to deliver and discuss such news with clinical detachment, but in this case, she couldn't help but grieve and be anxious about the prognosis.

Lars cradled his head in his hands and didn't speak for several moments. When he finally looked up at her, his eyes were wet with tears. "Do you know Maggie's pregnant?"

❖

Fairbanks

After Bryson secured the cargo door of the Cub, she stood in the doorway of the hangar staring toward the terminal. Should she go inside to track down Sue Spires and set up a time they could get together for a few hours of fun?

She wasn't as tempted as she was last night, and not because she'd been sexually satisfied in the interim.

Geneva hadn't tried very hard to coerce Bryson to rekindle their affair. She pouted a bit when Bryson repeated that she wanted to remain friends, and *only* friends, but soon curled up on her side of the queen-sized bed and went to sleep.

Bryson was the one who somehow managed to drift over the invisible line between them as they slept, for when she woke she was spooning Geneva from behind, their bodies tight together and her hand cupping Gen's ample left breast.

She lay like that for a long minute, listening to Geneva's deep breaths and imagining she was waking at home in the arms of a loving partner she was madly passionate about. Her series of transient liaisons satisfied her less every day, and as much as she tried to tell herself she was comfortable with her life, at moments like this she couldn't keep her loneliness at bay.

She longed for a woman to wake up to every morning, to share coffee with as the sun rose over the mountains, to laze with drowsily in bed on stormy days. Someone who would worry if she was overdue from a flight and welcome her home with kisses and caresses. Lately the prospect of spending the rest of her life alone left her feeling incomplete and not as happy in this wilderness as she had once been.

We all have to make choices, and you've made yours. She couldn't be happy somewhere else, and sharing her days with someone she wasn't in love with wouldn't fill her inner void. She gently withdrew from Geneva and dressed, ignoring her small groan of protest.

The whole experience with Geneva had dampened her desire to

spend an evening with Sue, and she needed to get back to Bettles to deliver the rest of her supplies. As she towed her plane back out of the hangar, she discovered one more reason she didn't want to linger long in Fairbanks. She was curious about Karla Edwards and why she'd come to see Maggie and Lars.

CHAPTER EIGHT

Bettles

"Pregnant? Oh, God. I had no idea." Karla knew Maggie would already have plenty to deal with—the revelations she was adopted, had a sister, and had just lost her biological mother without ever meeting her. And especially that she was at high risk for one of the most insidious and awful diseases imaginable. But to learn that the child she was carrying might suffer the same fate, and that she might lose her mind before that child even started school… "Lars, I'm so sorry. I knew all of this would be difficult enough. I shouldn't have come."

"Don't say that." Lars put one of his hands over hers again. "You did the right thing." He took a deep breath and straightened, setting his jaw. "I need some time to think how best to tell Maggie. Oh, she'll *seem* to take it well. She always puts on a brave face when the going gets rough. But she'll be afraid, inside. She's a worrier." He gave a half-hearted smile. "At least that's her normal reaction. But these days, her hormones are goin' nuts. No telling sometimes what she's gonna say or do next."

"When is she due?" She was going to be an aunt. That is, if Maggie accepted her the way Lars seemed to have. But even if Maggie embraced the idea of suddenly having a sister, she certainly wouldn't welcome all of Karla's news. That worried her most.

"Less than three weeks left. November sixteenth. The baby's a girl." The softness in his eyes told Karla how devoted this man was to her sister and how very much he wanted this child. "We haven't decided on a name yet. Maggie wants to see what suits her when she arrives."

"I love the idea I have a niece on the way. When Mom died, I didn't think I had any family left at all."

"You're not married? No children?" Lars asked.

"No. I live alone." *And hate it.* She considered telling him about Abby. She'd *felt* married, even if their union hadn't been legal or even the mutually devoted commitment she'd thought it'd been. But the last thing she needed right now was to voluntarily unearth those memories in vivid detail. She thought about Abby too much as it was, and the recollections just depressed her and made her feel inadequate. Time, she hoped, would help her understand what had gone wrong, and why. Lars's question had given her an opening to tell him she was gay, however, and she didn't mind getting into that. From the way Lars acted around Bryson, she was pretty certain he wouldn't have a problem with it. "I'm not seeing anybody right now. But I have had one serious relationship...with a woman." She watched for his reaction.

His eyebrows lifted in surprise, but his expression showed no hint of disgust or disapproval, only curiosity. "You're a lesbian?"

She nodded.

"Bryson is, too. And Geneva, one of the waitresses at the Den."

"Yeah, I gathered that."

He laughed. "You got that gaydar Bryson talks about? I swear, how you can all recognize each other is beyond me. I'd never be able to tell with any of you."

"So I gather you and Maggie don't have any problem with it?"

"Oh, hell no. Bryson's family. And hey, we may live out in the sticks and all, but that doesn't make us narrow-minded. We live in Alaska partly because people here are generally more tolerant of each other's lifestyles. You get all kinds."

"Good to know. Lars, I'd like to tell Maggie myself about our connection. Unless you think it would be better coming from you?"

"I've been pondering that. How long are you in Bettles?"

Karla looked out at the runway. A plane was coming in, the Wright Air flight the gate attendant had offered to book for her. The Cessna was only marginally bigger than the Cub. And though the pilot looked capable in his starched white shirt, navy slacks, and bomber jacket, she was glad she'd flown with Bryson. The woman exuded calm self-confidence and had gone above and beyond in her efforts to help her through a troubled night, even if she had been reluctant at first. "I'm not sure how long I'll stay. I guess that's up to you and Maggie. I'm on an open-ended leave of absence from my job."

"What do you do?"

"I'm a registered nurse. I work in the ER at a hospital in Atlanta."

Lars's eyebrows rose. "That's great. Don't mind telling you, it's reassuring to think you might be around a while, with Maggie getting so big. The nearest doctor's in Fairbanks."

"Are you planning to stay there when she gets closer to her due date?" A lot of airlines hesitated to let a pregnant woman fly when she was more than eight months along, primarily because they were afraid she'd go into labor en route or have problems with deep-vein thrombosis—blood clotting in the legs. Bryson probably wouldn't let that stop her where Maggie was concerned, but the flight to Fairbanks was long enough that it could be perilous to wait until she went into labor to leave.

"She wants to have the baby at home. A midwife in Evansville is willing to come out when the time comes. But of course, at her age, I worry about complications, or that she might go into labor during a snowstorm or something and I'd be alone with her." Lars sat up straighter and rubbed sweaty palms along the top of his jeans. "I'm reading all the books I can get my hands on about what to do, but I'd sure appreciate any advice you can give me. We don't have any of those birthing classes around here."

"I'd be happy to. Has Maggie been seeing a doctor?"

He nodded. "Every month. She's got an appointment next week."

"Great. So, who tells her about me? What do you think?"

"Well, we shouldn't just spring you on her without any warning. She's been alone for a couple of days, so no telling what the cabin looks like and what kind of mood she's in. She's a stickler about having everything neat and tidy when people visit." He glanced at his watch. "Bryson should be back soon. I say best thing is to let her fly me home, give me some time to make everything presentable. I'll just say we're going to have a guest for a while. You can tell her about everything, except the Alzheimer's. We should leave that until after the baby's born."

"Probably wise. No need to stress her any more right now."

"While I'm doing that, Bryson can come back for you, and I'll pick you up at her place in the skiff." He squeezed her shoulder. "Provided Maggie takes the news well, as I think she will, you're welcome to stay with us as long as you like."

"Thank you, Lars. I'm really looking forward to getting to know you both. And helping Maggie any way I can." Her stomach churned at the thought she'd finally be meeting her sister in just a few hours. *Please, God. Let her want me in her life as much as I want her in mine.*

❖

Bryson knew before she'd even shut down the Cub's engine that Karla and Lars had talked. In all the years she'd known Lars, she'd rarely seen anything except calm complacence on his face. He was the kind of guy you'd want beside you when all hell was breaking loose, entirely unflappable in a crisis, and he'd been tested on more than one occasion.

Once a grizzly, fresh out of hibernation and desperate for food, stormed his camp during the night and clawed through the wall tent he was sharing with two fishermen. His clients had bolted screaming from the tent; it was only luck the bear hadn't chased them. But Lars kept his head, rolling under his cot to retrieve the can of Mace and the Ruger Super Redhawk Alaskan .454 Casull he carried. The noise of the gun stopped the bear, and the Mace ran him off, though the spray also made Lars profoundly uncomfortable the rest of the day.

But whatever news Karla Edwards had brought to Bettles had certainly rattled Lars. Though an icy mist had descended on the village during Bryson's trip to Fairbanks, she'd barely touched down on the runway when he came trotting out of the Den without his coat, looking concerned and frowning.

Damn it, I knew that woman was trouble the minute I spotted her. If she's here to stir up trouble for them...

She flipped open the window of the Cub and turned up the collar of her coat. "What's up?" she hollered over the drone of the propeller as it began to die. "Everything okay?"

"Big news." He shook his head as though he was still having trouble absorbing it. "Big news."

She climbed down and faced him. "Bad?"

"Well, yes and no. I'll tell you all about it on the way home. Like to get you unloaded pronto, so we can get going. And I hope you don't have other plans for the day, 'cause I'd like you to come right back here and pick up Karla Edwards. She'll be staying with us for a while." The uncertainty on his face deepened. "Least I think she will. Like I said, I'll explain on the way."

"Sure, Lars." She forced herself not to press him for answers as they walked to the cargo hold and began to remove the supplies. She hated to see him so distressed, and the last thing she wanted was to have Karla as a passenger again, but the announcement that she would be staying with the Rasmussens piqued Bryson's curiosity. They rarely had overnight guests who weren't close friends, and with Maggie so volatile lately it was especially strange for them to extend such hospitality to a stranger.

When it was time for them to leave, it was even more peculiar that Lars embraced Karla and spoke to her in low tones, like she was an old friend who needed comfort. Karla had stood off to the side, watching them expectantly as she and Lars brought in their cargo and distributed it among the townspeople who'd congregated in the bar when they heard her plane come in.

Lars put his arm around Karla and led her over to Bryson when they finished their quiet tête-à-tête. "Karla's all checked out." He squeezed the woman's shoulder reassuringly. "She's planning to walk around a bit and see the town, but she'll be back here by the time you make the round trip."

"Fine. Shouldn't take more than an hour or so."

Karla was obviously impatient to leave. She chewed on the inside of her cheek and glanced around, shifting her weight from foot to foot, her hands jammed in her pockets. She didn't seem the type to subject herself to the chill weather voluntarily, but probably needed to work off her restlessness instead of sightsee.

"Don't worry," Lars whispered as he kissed Karla on the forehead. "It'll be fine."

"I sure hope you're right," Karla replied in a quiet voice.

As soon as they were airborne Lars's air of confidence faded, and he seemed troubled again. It took him a few minutes to share his news.

"Karla is Maggie's sister."

"*Sister?* Wait a minute…I thought Maggie's—"

He held up a hand. "Yeah. She doesn't know." The whole story spilled out, everything that Karla had said, including the revelation about the rare form of Alzheimer's that Maggie and their unborn child might be carrying.

Bryson's heart ached for him and the possibility that Maggie might suffer such a debilitating illness soon. Suddenly, all of Karla Edwards's frantic and bizarre behavior the night before made sense.

"We're not planning to tell her about the Alzheimer's until after the baby's born," Lars said. "And Karla wants to tell Maggie the rest herself. I'm going ahead to get everything ready for her to stay with us."

"How you gonna explain to Maggie you're putting up somebody you don't even know? I'm sorry, Lars, but she hasn't even been happy to have *you* underfoot sometimes these days."

The comment brought back his familiar smile. "Yeah. I better hide all sharp objects and breakable keepsakes as soon as I hit the door." His grin faded. "I don't know what to tell her. I don't want to lie to her, but I also want to respect Karla's wish to break the news. Any suggestions?"

"Hmm. That's tough. Well, you did say she's a nurse. Maybe you could just tell Maggie you thought it'd be a good idea to have her out to the house for a couple of days, to help you both know what to do when the baby comes."

"That's not bad." Lars appeared to mull over the suggestion. "Not the whole truth, but not a lie, either."

"She still won't be too happy about it."

"No lie."

As they neared her cabin, a thin layer of ice was beginning to accumulate on the plane. Visibility was still tolerable, and since the cargo hold was empty except for her own supplies, the added weight of any ice buildup wouldn't become an issue right away. But she'd better hustle right back to Bettles and check the plane over carefully before they got back in the air. Maybe ask Skeeter if the weather was expected to deteriorate any further.

Karla was already wound up tight, and hadn't much liked flying in the Cub when conditions were good, let alone through narrow canyons in a pea soup of icy mist. Hopefully her preoccupation with meeting her sister would distract her.

"Good luck," she told Lars as the Cub rolled to a stop on the gravel bar in front of her home. Lars's skiff was anchored just upstream.

"I'll need every bit of that." He climbed down and automatically went to the back of the plane. Bryson had to make a tight turn to be able to take off again from the short strip of gravel, and the fastest and easiest way to accomplish that was for Lars to lift the rear fuselage and pivot the plane by hand.

She watched him hurry toward his boat in her rearview mirror as she released the brake. Two minutes later, they were headed in opposite directions, she through the narrow canyon to the south, and Lars north at full throttle in the skiff.

❖

Karla bit her lip as she stared out the window of the Den, absently caressing the rim of the cold cup of coffee before her. She hadn't explored Bettles long because of the chill wind and icy mist, though she had wanted some time alone to think about what to say to Maggie and walk off the tension that coiled between her shoulders.

The lounge had emptied considerably after Bryson doled out her supplies, but Karla had barely settled into her booth when Grizz materialized, sliding uninvited into the bench opposite. He offered coffee and a sandwich in exchange for news from the lower forty-eight.

Too polite to brush him off after his kindness last night, she forced down the sandwich and answered his queries about urban life and crime, politics and grocery prices, must-see movies and current fads. He left only when his wife beckoned from the kitchen to help her prep for the evening rush.

When Karla returned her attention to the runway outside, looking for Bryson, she was alarmed at how much the weather had worsened.

The chilly mist had changed to a thick sleet that clung to the window and partially obscured her view of the mountains.

Maybe Bryson wouldn't be able to make it back. And even if she did, surely they wouldn't be able to take off again. She was both relieved and saddened that she'd most likely have to put off meeting Maggie yet another day. She was getting more anxious by the hour and waiting wouldn't help her break her news more easily.

She was about to find Grizz and reserve her room again when the familiar small plane emerged from the gloom at the end of the airstrip. Bryson hopped down and circled it for a couple of minutes, checking it over, then hurried toward the roadhouse. Karla met her at the door.

"Ready to go?" Bryson shook the sleet from her shoulders and ball cap. "Where's your bag?"

"In *this*? You can't be serious. Is it safe?"

"We'll be fine. Skeeter says the worst of it is still a good bit west and we don't have far to go, but we oughta hustle."

"If you're sure." Trying not to worry, she retrieved her bag from the back of the bar where Grizz had stashed it and followed Bryson to the plane.

CHAPTER NINE

"What has Lars told you?" Karla asked as they strapped themselves into the Cub.

"Pretty much everything." Bryson got clearance for takeoff from Skeeter and quickly headed north. Thin ice now coated the plane, and the sleet was still coming down, but the prop was spinning smoothly and she couldn't detect any sluggishness in her controls yet. Certainly not optimum flying conditions, but she'd seen worse. "That you're Maggie's sister, and she was adopted. And about the Alzheimer's. Sorry about your mother."

"Thank you."

"Hope you don't mind that he told me, but I'm close to both of them, and Lars wanted some advice on what he should say to Maggie."

"No, it's okay. What's he going to tell her?"

"That you're a visiting nurse, and he thought it'd be a good idea to invite you out to stay for a few days so you could help them know what to do when the baby comes."

"That's good."

Bryson glanced into her mirror. Karla was staring out the window, looking anxious. Bryson wondered whether it was due to her imminent meeting with Maggie or the storm raging outside. Probably both. They were flying only a couple hundred feet off the ground because of the low cloud ceiling, and occasionally a wind gust shook the plane like an angry fist. In a few minutes, they'd be navigating through the narrow canyons of the river, which would do nothing to help calm Karla's distress. She felt sorry for the woman and a little ashamed at how quickly she'd jumped to conclusions about her during their first meeting. Karla was dealing with a lot. No wonder she'd been so self-absorbed and agitated about getting to Bettles. "Nervous about meeting your sister?"

"Very. How do you think Maggie will react?"

"Hard to predict," she said honestly. "Under normal circumstances, Maggie's real even-keeled. She doesn't make snap judgments. She weighs things in her mind before she acts. And I know family is real important to her." A sudden downdraft dropped the plane ten feet. She heard Karla gasp, but continued in a calm voice, as if it'd been nothing. "I'm sure Lars told you she's kind of touchy these days. Sobbing like crazy one minute and throwing things the next. Guess that's something you're familiar with, huh?"

"Yeah. Very common with pregnant women," Karla said distractedly as another gust shook the plane. "Are we okay? I mean, is this normal?"

"Nothing to worry about. Just a little turbulence."

"I don't know how you can do this every day." Karla leaned forward and stared over Bryson's shoulder through the front windshield. They were coming up fast on the first narrow valley. "Holy shit! Watch out."

"Chill, huh? It's scary the first time, but we gotta fly through the canyons because of the clouds. I've done this route hundreds of times, and believe me, I could do it in my sleep." The Cub entered the deep gorge, the cliffs on either side no more than thirty feet from each wing tip. Bryson was too busy steering the plane to be able to look back at Karla. "Try to think of something else. We'll be through before you know it."

Bryson heard an obscenity from behind her, then another sound that disturbed her even more: a change in the whirr of the prop, a slight laboring in its normally smooth rhythm. The buildup of ice was getting worse.

"I hate this, hate this, *hate* this." Karla's voice betrayed the extent of her alarm. "This is what I get for jumping headfirst into something without thinking it through. I must be crazy."

"Maybe it's not something you ordinarily do." Bryson kept her voice matter-of-fact. "But if it works out, it'll be worth it in the long run. You won't find a better family than Lars and Maggie."

The irregular cadence of the propeller worsened, and Bryson

was sure that even Karla could detect the change, though she didn't comment on it. Probably was too afraid to.

Her wipers were barely able to keep up with the accumulation of sleet, and her GPS told her they still had ten miles to go to reach her cabin. Bryson took a deep breath and let it out. They wouldn't get there a minute too soon.

❖

"Are you insane?" Maggie's face contorted in anger, and she'd turned such a deep shade of crimson Lars worried about her blood pressure. She lay propped up on pillows on their bed, which occupied the northeast corner of their large, one-room cabin.

"Maggie, sweetheart—"

"Don't you *sweetheart* me, Lars Rasmussen. If you think for a *second* I'm about to allow anyone in here. *Look* at this place!" She spread her arms as if in supplication, and Lars had to admit the chaos was even worse than he feared. Dirty dishes were stacked high in the sink and on every counter. The trash bin overflowed, as did the hamper of dirty clothes, and magazines littered the coffee table and rug beside the bed. The bin of firewood was empty, and the wood floor covered with mud tracks. Maggie had gotten so big and was so easily exhausted she simply couldn't handle anything when he was away beyond keeping herself fed and warm.

"I won't go get her until I have everything all spic-and-span, just the way you like it," he promised. He knew her throwing range so he remained by the door, the only interior spot outside that perimeter. The trio of heavy mugs on the nightstand could do some serious damage to his head.

"Do I *look* like I want to play hostess? I'm a beached whale who sleeps fifteen hours a day and farts uncontrollably. I'm not about to let even a stranger see me like this."

"But honey, she can help us get ready—" The first mug came flying at him, but he ducked in plenty of time and it shattered when it slammed into the heavy wooden door.

"You try to appease me with one more *honey*, *sweetheart*, or *darling*, and your ass is grass, Lars. You'll be sleeping in the shed, I swear to God." Maggie reached for another mug and glared at him, tight-lipped with fury.

Anything he said would only result in more broken crockery, and she'd already busted half of what they owned, so he kept his mouth shut and began to clean up, careful to stay well away from the bed.

Every chore completed seemed to lessen her rage. Once the dishes were done she put down the mug, and she relaxed back against the pillows when he returned the floor to its usual spotless perfection. By the time he finished the laundry, she was sound asleep and snoring lightly. The tasks took three hours, and Bryson and Karla would be wondering what had happened to him and whether he'd be coming back in the skiff. But he didn't dare leave until Maggie gave him clearance. It wouldn't do for her to fling the rest of their dishes at her sister before they were properly introduced.

He approached the bed on tiptoes, like a bomb-disposal expert venturing unprotected toward a case of unstable TNT.

She looked so serene in sleep that at least for the moment she resembled the woman he'd married, and he tenderly stroked her hair away from her face. The thought that within a few years she might lose her memories of their life together made his chest ache. It couldn't be true. He'd always been optimistic, facing any challenge that came his way with hope, resolve, and a deep faith in the power of prayer. He sank to his knees beside the bed and bowed his head, asking God to spare his wife and child this awful future. Tears formed when he imagined looking at Maggie and finding no hint of recognition in her eyes, and a steady stream poured down his cheeks when he pictured himself raising their daughter alone.

When he lifted his head, Maggie was awake and watching him. His obvious distress was so rare that her anger vanished.

"Lars, please don't let my mood swings upset you so. You know I love you. I can't help flying off the handle like that, and you always take the brunt of it. I wouldn't blame you if you're getting fed up with me." She began to cry, which was another frequent side effect of her body's raging hormones. Normally he simply held her when it happened, murmuring reassurances that she'd be back to her old self in no time.

On this occasion, though, he moved into Maggie's arms and rested his cheek against her swollen belly, letting the tears come. Time might not be their friend after all. "I'm just worried about you, Mags." His voice broke.

Maggie's hand caressed his back. "Aw, honey, if it means that much to you, you can bring that nurse here to stay with us."

❖

The groaning of the engine's battle to turn the icy prop worsened every minute, and the controls grew increasingly sluggish with the added weight on the fuselage. Bryson's biceps strained with her effort to keep the plane steady, as she mentally ticked off the familiar landmarks passing beneath the Cub. When they emerged from the canyons and into the final stretch of river leading to her cabin, she breathed only a little easier. Setting down on the short gravel bar with the plane responding so poorly would be a challenge.

Karla either hadn't uttered a word in the last several minutes, or the noisy engine had kept Bryson from hearing. And she'd been concentrating so intensely on getting them down in one piece that she hadn't made any further effort to talk.

"We're here," she hollered back over her shoulder as they descended the final fifty feet. "Fasten yourself in tight. Gonna be bumpy."

That turned out to be an understatement, for in the days she was away, the river had risen, depositing a variety of branches and a medium-sized spruce on a smaller-than-usual landing strip. Steering over the obstacles that the plane's turbo tires could handle, and around the ones they could not, was like trying to drive a cement truck full speed through a short and narrow, twisting hallway.

One of the bumps was so bone-jarring only their seatbelts kept their heads from hitting the roof. Karla cried out, and Bryson cursed. But they came to a stop finally, with the front tires inches from the water's edge.

Neither of them moved for several seconds. When Bryson cut the engine, she could hear Karla's loud, erratic breathing behind her. She loosened her belt and turned to face her. Karla's face was white and her eyes were glassy, as if she was in shock. "You okay?"

"You...you..." Karla licked her lips. "You can't tell me that was a normal landing."

"Well, no. But we're fine. Sit tight for a minute and I'll get you inside."

She retrieved Karla's duffel bag, towed her Cub away from the water's edge, and secured its tie-downs with some hefty rocks. By the time she went to help Karla out, her color had returned to normal. But she still looked so unsteady on her feet that Bryson kept an arm around her waist as they waded the shallows and headed up the trail to the cabin.

As they neared the front door, Bandit appeared out of the mist and dive-bombed them with a loud *croak*. Karla screamed and buried her face against Bryson's chest.

"Don't mind him. He's a pest, but not dangerous, just hungry."

She settled Karla on the couch and went out to start up the generator and gather a load of wood. Once she got the lights on and a fire blazing in the woodstove, she helped Karla out of her coat and boots and wrapped her in a thick quilt. "Some tea?"

"Yes, thanks." Karla rubbed her hands together beneath the quilt to warm them, grateful to be out of the Cub and on safe ground again. She'd never been more afraid, and her heartbeat had only just returned to normal.

She studied the cabin and its owner. While Bryson looked every bit a modern-day woman, albeit the outdoorsy type, her home resembled something out of *Little House on the Prairie*. The entire living space was not much larger than the living room of her Atlanta apartment, and most of the furniture and cabinetry was of the primitive, hand-hewn variety, though a skilled woodworker had crafted it. The couch on which she sat was rough pine, padded by a futon mattress. Simple pine end tables flanked it, and a matching low coffee table in front held a small stack of books and copies of *National Geographic* and *Alaska Magazine*. A pine chair with a smaller futon sat perpendicular to the couch, opposite a rocker.

A small square table and three chairs created an intimate eating area in one corner of the room, in front of an L-shaped counter with a sink and several cabinets. As she expected, there was no refrigerator, microwave, or conventional oven, only the woodstove at the end of one of the counters. But something else was missing in the tiny kitchen—a faucet above the sink. No running water, either? Unimaginable. How did Bryson do her dishes, wash her face, take a bath?

Bryson lifted a stout iron teakettle from the woodstove and filled it with a dipper from a large oak barrel by the door. When they arrived, Karla saw a massive galvanized tub leaning against the porch, which evidently explained the bathing aspect, and the laundry one too.

Bryson had told her she liked to read, which was certainly evident. In lieu of a television, the wall opposite the couch was filled with built-in bookshelves. Pine again, and jammed with several hundred books and a few animal figurines.

There were other primitive touches. Though an electric floor lamp behind the couch and a ceiling lamp in the center of the room provided the current light, Karla also spotted a trio of old-fashioned kerosene lamps, their blackened chimneys indicating they were well-used. The quilt Bryson had covered her with looked Amish-made, and the cookware hanging from pegs in the kitchen was cast-iron, like the stuff carried on covered wagons in old Westerns.

Bryson either slept on the futon or somewhere in the loft, which took up half the cabin and was accessed by a plain wooden ladder.

The home was unlike any she'd ever been in, but it was cozy. The fire in the woodstove was cheery and efficient, and colorful rugs adorned the wood floor. One wall featured a grouping of photographs, nearly all of them aerial views of the Alaskan landscape, and another held ornate masks presumably carved by local natives.

"What you expected?" Bryson sat beside her holding two steaming mugs of tea and a small jar of honey.

"Kind of. It's pretty much fits the lifestyle you described. But I didn't imagine it would feel so...I don't know...snug."

Bryson smiled. "Glad you think so. Have to say, you get a special satisfaction from living in a place you built yourself."

"You built this cabin?" She glanced about again, viewing the structure in a new light, critically assessing the tight construction of the walls and roof and the smooth perfection of the floor. Bryson must have done a lot of backbreaking work and have considerable skill in carpentry.

"Lars helped move some of the big logs. But, yeah, I did most everything alone. Took most of a year."

"I'm impressed. I can hardly drive a nail in straight."

"My pop taught me." Bryson sipped her tea. "He was a hell of a craftsman. Built the cabin I grew up in, which was a good bit bigger than this one. And during breakup and in bad weather, he made furniture. Almost everything in here is his, 'cept the rocker. That's an heirloom handed down to my mother."

"You're lucky." Karla well understood what a comfort such treasures could be in dealing with the loss of a parent. She kept her mother's tigereye necklace with her always, in her pocket, and pulled it out often to caress its smooth surface. Doing so gave her strength and a sense of calm, as though her mother had somehow endowed the stone with her energy and love. "Must be nice to have all this to remember your father by."

Bryson ran her hand lovingly along the polished armrest of the couch. "Sure is. I can remember him making every single piece. One of my favorite things used to be watching him take a rough log and turn it into something."

"So you're a pilot and a carpenter. Any other hidden talents?"

Bryson's cheeks colored slightly. "If you mean what else occupies my time, mostly music. I play drums now and then with a little group at the Den and also dabble in photography, but I'm still learning."

"Did you take those?" She indicated the grouping of aerial photos. "They're quite good."

The blush deepened. "Well, it's hard not to get a few keepers when you have these awesome views. What do you do, besides your work as a nurse?"

"Nothing worth mentioning. My friend Stella and I play tennis and golf, though neither of us is very good at either. It's just an excuse to get outside and exercise."

"Lots of good places to hike around here. You should see some of the scenery."

"I may do that if I stick around a while. Which all depends on whether Maggie will want me to." The room had warmed enough for her to comfortably shed the quilt. She rose and walked to the front window. It was growing dark, but the storm was still intense. "Do you think Lars will make it back to get me?"

"Sleet won't stop him. The skiff has lights and a covered cockpit, and he's seen a lot worse, believe me."

"Shouldn't he be here by now?"

"Give him time. He's gotta smooth things with Maggie, and I bet he has to pick up the place. She's kind of a neat freak, and it's been tough for her to keep up with everything the last month or so."

"The cleanliness bug must be hereditary." Karla chuckled. "Mom was, too, and I tend to be that way myself."

"I'm curious to see what else you two have in common."

"You and me both. You can't imagine how weird it is to suddenly find out you have a sister you never knew about."

"Couldn't have a better one than Maggie. She's one of the sweetest women I know." Bryson smiled. "At least when she's not pregnant."

Karla returned to the couch. "That bad, huh?"

"Let's just say Lars has learned to tread *very* lightly around her these days. She's become fond of throwing dishes and food at him."

"I hope she's okay with the idea of my coming to stay with them."

Bryson leaned her head against the back of the futon and stretched out her legs. "Lars'll make it all right."

Maybe Karla had judged Bryson a little too harshly. Her home and interests reflected an artistic, sensitive soul, one who cared deeply about animals and the environment. She was evidently very loyal to her friends, and now here she was, putting up a stranger and helping pave the way for her meeting Maggie, without asking anything in return. Looking back on her own behavior the night before, Karla realized she'd practically bullied Bryson into taking her along. *And what right did I have to discount the importance of her supplies? Maybe fresh orange juice and Oreos don't seem like much to me, but I bet I'd feel differently if I couldn't run down to the corner store and get them whenever I wanted.* She'd give her the benefit of the doubt and chalk it up to a bad first impression, heightened by fatigue and preoccupation.

Why, then, didn't such an attractive woman have a partner? Sure, she lived primitively, and out in the middle of nowhere, but the cabin was warm and welcoming. Why hadn't someone snapped her up long before now?

The waitress at the Den and the gate attendant in Fairbanks both had shown a definite interest in Bryson, but neither seemed to have captured her attention. Had she had an Abby in her life too, someone who'd broken her heart and left her unable to trust again?

CHAPTER TEN

Looks like he's been held up," Bryson said, when an hour had passed with no sign of Lars. "I'm starving. You?"

"No, thanks. I had a sandwich back at the Den, and my stomach is in knots from the thought of meeting Maggie."

"Understandable." Bryson went to the kitchen and pulled down a deep iron skillet hanging from a peg over the sink. She poured some oil into it and set it on the woodstove. "Think you'll change your mind, though, when you get a whiff of this. Nothing like moose stew to warm you up on a chilly night."

"*Moose*?"

Bryson knelt by a trapdoor in a corner of the cabin and pulled out a square plastic food container. Bits of hay were stuck to it. "Made a batch the other night that'll warm up quick. Moose tastes kinda like beef, only more tender, and it's better for you than any steak you'd buy. Not much fat. No additives."

"If you say so. But I still think I'll pass."

"Suit yourself. Don't know what you're missing." Bryson dumped the contents of the container into the skillet and stirred it with a big wooden spoon. "Up here we eat a lot of it, along with salmon and caribou. Regular groceries have to be trucked or flown in, so they're about double what you probably pay."

"Well, if you get a craving for something you can't find here, let me know. When I get home, I'll ship it to you. To say thanks for what you've done for me."

Bryson looked up from her cooking with a surprised smile. "Might take you up on that. How long you staying, by the way? Any chance you'll be here until the baby's born?"

"Probably not that long. But my job would be okay with it. I'm on a leave of absence right now, and I've accrued a lot of vacation time. It all depends on whether Lars and Maggie want me to."

"Bet they will. Not much in the way of trained medical help around. Lars would feel better having a nurse close by right now."

The moose stew smelled better than it sounded. Karla's stomach rumbled when Bryson returned to the couch with a large bowl of the stuff.

"Hungrier than you thought, huh?" Bryson grinned. "Come on, live dangerously. Least take a taste and see how you like it." She held out the bowl.

"Just to satisfy my curiosity." Karla scooped out a small spoonful. Then a larger one, just to make certain it was as fabulous as her taste buds said it was. "Okay, I'm sold. Do you have enough for me?"

"Plenty. Keep that. I'll get another." Bryson ladled herself a portion and they sat side by side on the couch, eating in easy silence until both bowls were empty.

While Bryson did the dishes, Karla perused the titles in her bookshelves. The wide assortment of nonfiction included books on flying, Alaska, wildlife, and the environment, but most were novels, sorted according to type. Four shelves of mysteries, five of suspense and intrigue, five more that appeared to be romances, and...*what do we have here?* Eight shelves of lesbian literature. The representation was impressive, especially considering where she lived. Most of Karla's personal favorites were included.

Bryson's extensive library indicated she was a bright, inquisitive woman with a definite fondness for old-fashioned romanticism, and once again Karla wondered why she didn't have a partner. She turned to study Bryson, who was stowing their bowls back in a cabinet.

It'd been years since she'd really looked at another woman with *that* kind of assessment, but it didn't take long to judge Bryson as prime material. She was easy to talk to, had a good sense of humor, and she exuded an open honesty that was refreshing, especially after Abby's duplicity. And it certainly didn't hurt that Bryson looked as though she'd just stepped off a recruiting poster for sexy hot pilots who can take you places you've never been before.

Yes, Bryson was quite a catch. Karla could see that now. And though her current scrutiny had been born out of a general curiosity about why Bryson was single, it was igniting something very personal. With everything else she had to deal with, Karla would not have thought herself capable of sexual fantasies about anyone right now. But there was something raw and intensely alive about Bryson that jerked her from the numb fog of her grief. She felt guilty enjoying a long, lingering look at Bryson's exquisitely toned physique, but she also felt a ripple of happiness. Something had stirred inside her, if only briefly, reminding her that it was possible to heal. She wasn't broken, just bruised.

"You said Lars told you pretty much everything. Did he include the fact that you and I have something in common?"

Bryson paused and looked at her, forehead furrowed. "We do?"

A sharp rap on the door precluded any further discussion. Bryson went to admit Lars, who shook a heavy coating of sleet from his clothes before he stepped inside.

"Hey, ladies."

"Wondering if you'd make it back tonight." Bryson took his coat and hung it from a peg by the door as Lars walked to the woodstove to warm his hands.

"It took a while to get Maggie to agree to have a houseguest." He smiled encouragingly at Karla. "Place was a mess, and I had to clean it up first. Plus I think she was a little stir-crazy, cooped up a couple days without me."

"But she's all right with it?" Karla asked as she and Bryson both reclaimed their seats on the couch.

"Yeah. I convinced her having a nurse around for a few days would make me more comfortable about having the baby at home." He took the futon chair and stretched his legs out in front of him. "I was thinking on the way, how will you avoid telling her about the Alzheimer's? She'll want to know how your mom died. She can't have been very old."

"No, she wasn't. She died just a couple weeks before she would have turned fifty-seven." The memory of her mother in the coffin, dressed in her cream-colored birthday dress, flashed into her mind, and she prayed that one day it wouldn't be the first image she recalled at the mention of her name. That she could remember first the way she laughed at Karla's adolescent knock-knock jokes, or the proud look on her face whenever she brought home a report card with straight A's.

"Even though it was the Alzheimer's that really killed her—it shuts down the functions of the brain, which impacts the rest of the body—the cause of death was listed as probable heart failure. I didn't want to have an autopsy done. It wasn't necessary. So that's all I'll tell Maggie for now. That she passed away in her sleep, very suddenly. If she asks me questions about the last few years, what Mom was like, or anything—well, I'll just have to deal with those as they come."

"Okay," Lars said. "I hate having to hide this from her. It tears me up, really, because we've always been completely honest with each other. But I don't want her worrying about this right now. It might hurt her or the baby. Could it?"

"Stress can profoundly impact the body. It can compromise your immune system, disrupt sleep, impact the digestive tract, cause all sorts of other issues. It's definitely best to wait to tell her."

"Anything I can do?" Bryson offered.

"Not for me," Karla said. "Thanks for the ride and the hospitality."

"I'll give you a ring if I can use some backup with Mags," Lars told Bryson as he got to his feet. "Karla, you ready to do this?"

"Guess I better be." Her heart began to pound. The time had finally come. She took her coat and bomber cap from the peg by the door and put them on, trying not to appear as nervous and unsteady on her feet as she felt.

"I'll walk you down." Bryson reached for her coat as Lars did the same.

They trooped down the trail in silence, Lars in the lead carrying Karla's duffel. The ground was white, and the sleet was still pelting down hard.

As Lars tossed her bag on deck and climbed up to start the engine, Karla felt a tug at her elbow and turned to face Bryson. It was too dark to make out her features clearly.

"Good luck," Bryson said. "I mean that. Sorry we kinda got off on the wrong foot."

"That was much more my fault than yours, Bryson." Karla was grateful for the darkness, because she could feel the burn of shame and embarrassment on her face and neck. She'd so misjudged Bryson. "I can see why Lars and Maggie think so highly of you. Sorry I was such a bitch last night. Got a lot on my mind, not that that's any excuse."

Bryson's voice softened. "No problem. I know you've had a rough go lately, but keep your chin up. Maggie's the best. So's Lars. Things are looking up for you. I know it."

Karla let Lars help her into the skiff and waved good-bye to Bryson as they headed upriver, feeling a bit like she was letting go of a life preserver before she'd reached safe water. She hoped to God Bryson was right.

❖

Bryson stood at the edge of the river long after the skiff had disappeared from view. *You're not so bad after all, Karla Edwards.* Except for Lars and Maggie, Karla had been the first person she'd had in her cabin in months, and though brief, the visit had reinforced her growing sense of isolation and loneliness.

She wasn't looking forward to freeze-up, the fast-approaching period when flying home would be impossible for days, perhaps weeks. She could stay in Bettles for the interim as she usually did—certainly the best option business-wise. Though all backcountry travel was suspended, she could continue to run flights to any improved airstrips. And staying in the Den gave her limitless opportunities to socialize with friends.

Or she could remain at home, where her only possibility for interaction with others would be a long hike to see Maggie and Lars. And Karla, if she stuck around. They might need me, she told herself. Not that she'd had any medical training beyond basic first aid, or any experience whatsoever with babies. But with Maggie virtually incapacitated, perhaps Lars could use a hand with cooking or cleaning. Or chopping wood and doing laundry.

The decision came more easily than she expected. Lars and Maggie had been there for her more times than she could count, and she would stay put and return the favor. As she trudged back up the trail to her cabin, she realized that sticking close to home would also likely entail spending more time with Karla, and that prospect wasn't quite as disagreeable as it had been. *Darn. Meant to ask her what it is we have in common.*

❖

Karla huddled near the boat's tiny heater as they sped toward the Rasmussen cabin. Lars's boat was a well-equipped skiff more than twenty feet long. Fishing rod mounts ringed the open rear half of the vessel. The front half, containing two padded chairs and twin side benches, was protected by a hard top—a rigid metal-and-glass enclosure that shielded its occupants from inclement weather on all sides.

"How're the nerves?" Lars had to speak up to be heard over the sound of his outboard motor.

"I'm about to jump out of my skin. It seems like months, not days, that I've been thinking about meeting Maggie."

"Well, the time's come. Just around the next bend. You going to tell her right off the bat you're her sister?"

"I kind of want to get it over with. What do you think?"

"Play it by ear. See how she is. One thing to think about, it's getting kind of late, and she'll have a lot of questions. Don't want her up all night, she needs her sleep."

"Good point." They rounded a curve, and Karla saw a vast black stretch of open water ahead.

"Wild Lake," Lars announced. "We're almost there."

Karla spotted the welcoming beacon of lights from a cabin in the distance now, on the left bank of the massive lake, nestled among the trees a short hike from the shore. The valley was wider here than at Bryson's place, the tall mountains on either side more than a mile apart. The pitch-black of the forest that surrounded the lake seemed absolute and impenetrable.

"Home, sweet home." Lars cut the outboard and the skiff came to rest against a pair of log posts that had been set a few feet from the shoreline. Tires had been fixed to the posts to protect the boat, and large metal rings were set on top to secure rope lines fore and aft.

Lars got the skiff squared away, then helped Karla down onto a ramp of rough boards that led to shore. The sleet had turned to snow, fat heavy flakes that clung to her face, but she barely noticed. They stood staring up at the cabin, perched on higher ground a few hundred feet in the distance. Was Lars as nervous and apprehensive as she was? Karla's heart had become such a runaway jackhammer in her chest she found it difficult to breathe.

She reached into her pocket and palmed the tigereye necklace. It gave her courage. "Let's do it."

Her first glimpse of her sister as she came through the door behind Lars was of Maggie in profile. She was sitting in an overstuffed chair, feet propped up on a padded stool and head slightly to the side because she'd obviously fallen asleep while waiting for them. Lars had said he'd left Maggie propped up in bed in a bathrobe, but she must have been determined to greet her new houseguest properly, for she'd dressed in green sweatpants and a sweatshirt, the latter embroidered with Michigan State Spartans. Both garments clearly belonged to Lars, because Maggie had rolled up the cuffs and sleeves, and they were still baggy on her except for the material stretched tight around her extended belly. On her feet, beneath badly swollen ankles, was a pair of thick, fuzzy, pink socks.

Karla registered several facts at once. Maggie's hair, which cascaded below her shoulders, matched the curly red locks she'd found among her mother's things. Her forehead was higher than her mother's, but the nose was the same—long and straight, with a slight upturn at the end.

And she and their mother shared another trait—both were sound sleepers. The door squeaked loudly when Lars shut it, and he spoke in a normal tone of voice when he asked to take her coat and hat and told her to make herself at home. But Maggie didn't stir until Lars knelt beside her and caressed her arm. "Honey? Mags?"

Karla crossed the room slowly toward them, her gaze fixed on Maggie's face. She tried to will her hands to stop trembling, and when they refused, she thrust them into the pockets of her jeans. Her palms were slick with sweat but her mouth was dirt dry, and she was having trouble thinking clearly. The whole experience seemed surreal, like she'd stepped onto a movie set. Time seemed to freeze in those few seconds while Maggie came awake.

And then she was looking directly into a pair of eyes with that same unusual color—hazel with tiny gold flecks—that all the women in her family had been born with. *Grandmother, Mother, Maggie, and me. Sounds like a child's nursery rhyme.* Maggie had the oval face, too.

Karla's breath caught in her throat when Maggie smiled and she saw her mother's dimpled left cheek. They were definitely sisters.

"Mags, this is Karla Edwards." Lars was still on his knees beside her. "Karla, I'd like you to meet Margaret June Rasmussen. My Maggie."

Maggie flashed him a look of annoyed bewilderment, which told Karla he rarely, if ever, introduced her by her full name. Then she turned her full attention back to Karla. "Hi, Karla. Welcome." She leaned forward and stuck out her hand, and Karla wiped the sweat off her palm as she withdrew hers from her pocket to shake hello. She wanted so much to prolong the contact, but forced herself to keep it brief and casual.

"It's great to meet you, Maggie." Her voice sounded several notes higher than normal. Not surprising, she thought, since her throat, like the rest of her, was as tense as a bowstring. "I really appreciate your letting me stay with you."

"We should be thanking you." Maggie smiled, showing that dimple again, and rubbed her swollen belly. "I'm getting so close now, it'll be nice to have someone around who can answer our questions. Oh, we've talked to the doctor and the midwife. But we're always thinking of something we forgot to ask."

"I'm glad to help in any way I can." Karla had to force herself not to stare at Maggie for more evidence of their family linkage. She didn't want her to suspect she was anything but a random visitor, yet. The fact that Maggie had been asleep when they'd arrived convinced her they should keep her news until morning. So she glanced around the cabin instead, taking it in, comparing it to Bryson's.

It was larger by several feet and similarly constructed, one large room with a kitchen in the corner, a woodstove, and a loft. And like Bryson's, a large portion of the space was dedicated to the "living room," with a couch, two chairs, and accompanying tables. But their bed was on the ground floor, tucked into a corner, and they had more modern amenities than Bryson: a stereo, small refrigerator, and stove. Far more electric lights—their pair of kerosene lamps was on a high shelf, as though rarely used. And there was a second door, at the rear of the cabin. It looked far less formidable than the front door and had louvers along the length of it, which indicated it didn't lead outside. *A bathroom?*

The warm, homey touches everywhere gave her some insights into the Rasmussens and their interests. Native Alaskan handcrafts dominated: the rugs, pottery, and masks hanging on two walls fine examples of unique totem art. Several carved ivory figurines stared up at her through a glass dome in the middle of the coffee table, all of them denizens of the north: otters, walrus, polar bear, snowy owl, moose, caribou. Several small framed photographs, mostly of the couple with various nature backgrounds, sat here and there on available surfaces.

Like Bryson, the Rasmussens were evidently avid readers, though they'd devoted about half as much shelf space in their cabin to books, the rest occupied by an extensive CD collection. "You have a lovely home. I didn't know it was possible to have so many modern conveniences, living so far away from everything."

"We have to burn a lot of fuel to keep the generator going all the time," Lars said. "But unlike Bryson, we want to make life up here as easy as we can. Especially now."

"Speaking of, Lars, can you brew me some chamomile tea?" Maggie asked. "Make yourself comfortable, Karla. What would you like? Tea? Coffee?"

"Chamomile tea sounds wonderful." Karla settled onto the end of the couch by Maggie's chair as Lars went to the kitchen.

"Is this your first visit to Alaska?"

Maggie's voice didn't betray that anything was amiss, but Karla was watching her so intently, she noticed her small wince of discomfort when she shifted her weight to turn in her direction.

"What's wrong, Maggie?"

"I've started getting cramps in my legs, especially at night." Maggie grimaced. "They wake me up sometimes."

"How bad are they? How often do you get them?" While such muscle spasms were not uncommon in the latter stages of pregnancy, they could indicate a blood clot somewhere deep in the body.

"Now and then, maybe one or two a week. They're not that bad, they go away pretty fast. But it always takes me a while to get back to sleep."

"I don't think they're anything to be concerned about unless they get worse or more frequent." Karla knelt down beside her. "Where is this one?"

"Left calf."

"Flex your toes toward your head," she instructed, as she began to massage the area. "Sometimes an ice pack will help, or heat. And you should make sure you're drinking plenty of fluids. I can show you some stretching exercises tomorrow you can do before bedtime that might help you sleep through the night."

"That's better already." Maggie leaned back in the chair and sighed. "I think I'll be really happy you're staying with us."

Karla hoped to hell Maggie felt the same when she found out who she really was. "Glad I could help." She returned to the couch as Lars came over with two mugs of tea.

"Told you, Mags." He leaned down to kiss her forehead as he handed Maggie her mug. "And it gives Karla a nice chance to see some of the real Alaska. I bet Bryson will take her out. Show her around." He returned to the kitchen for his own mug and sat beside Karla.

The words *Bryson will take her out* conjured up a host of pictures in Karla's mind, none of which involved hiking in Alaska. Instead, she envisioned them on a real date, laughing together over a nice meal, going to a movie, and ending up naked somewhere. She rubbed her eyes, trying to shake off the images and return her attention to the conversation at hand. She was just exhausted and confused, she told herself, that was all, and seeking some balm for the ego Abby had shattered.

"Oh, that'd be nice," Maggie was saying. "No one knows the area better. So it *is* your first time here, then?"

"Yes, and it's certainly been an eye-opening experience so far. So different from home—I live in Atlanta."

"What made you decide to visit Bettles? And at this time of year. Most folks tend to come during the summer."

Good question. How could she answer without giving away her real reason? She fumbled for an answer, realizing she was taking longer than she probably should have. "I needed to get away for a while and sort out some recent changes in my life." She shrugged. "Choosing to come here was kind of an impulse."

"A lot of people find the wilderness a good place to think things out." Maggie fought back a yawn. "Lucky for us you picked where you did."

"Honey, you look exhausted," Lars said. "Why don't you let me help you to bed, and I'll get Karla settled upstairs."

"I'm not being a very good hostess, I'm afraid." Maggie frowned apologetically.

"Nonsense." Karla smiled at her, once again struck by the similarity in their unique eye color. Maggie hadn't seemed to have noticed. "You've been splendid. I'm very grateful for your hospitality. And Lars is right, you should get your rest. We'll chat some more tomorrow."

"I look forward to it." Maggie allowed Lars to support her as she rose and walked unsteadily to their bed.

Karla slept fitfully. The twin bed Lars showed her to in the loft was comfortable enough, but her mind churned for hours, mulling over what she was going to tell Maggie. She had been so warm and welcoming, but would she remain so when she found out her parents had lied to her all her life? Karla certainly knew firsthand how upsetting that could be.

And she couldn't get over the physical similarities between Maggie and her mom. Finding so many had been bittersweet. Though it was wonderful to see traces of her mother in Maggie's face, the grief she felt was still so fresh they made her miss her all the more.

What disturbed her sleep the most, however, were the visions of Bryson that invaded her dreams. However briefly, they were able to dispel all the worry and sadness that crowded her waking hours, but they stirred up other feelings that were equally disquieting. How could she feel such longing for a woman she barely knew?

The howling of wolves near the cabin awakened her shortly before dawn, a cacophony of yowls and yipping sounds, like they were on a chase. Karla buried herself beneath the thick comforter. They sounded very close. As anxious as she was to see some of the local scenery, how safe could it be with grizzly bears and wolves and who knew what else lurking about? Perhaps Lars was right. Maybe it was best to have a guide like Bryson along. And maybe spending more time with Bryson would help her sort out why she couldn't get her out of her mind.

CHAPTER ELEVEN

The cabin was still dark when Karla heard the first sounds of movement from below. A light came on in the kitchen, and she was able to see the top of Lars's head from where she lay. She dressed in the clothes she'd worn the night before and climbed down the ladder to find him brewing a pot of coffee.

"Good morning." She kept her voice low, because Maggie's soft snores indicated she was still asleep. "What time is it?"

"Morning to you, too." Lars yawned and scratched his stubble of blond beard. "Almost nine, and you don't have to whisper. Maggie can sleep through a tornado. Coffee?"

"Love some. With milk or cream if you have it." She looked out the window, but it was still pitch-black. She couldn't tell whether the snow had stopped. "I can't believe how late the sun rises here."

"Dawn's not for another hour." Lars poured two cups and brought one over to her. "In a couple of months, it'll be dark until noon, and sunset's only a couple hours later. Those are our hardest months. Not a lot to do and too cold to be outside much. Real easy to get cabin fever."

"You'll have a lot to keep you occupied this winter with a new baby." Karla glanced over at the bed to reassure herself Maggie was still sleeping. "Did Maggie say anything about me last night after I went up to bed?"

He grinned. "Yeah. She said she liked you right off, and that she shouldn't have given me such a hard time about letting you come. Getting rid of her leg cramp was a nice way to break the ice."

"I hope she still likes me when she finds out we're sisters."

Lars laid a hand on her shoulder. "I don't think you have to worry. But just to make sure you have as much going for you as possible, I'd say wait until after breakfast. She wakes up like a starving bear coming out of hibernation."

"What can I do to help? I really want to pitch in while I'm here."

"If you know your way around a kitchen, you're hired, 'cause I can barely boil an egg. How're you at making pancakes?"

❖

"If Lars had told me you could cook like this, I'd have begged him to bring you." Maggie sighed with contentment as she pushed her plate away, no trace remaining of the large stack of pancakes and reindeer sausage Karla had whipped up. "How long can you stay?"

Karla laughed. "I'm no Rachael Ray, but I'm glad you liked it."

"Who's Rachael Ray?" Lars and Maggie asked in chorus.

No television, idiot. "Not important."

"I'll take care of the cleanup, if you two want to adjourn to the comfy chairs and get acquainted," Lars said, smiling encouragingly at Karla.

"Sounds like a great idea to me." Maggie braced her hands on the table and pushed herself up. "And it's not looking like a good day for you to be out sightseeing, anyway."

Karla followed her gaze to the front window. The sun had come up but the sky was overcast, and it was snowing heavily. There seemed little chance she would be seeing Bryson soon, and she couldn't help feeling disappointed. "How long do you think it will last?"

"No telling." Maggie shuffled slowly toward her overstuffed chair, rubbing her stomach. "An hour, a day, a week. Weather forecasts here are virtually useless."

Karla went to the window to try to gauge how much snow had fallen. At least four or five inches, she guessed. She saw no trace of their tracks from the night before, and the branches of the spruce trees around the cabin were bending under the weight of the accumulation. With the surrounding mountains providing a majestic backdrop, the scene was serenely beautiful, a Christmas card come to life.

Though the weather might keep her from spending time with Bryson, even if Maggie wanted her to leave, travel was impossible.

Nature was allowing her time to convince her sister to accept what she'd come to tell her.

As she turned from the window and walked slowly toward Maggie, she was startled by how calm she felt. In the blink of an eye, her trepidation had melted away. Her palms were dry, her head was clear. She felt no trace of the trembling that had seized her every time she'd imagined this moment.

She sat on the edge of the couch facing Maggie, but looked behind her at Lars. He was keeping himself busy at the sink, watching them both. He met her eyes and gave a little nod and smile of encouragement.

Maggie half turned to look at him, then back to Karla. "What's going on?"

"I haven't been entirely honest with you," Karla said in a soft voice. She placed a hand on Maggie's knee. "And Lars agreed to keep my secret until I could tell you myself. I waited until this morning because I know you'll have lots of questions, and I didn't want you to lose sleep over it."

Fear came into Maggie's eyes. "Is this about the baby? Is something wrong?"

Lars hurriedly reassured her. "No, no. Nothing's wrong with the baby." He wiped his hands on a towel and came to stand behind Maggie, placing his hands on her shoulders. "Tell her, Karla."

She took a deep breath and let it out. Simple was best. "Maggie, I'm your sister." She sat back and let the news sink in.

Shock. Bewilderment. Maggie's face registered both in quick succession. "What are you talking about? Is this a joke?" She craned her head to look up at Lars. "This isn't funny, Lars. I don't know what you two are up to, but you know damn well I don't have much of a sense of humor right now."

He stooped until they were eye to eye. He wasn't smiling. "It's not a joke, Mags. Karla is your sister. If you just give her a chance to explain—"

"I don't have a sister," Maggie insisted, glaring at him. "You *know* that."

"You were adopted, Maggie." Karla kept her voice as soft as Lars's had been, the same tone she used when giving a patient news they wouldn't want to hear. Maggie's head whipped around and she started to open her mouth in protest, but Karla cut her off. "The Van

Rooys adopted you when you were a baby. Our mother had to give you up. She was very young, just sixteen, and in those days—"

"Stop!" Maggie was red in the face. "Just stop. I don't know where you got this information, but it's not true. I wasn't adopted, and I don't have any brothers or sisters. I had a great relationship with my parents. We were very close, and they wouldn't have deceived me about something like that. Not something that important."

"Believe me, I know how hard all of this to absorb," Karla said. "Especially the idea that your parents lied to you. My mother—*our* mother—lied to me, too, and I would never have thought her capable of it. I didn't find out about you until a week or so ago."

"What's a lie is any claim by *your* mother that I'm not who I *know* I am." Maggie turned to look at Lars. "Get the satellite phone. Let's call her right now. We'll settle this, find out what her motive is."

"We can't do that, Mags." Lars started to stroke her arm, but she jerked away from his touch.

"Get the damn phone!" Maggie was shouting. "I won't listen to any more of this bullshit. I'll get her to tell me the truth."

"Maggie, she died three weeks ago." The image of her mother in the coffin rose again in Karla's mind, and tears sprang to her eyes. When they overflowed, she wiped them away absentmindedly.

Maggie went quiet, her rapid, loud breathing the only sound in the room. She slumped back in her chair and all the fight went out of her. Her eyes were fixed on Karla's. When she finally spoke, she sounded in pain. "I'm sorry for your loss. But I still don't believe this. How are you so sure it's true?"

"My mother left behind a letter explaining everything. It was pretty convincing on its own, but I was certain it was true as soon as I saw you last night. She kept a lock of your hair. It matches. And you have so many of her features. Nose. The shape of your face. That one-sided dimple when you smile. And the color of your eyes. It's the same as hers. As our grandmother's. The same as mine."

Maggie leaned forward, as best as she was able, to compare them for herself, and Karla shifted toward her, until they were only a foot or two apart. Maggie looked intently into her eyes for what seemed like an eternity. Then she leaned back again, her face expressionless. "Exactly what did this letter say?"

Karla had expected this question, so she'd made a photocopy of her mother's note before she left Atlanta. She didn't want anything to happen to the original so she'd put it in her safety-deposit box. And when Lars and she'd decided to withhold the news of her mother's Alzheimer's, she'd tucked away the first of the three pages and torn the second in half. She pulled the remaining portion from her back pocket, unfolded it, and handed it to Maggie, who began to read.

Karla had read the note so often, she'd committed it to memory.

> *I hope you will seek to understand what I have to tell you, and forgive me for not telling you until now.*
>
> *You have a sister.*
>
> *Five years before I met and married your father, I became pregnant. I was only sixteen, still a child myself and naïve about such things, but I fancied myself in love with a boy at school named James O'Hara.*
>
> *After talking with Jim's parents, mine sent me immediately to a home for unwed mothers to have the child and convinced me that it was best for both me and for the baby to give it up for adoption as soon as it was born. It was what girls did then, especially those from Catholic families. I knew from my brief glimpse of her that I'd had a daughter, born healthy and with curly red hair, like her father. Then the nuns took her away.*

Maggie began to cry silent tears halfway through the letter and her hand began to shake. She was completely absorbed in the words, her face registering confusion and incredulity. Karla soon stopped mentally reciting the letter and lost herself in empathy for Maggie.

Neither Karla nor Lars spoke, but Lars, still stooping beside Maggie's chair, put his arm around her shoulders. It took her so long to finish that Karla was certain she'd read it through at least twice.

Finally she looked up at Karla. "My God. It's true."

Chapter Twelve

"Yes, Maggie." She held her breath, studying her sister's face. Maggie looked away, staring off into space, her gaze unfocused. Clearly, she was stunned by what she'd heard and read, and Karla certainly empathized with that reaction. The memory of how she'd felt when she opened the letter was still fresh. What now, she wondered. Did Maggie want her in her family? She couldn't speak the words. It would probably take time for Maggie to come to terms with everything. "Look, why don't I take a walk and give you two some time alone. I realize you have a lot to think about."

Maggie didn't reply or react. Lars put his mouth to her ear and whispered something, but she acted as though he wasn't there.

Karla climbed up to the loft and dug the photo album out of her bag. Then she put on a set of long underwear and redressed, adding a new woolen sweater to her ensemble that she'd forgotten to take the price tag off of. By the time she descended the ladder, Maggie was back in bed and Lars was seated beside her, speaking in low tones.

She gingerly approached them. Maggie still wouldn't look at her, so she offered the album to Lars. "Pictures of our mother."

He took it with a half smile, but his eyes were dark with worry. He set the album down on the bed and turned his attention back to Maggie.

Karla retreated, donned her coat, hat, and boots, and stepped outside, feeling oddly more relaxed than she'd been in ages. Her part was over. The rest was up to Maggie.

She inhaled the crisp, clean air and stepped off the porch into ankle-deep snow. Thick flakes were still showering down and the sky was gunmetal gray. It was eerily quiet, with no hint of movement in the sky or forest around her.

The Rasmussens had an outbuilding like Bryson's, though much larger, nearly half the size of their cabin. The roof on one side extended several feet beyond the building to cover an enormous pile of stacked firewood. And like Bryson, Lars and Maggie also had an outhouse and a small log structure built high off the ground on four long posts, with a narrow ladder leading up to it. A large round thermometer nailed to one of the posts told her it was a couple of degrees below freezing.

The ground had been cleared in a wide circle around the homestead, and the snow cover was nearly pristine, unmarked except for a single set of fresh tracks that ran along one side of the outbuilding and down the trail to the river. She walked over to examine them. Up close, they looked like cat tracks. Smudge, the gray tabby she'd had growing up, often left muddy prints on the kitchen floor and she'd had to clean them up. But these seemed quite a bit bigger than the ones she remembered, at least five inches long by five inches wide.

She followed the paw prints down the trail to the water, where she stood transfixed. Wild Lake was oblong, nearly a mile across and more than six miles long, framed by majestic peaks in all directions. It was snowing so hard the mountains were partially obscured, as though seen through a veil of lace. She detected no sign of any other human habitation.

The tracks led to the water's edge, as if whatever had made them had taken a drink and lingered a moment before heading off to the right, along the shoreline. It seemed as good a way as any to go off exploring a bit. At least she couldn't lose her way. The memory of the wolves howling only hours before made her hesitate briefly, but she felt relatively safe in the daylight. And it was so quiet she was sure she'd be able to hear anything moving toward her from a good distance away.

Though the trail from the cabin had been easy walking, once she got off it the going was more difficult. The snow cover hid an uneven terrain dotted with large rocks and spongy mounds of grassy tundra that hadn't completely frozen, so she had to walk gingerly to avoid twisting an ankle. Every couple dozen steps, she paused to look around because the view was so breathtaking. She'd gone about a half mile when she saw her first sign of movement—a bald eagle, startled from its nest in a high tree near the shoreline ahead. It spread its massive wings and soared gracefully over her, giving her a clear view of its startling white head and tail feathers. She was beginning to understand why Bryson loved Alaska so much, and Lars, and Maggie, too. Why hadn't she remembered to bring her camera?

Karla glanced at her watch. She'd been gone forty minutes and should probably think about starting back. She hoped Maggie cared enough to be concerned about her welfare, even if she wasn't ready to embrace her as family.

The return trip was uneventful until she got within a quarter mile of the cabin. A high-pitched shriek, off in the trees to her left, shattered the quiet that had accompanied her entire journey. She'd never heard anything like it before, but was certain no human had made it. Suddenly uneasy, she hurried as fast as she could, her attention half on the uncertain ground in front of her and half on the woods, seeking any movement. By the time she reached the cabin she was winded.

Karla stepped onto the porch and leaned against the front rail to catch her breath, berating herself for panicking at the first unfamiliar sound. She was tempted not to say anything about it to Lars and Maggie, but she was too curious about what might have caused it not to.

The door opened behind her and Lars stepped out, his coat in his hand. He shrugged into it and joined her.

"How is she?" Karla asked.

"Doing okay, I guess, all things considered." He stared out at the view. The snowfall had diminished to just a few intermittent flakes. "Her emotions have been all over the place anyway, and this yanked the rug right out from under her. She's numb, confused, furious—at her parents, not you. That's the big focus right now. How they could have lied to her about this. She's in there reliving everything they ever told her, calling it all into question."

"I certainly understand how that feels."

"I bet. And that's a good thing. Once she's ready to talk to you about it, maybe your common ground will help her come to terms with it." He faced her. "It may take a while, though. She's got a lot to sort through."

"I spent a good two weeks locked up in my apartment after Mom died because I didn't want to talk to anybody, so I totally relate. And even after all this time, I'm still in kind of a fog, not knowing how to process everything that's happened. Part of my reason for coming here was just to get as far away as I could from everything that constantly reminded me how much my life had suddenly changed. I was hoping distance could give me some perspective."

"Has it?"

"Time will tell. I've been so preoccupied with meeting Maggie, I haven't thought of much else." That wasn't entirely true. The last several hours, anyway, thoughts of Bryson had begun to compete for her attention, but they were largely out of her control. And if anything, they were only adding to her confusion. "I suppose it's too early to ask what Maggie thinks of having me as a sister."

He gave her an apologetic half smile.

The snow had stopped now, and the clouds were thinning enough to let some sunshine through. The thermometer had risen to thirty-three degrees. "Do you think I should make myself scarce? I was thinking about your suggestion to ask Bryson to show me around. Looks like it might turn out to be a nice day after all."

"Maybe not a bad idea. I can call her and see what she's got planned." Lars's gaze followed her tracks down to the river. "So your walk made you want to see some more of our little corner of paradise?"

"For sure." And more of Bryson. "Oh…I was meaning to ask you a couple of things." She pointed to the now-faint impressions that led from the corner of the outbuilding and paralleled her footprints. "I was following some tracks. They looked like cat paw prints, but were bigger than any I've ever seen. About like this." She held up her hand and approximated the distance between her thumb and fingers.

"Probably lynx. We have one that comes through now and then, checking out our woodpile for mice, though we've never seen it. Their paws kind of spread out, to act almost like little snowshoes to keep them from sinking in the snow."

"A lynx?" She vaguely knew what one looked like, but had no idea how big they could get. Cougar sized? "Are they dangerous?"

"Not to people. They're very shy and solitary. Generally they go for things like snowshoe hares, birds, fish. Although now and then they can take a young Dall sheep or caribou, if smaller prey is scarce."

"I heard this really weird noise coming from over there." She pointed. "It was an animal, I think. Kind of a shriek, kind of a scream. Eerie."

"Hmmm. Porcupine, maybe. It's their mating season. Or could have been a raven. They make all sorts of oddball sounds."

A bird or a porcupine, and she'd let it scare the shit out of her. She felt foolish. She had a lot to learn about Alaska and the wilderness, apparently. And a ready teacher was available. "Shall we call Bryson?"

❖

The bath wasn't the long, luxurious soak Karla was used to, but considering the locale, she was grateful for the opportunity to warm up from her walk in a real old-fashioned tub that allowed her to immerse herself completely. Although in terms of bathroom conveniences the Rasmussens had only the traditional outhouse and honeypot—an indoor bucket with seat used in extremely cold weather and emptied frequently—they had the luxury of running water and a bathtub, set up in a small room accessed through the door at the rear of the cabin. Of course the water from the tap was always frigid, since it was piped directly from the river bottom, but it didn't take long to boil enough on the stove to make things comfortable.

Though Maggie wasn't apparently ready to talk to her, Karla had been encouraged to see her going through the photo album. And Maggie had at least said "Good morning" as Lars and she came back inside. *Give her time.*

Spending the day with Bryson would be a welcome distraction from her apprehensions about Maggie's reaction to her news. Her whole Alaskan experience so far had been surreal. To be expected, she supposed, with her emotions all over the place and her surroundings so alien. But most bizarre was the turnaround in her perception of Bryson Faulkner.

Bryson had taken the brunt of the frustration, fatigue, anger, sadness, and grief that had transformed her into some bitch cousin of herself. She replayed in her mind how she'd acted at the Bettles Air gate. No wonder Bryson had been reluctant to take her on as a passenger. She owed that blond gate attendant an apology, too.

She wanted to kick herself because she didn't usually make snap judgments about people. Her appraisal of Bryson as an ass had been incredibly unfair and irrational. Fortunately, she seemed the forgiving type. And the hours ahead would give Karla the opportunity to try to make amends and give Bryson a better impression of who she really was.

Like Bryson, Alaska was really growing on her, much to her surprise and despite the frigid weather, the white-knuckled flying, and the lack of some of the modern conveniences she'd always considered essential. She didn't miss her television or the Internet when there was such a feast for the eyes everywhere she looked. Now she had an idea how humbled the early explorers must have felt at seeing the vast, pristine wilderness of an unexplored and largely uninhabited land. She couldn't wait to see more of it, especially in Bryson's company.

Abby would have hated all of this. She didn't appreciate a beautiful sunset or a simple walk in the park. She'd bitched when the power went out for more than a few minutes or when the satellite reception pixilated because of storms moving through. They had chosen their apartment partially because Abby insisted there be several good restaurants in the area that delivered. And the one time Karla suggested they spend their vacation at a lodge in Yosemite, Abby thought she was kidding. *Are you crazy? What would we do all day? Fight off mosquitoes and stare at trees? I say Vegas or New York. San Francisco. Somewhere with some nightlife and great places to shop.*

Perhaps being here *was* helping her put some things into perspective. Why had she always acceded to Abby's desires, often at the expense of her own wishes and dreams? Abby had been so strong-willed she'd been afraid if she didn't give in, Abby would find someone who would. And Abby had left her anyway. She felt like a fool.

Karla lingered until the water turned lukewarm, then hurriedly toweled off and dressed. The louvers in the door allowed some of the heat from the woodstove to penetrate the inner room, but it was several degrees colder here than in the main living space.

Maggie was still in bed leafing through the photo album when she emerged from her bath. Lars, in the kitchen brewing tea, turned Karla's way and beckoned her with a tilt of his head. "Finally reached Bryson. She's got no plans today and will be happy to take you out and show you around. I'll run you over in the skiff whenever you're ready."

"Great. I'll take a mug of that and then I'm good to go." She glanced over at Maggie as Lars poured her tea and whispered, "Has she said anything more?"

"She sees the resemblances you pointed out between her and your mother. I think it's made it all more real. Here, why don't you take hers over to her?" Lars handed her a second mug.

When she set the chamomile tea down on the nightstand beside the bed, Maggie looked up at her. Her eyes were swollen and red, but she'd dried her tears, and she was contemplating Karla intently in a way she hadn't before, curious and…hopeful? Karla's spirits lifted as she stood patiently waiting under the long scrutiny.

"Sit," Maggie finally said, patting the bed beside her. Karla settled carefully onto the edge within arm's reach and put her mug beside Maggie's.

They studied each other without speaking for several seconds.

"So…sisters, huh?" Maggie said finally, smiling tentatively.

She smiled back. "Yeah. Still sinking in?"

Maggie nodded. "I always wanted a sister."

"Me, too. So much I invented an imaginary one when I was little. Her name was Emily."

"Did you tell your parents about her?"

"Oh, yeah. They used to set a place for her at the table and pretend to tuck her in next to me at night."

Maggie let a long pause elapse as she seemed to mull that revelation over. "So it must have been especially tough on you to find out all these years later you've had one all along."

"I imagine it's pretty much the same as you're feeling. Both our parents lied to us. About things we had a right to know. And I get the impression you didn't think it possible of yours, any more than I did of mine."

"No."

"They've both passed away?"

"Yes. My father was a logger. He was killed in an accident on the job not long after Lars and I married. My mother…" Maggie looked away. Karla knew she'd never view that word again quite the same. "My mother had ovarian cancer. She died four years ago."

"I'm sorry."

When Maggie's eyes met hers again, they were moist with tears, but full of compassion. "Those first few weeks after the funeral were so tough to get through. I imagine you're still feeling like you're on an emotional roller coaster."

"Good way to describe it. The smallest things set me off. A piece of music or picture of someplace we went on vacation. The scent of patchouli. It all comes rushing up and just overwhelms me."

"I know it's a cliché, but time does help," Maggie said. "God knows I still think of them both often and miss them terribly, but with not the same kind of raw ache and terrible emptiness I felt in the months right after."

"I'm sorry you'll never get the chance to meet Mom. Not that I'm excusing what she did. But she was a wonderful woman with a big heart. Smart, and with a wicked sense of humor."

Maggie glanced down at the photo album, which was open to a snapshot of their mother taken when she was in her early forties, just before she'd started showing signs that something was wrong. She was holding a camera up near her face, evidently about to take a picture, but someone had snapped a photo of her instead. She was looking sideways at the photographer with an annoyed but endearing scowl, an expression that said *Oh, don't take that!* "She apparently had her reasons for doing what she did." Karla detected an unmistakable note of bitterness in her voice.

She didn't know how to respond, so she reached for her tea and sipped it, and Maggie did the same.

"I'm so *angry* at all of them," Maggie volunteered. "My parents, and yours." She ran a hand protectively over her swollen belly. "A part of me realizes they were all acting in what they thought were my best interests, at least in terms of the adoption. But the *deception* afterward. The hypocrisy. That'll take a while to accept."

"I certainly understand, I think. If there's anything I can do—"

Maggie put her hand over Karla's. "You came all the way here to tell me this. To meet me and get to know me. That's so much."

"You make me sound unselfish. But I assure you I'm not. I have no family but you now, Maggie."

Maggie smiled broadly for the first time that day, her smile so much like their mother's that Karla's heart ached. "That's not true. Now you have Lars, too. And very soon, a niece." She opened her arms, and Karla slipped into her embrace. They hugged each other tight. "We've lost too many years already," Maggie whispered in her ear. "Let's not waste any more, sis."

❖

Two hours passed in a flash. Karla climbed up onto the bed beside Maggie and went through the photos with her, telling her stories about when and where they were taken, interspersed with other memories of her childhood. They laughed as much as they cried, until finally Lars interrupted them.

"Want me to call Bryson and tell her you'd like to make it another day?" He smiled down approvingly at them.

"Oh, gosh. I completely forgot." Much as she wanted to continue getting to know her sister, Karla was looking forward to seeing Bryson, too, and who knew when the weather would provide her another opportunity. Besides, she wasn't about to be rude to Bryson again. She started to look at her watch but it wasn't there. She'd left it next to the tub. "What time is it?"

"Nearly two," he said. "You have about four hours of daylight left."

Maggie yawned loudly beside her, and Karla remembered that Lars had mentioned she often needed an afternoon nap.

"Since she's expecting me, and since you could probably use a little rest, Maggie, I'll go over for a short visit. But I'll be back in time to cook dinner."

That got a *great* out of Maggie, and a *thank God* out of Lars. They all laughed.

She hugged Maggie, relishing the warmth of her return embrace, and hopped off the bed. By the time she and Lars were suited up in their outerwear and boots, Maggie was settled into the pillows and comforter on her side, her eyes closed and her expression serene.

"I'm happy you two seem to be hitting it off so well," Lars said as he started the engine to the skiff and they started downriver to Bryson's cabin.

"Better than I dared hope." The clouds had fled, and the sun had already melted most of the recent snow. It felt warmer out by several degrees than when she'd returned from her walk. "She asked me how long I can stay."

"And you said?"

"I told her I can probably be here until the baby's born, maybe a little after, if that's what you both want."

He grinned broadly, the relief on his face unmistakable. "I wager she was as delighted to hear that as I am."

On impulse, Karla hugged him. She felt better than she had in weeks. Not only were things going wonderfully with Maggie, she was about to get some quality time to get to know Bryson better. "No happier than I am, Lars. No happier than I am."

CHAPTER THIRTEEN

Bryson was extraordinarily patient under most circumstances, as imperturbable as one of the hundred thousand glaciers that dotted the landscape of the state she loved. The ability to tolerate any lengthy delay with good humor was necessary if you wanted to thrive in Alaska. Every year, she had to endure weeks of breakup and months of minimal sunlight. And she had to wait for endless intervals for the weather to clear so she could take to the air.

But all her patience abandoned her today, and she was pacing back and forth in front of her cabin window. Why was she so anxious for Karla Edwards to arrive? Her initial impression of Karla had been as bad as possible. She'd assessed her as a self-involved, petulant annoyance. But she'd been so damn tired she'd been less than charming herself. And who wouldn't be edgy and preoccupied with herself after flying halfway across the world to meet a long-lost sister, unannounced, still grieving for her mother? She'd actually been quite pleasant during her visit at the cabin. And she was related to Maggie, which somehow made her all right.

It had been a long while since Bryson had looked forward to something so much, felt such a heightened excitement at the thought of spending a few hours in the company of another woman.

But she was being ridiculous. This wasn't a date. Karla hadn't indicated she was even gay, let alone that Bryson was on her radar. And their first meeting had certainly been less than auspicious. Regardless, she hadn't been able to get Karla out of her mind. Why had she remembered things about Karla in vivid detail so often lately? What she looked like, sounded like, even smelled like, for God's sake.

Bryson didn't wear perfume, so she'd immediately picked up Karla's clean citrus-floral scent in the enclosed cabin of the Super Cub.

Had something happened with Maggie? It had been nearly three hours since Lars telephoned, and she'd expected the skiff long before now. On her next pass by the satellite phone, she paused and stared at it, willing it to ring. When it didn't obey, she reached for it and started to punch in Lars's number, then thought better. Things were probably pretty intense over there, and the last thing they needed was an interruption. Karla and Lars would either show up or call. It wasn't like she had a lot else to do. She set the phone back in its cradle.

Too restless to confine her pacing indoors any longer, she grabbed her coat and headed down to the river.

The sun was shining bright against the mountains, but even at its height it rose only fifteen degrees above the horizon these days, so it cast deep shadows over the white-tipped peaks, outlining every jagged outcropping. In addition to the track of the sun, she measured the coming of winter in the amount of snow on her part of the Brooks Range. Each significant snowfall lengthened and stretched the blanket of white, until finally it covered everything above and below: first the mountains, then the forest and tundra, and finally, the rivers and lakes.

Interior Alaska was in that capricious phase of transition, the nights routinely below freezing, the days warm enough to melt any snow that had fallen. The ground had been mostly frozen that morning when she went outdoors to quiet Bandit's noisy tirade with a handful of seeds, but now it was spongy again beneath her feet.

She walked upstream a hundred yards to a large, smooth boulder that frequently served as her perch for casting a line into the water. The rock had a natural depression similar to the curve of a semi-reclined lounge chair, allowing her to relax comfortably for long hours without needing additional padding.

The granite had absorbed enough of the sun's rays to warm her through the thin layer of her jeans. She unzipped her jacket and leaned back against the rock, closing her eyes but attuned to the sound of the skiff's engine.

Where should she take Karla? If the choice were entirely hers, they'd be up in the Cub, flying low over glaciers, seeking a glimpse of caribou. This time of year, the massive Porcupine Caribou Herd, numbering a hundred thousand animals, was often split into two major groups, the nearest one wintering some 180 miles northeast of Bettles near Arctic Village. Seeing the animals up close, whether on land or from the air, never failed to impress outstate visitors. But the round-trip flight would take four hours, which was about how much daylight was left and allowed them no time to find and admire the herd.

Besides, considering Karla's attitude toward bush flying, it was probably better to choose a location within easy walking distance. That still left several possibilities. They could scale Mathews Dome, a relatively easy climb with an amazing panoramic view, or follow the Flat River up to Icy Creek, where the canyon was so narrow the sheer cliffs on either side rose claustrophobically close to the hiker beneath. Another option would be to follow the Wild River south to Madison Creek. She'd often seen moose there in the swampy areas, but that was probably too far away to make it back before dusk.

She caught the subtle chop of the skiff's engine long before the boat came into view. By the time it motored around the bend, she was standing offshore near Lars's usual tie-off spot.

She recognized the royal blue of Karla's down jacket long before she could make out her face; she was standing in the open rear of the skiff. Just as Bryson raised her hand to wave, Karla did likewise, and it warmed her from within to imagine that Karla might be anticipating their visit as much as she was.

The broad smile on Karla's face when the skiff pulled up reinforced that hope and reassured her that things had probably gone well with Maggie.

"Hi," Karla hollered as Lars cut the engine.

"Hi yourself. You look like your visit's been a positive one."

"Couldn't be better." Karla appeared so relaxed and happy she might have been a different woman entirely.

"Maggie's still dealing with the whole adoption thing," Lars said as he secured the boat. "But the two of them were having such a good time getting acquainted, time kind of got away from them."

"Great to hear." Bryson waded across the shallows and offered a hand to help Karla out of the skiff. When Karla took it, she felt a moment of regret that both of them had gloves on. It was silly to be wanting to touch her, even like this. *Get a grip.*

Karla hopped off the skiff, splashing water onto Bryson's jeans, but Bryson didn't care. Karla's expression was so pleased and expectant that it seemed she, too, was determined to push aside their initial friction and start fresh. Bryson was really looking forward to their afternoon together.

❖

"It's impossible to describe this with words." Karla's voice was full of awe as she surveyed the endless wilderness that stretched before them. "Certainly worth the hike getting up here."

The view from the 4,600-foot peak of Mathews Dome was one of Bryson's favorites, for it enabled her to see many miles in all directions: the vast valley of the Wild River as it stretched toward Bettles to the south, the Flat River gorge to the east, and Wild Lake, more than six miles to the northwest. She handed Karla her binoculars and pointed. "You can make out Maggie and Lars's cabin, there—up from that little inlet. See the glint of reflection on the water? That's the skiff."

Karla put the binoculars to her eyes and adjusted the focus. "Oh, yeah, I see it." She followed the shoreline north, surveying the entirety of the long body of water. "They have the whole lake to themselves?"

"A couple of primitive cabins are tucked up in the woods on this side. But only hunters use them, a few weekends a year. And a gold mine's just north of the lake, but it operates only in summer."

"The water is so smooth it looks like glass." Karla handed back the binoculars and sighed with contentment. "I bet you come up here a lot, don't you?"

"Great place to sit and think. You feel so small in such an enormous landscape. Yet still a very integral part of everything. That make sense?"

"Yes. Humbled, but embraced, like you're part of time immemorial. Experiencing the world as it was hundreds, maybe thousands of years ago."

"Exactly."

"Not many places like that left." She turned to Bryson. "With how much you obviously love all this, I bet you're pretty passionate about environmental issues."

"Oh, yeah. I don't pay a lot of attention to politics in general, but I keep up with anything that might impact the land, the water, the air, the animals. Especially efforts to drill in the Arctic National Wildlife

Refuge. Unfortunately, most Alaskans favor it because we all get checks every year based on state oil revenues. But drilling would have such a negative impact on the caribou herd and a lot of other wildlife that a lot of people oppose it. Skeeter keeps up-to-date on what's going on through the Internet and clues in the rest of us."

"Wow. Did you say everyone gets checks from the state?"

"Most everybody. You have to have lived here at least a year and intend to stay indefinitely. The dividends come out of something called the Alaska Permanent Fund. Usually it's about a thousand dollars, but last year I got a check for more than thirty-two hundred."

"Well, that's definitely one benefit of living up here."

"We also don't pay any sales taxes or state income tax. Just federal." Bryson leaned back on her elbows, legs stretched out in front of her. "But it doesn't amount to that much once you figure in how much more expensive everything is."

"I know that you and Lars are both part of an outfitters' group, but I didn't see Maggie's name on the Web site. Does she stay at home all the time?"

"No, she's taking time off while she's pregnant. She's a biologist for the NPS in the Gates of the Arctic National Park." Bryson gestured east. "Park boundary is only seven miles that way." Then she pointed north. "And two upriver of the lake. Maggie takes that way in, in the skiff, or I fly her where she needs to go."

"That sounds like a cool job. I'll have to ask her about it."

"Get her to tell you about the time a big ol' bull moose wanted to get a little too friendly during mating season." Bryson chuckled. The moose had been so convinced that Maggie was the hottest thing around she'd had to spend half a day up a tree.

"I will. I bet you've had a few misadventures, too, spending so much time in the bush."

"Hard not to." She didn't want to volunteer her own, however, as most had been life-threatening situations, not laugh-about-it-later moose encounters. And since Karla's statement seemed an attempt to get her to do just that, she thought it was a good time to change the subject. "Really glad you and Maggie are hitting it off so well. Have you decided how long you're going to stay?" During their trek up the mountain, Karla had elaborated on her morning with Maggie, but she hadn't mentioned her plans.

"Yes. They asked me to stay until after the baby's born, and I'm pretty sure I can arrange that with the hospital."

"That's great!" Bryson blurted, with the enthusiasm of someone who'd just won the lottery, and felt immediately self-conscious. She couldn't be more transparent about her hope that Karla extend her visit.

But Karla responded with a pleased and bashful smile. "I'm glad you think so, in spite of the fact I was kind of obnoxious when we met." She shrugged apologetically. "And I hope that means you'll want to show me more places like this," she added, "because I've had a wonderful day. I enjoy your company." Once more, she gazed out over the landscape, looking toward the Rasmussen cabin. "I'll never, ever forget this moment. For the first time in what seems like forever, I feel completely at peace."

❖

The expanded Rasmussen household soon settled into a comfortable routine that satisfied all of them. Karla took on all the cooking, Lars kept the place spotless, and Maggie got waited on hand and foot, so she had no reason to break pottery or throw food. Karla kept a close eye on her pregnancy, massaging her swollen feet and ankles twice a day and monitoring her blood pressure and the baby's heartbeat. Every daylight hour that Karla wasn't cooking and Maggie wasn't sleeping, they sat side by side on the bed or on the couch, trading stories of their lives.

Bonding with Maggie and sharing memories of their mother helped Karla deal with the grief that had haunted her since the funeral and Abby's betrayal. She cried on Maggie's shoulder during the moments it still overwhelmed her, finding solace in her sister's calming reassurance that time would mend her heart. And in her quiet moments alone she thought frequently of Bryson, reliving their time on the mountain, and that, too, helped erase some of her despondency.

On the sixth day of her stay, Karla's spirits lifted further when Bryson phoned and invited herself over to grill the caribou steaks she'd stashed in her cooler. She told Lars not to bother picking her up because she'd borrowed Skeeter's floatplane and would fly in. Maggie's doctor's appointment was the next morning, and taking the four-passenger Cessna would save Maggie a boat ride and allow Lars to accompany her on the flight to Fairbanks.

"Bryson said you're welcome to come along tomorrow," Lars told Karla as they headed down to the lake to meet the plane. "She sounded like she wasn't sure you'd want to."

Karla had to laugh. "Probably because both times I've flown with her I haven't been exactly the calmest passenger. I hate small planes." She still didn't care to repeat the experience, but with Maggie so close to her delivery date, it would be a good idea to force herself. "I'll go. Not happily, mind you. But I should ride along."

Lars pulled her up short and bear-hugged her. "Thanks. I know you're doing it for us."

Viewed head-on, Skeeter's orange-and-gold floatplane looked from a distance like a flying pumpkin with a hat and metal shoes. More whimsical than terrifying. She vowed to try to keep that image in mind when she boarded it the next morning for the two-and-a-half-hour flight to the doctor's.

Karla waved when the Cessna was still a long way off, though she doubted Bryson could make them out against the rocky bank of the lake. But the plane immediately tipped its wings to wave back and began to descend. The single silhouette at the controls became clearer as the plane touched down, spraying water in two wide streams on either side. Most of Bryson's features were concealed beneath the brim of her ball cap and oversized sunglasses, but the smile that dominated the lower half of her face told her she was just as happy to see them as Karla was to see her.

Bryson cracked her door as the propeller began to die. "Hi there! How's it going?"

"Great! Good to see you."

"Maggie's really missed you," Lars said as he helped Bryson tie off the Cessna. "Fair warning, she's gonna bend your ear a while."

Bryson laughed. "No worries. I've missed her, too." She reached into the Cessna and hauled out two grocery bags. "Brought her a bunch of new magazines. Imagine she's getting restless being cooped up in bed so much."

"It's certainly helped that Karla's been around to keep her occupied.

And," he added, opening his jacket to display a pristine sweatshirt underneath, "she's been feeding us so well Mag hasn't thrown anything since she got here."

Maggie was waiting in the open doorway. "Good God, woman, about damn time you hauled your ass our way for a visit."

Bryson trotted up the steps and carefully embraced her, then bent to put her mouth near Maggie's belly. "Your momma's such a sweet-talker."

Maggie swatted Bryson's head away, laughing. "Get in here and start cooking. I'm starved."

"Big surprise there, since she hasn't eaten in at least two hours," Lars mumbled under his breath to Karla as they followed them inside. "Hope Bryson brought a couple extra steaks."

❖

Once she'd caught up on all the Bettles gossip and her tummy was full to bursting, Maggie waddled off to bed.

"I'll get the dishes," Lars offered, "if you two want to have some coffee on the porch. I'll join you in a while."

"Shall we?" Karla asked Bryson. "It's become my nightly ritual. I love to watch the sun set from there."

"Sold. Lead on."

Seated side by side in hand-hewn Adirondack chairs, they admired the lowering sun in silence as it turned the mountains golden-orange. When darkness fell, Karla lit a kerosene lantern that hung near the front door. "Did Lars tell you I'm riding along tomorrow?"

"No, he didn't. And I gotta say, I'm surprised. Though happy about it, for sure. Long ways to Fairbanks, and Maggie's awful close to time." Bryson stretched out her legs. "Had a woman go into labor just after I got my license, and it wasn't an experience I'd like to repeat."

"What happened?"

"Once it got real clear the baby was coming whether we liked it or not, I set the plane down and helped her deliver. We were still a couple hours from anywhere. Thank God there weren't any complications, and she'd been through it before and knew what to do. I took first aid but I wasn't ready for that."

"Everything turned out okay, though?"

"Oh, yeah. In fact, she named the baby after me. A boy." Bryson grinned. "Bet she was happy I wasn't a Rebecca or Mary Anne or something."

"Bryson suits you." Karla studied her face. "Unique, for a girl. Strong. Down-to-earth. Where did it come from?"

"Pop was Brice. And he wanted a son." Her face turned melancholic, and her eyes filled with tears.

"Ah. I see." Bryson did seem the quintessential tomboy, though a very feminine one. She'd learned to fly from her father, and her fondest memories included watching him make furniture. The two had clearly been extremely close. "I suspect it didn't take long for him to appreciate how lucky he was to have been blessed with a daughter instead."

Bryson looked down at her feet as a slow smile spread across her face. "Well, yeah. I expect he'd have said that was true enough."

"How long has he been gone?"

"Five years."

Yet it was obvious Bryson still missed him deeply. "They say it gets better in time. Maggie claims it does. But I can't imagine thinking of Mom without getting this unbelievably terrible ache in my chest and knot in the pit of my stomach."

"It doesn't really get better," Bryson said. "Just more tolerable. The rawness scars over. I know right now it's hard to get past thinking about the end. Finding out they're gone, the realization sinking in. The painful acceptance. But eventually that fades, and what remains are the great, joyful times that made the deepest impressions. That's when you can let go of the grieving and move on." Her gaze was inward, her mind obviously engaged entirely on images of her father.

"How did he die?"

Bryson didn't answer right away. "I probably shouldn't tell you, since you're already not the biggest fan of flying and we're going up tomorrow. But Pop was killed when his plane crashed into a mountain. Ran into a williwaw, kind of a freak downdraft that happens sometimes here, mostly along the coast. Can't see 'em, can't predict 'em. It's like running into a tornado."

"I'm sorry."

"It was quick. And fitting, I guess. The way he'd have wanted it. Just too soon."

"It doesn't seem to matter how old you are," she said, "when your parents go, that word *orphan* takes on a whole new meaning."

"Yeah." Bryson's face was half in shadow, so her expression was hard to read. "But hasn't finding Maggie made it easier?"

"Oh, for sure. For now."

"For now?"

"Easier now, tougher later. Having gotten close to her, it'll be hard to go back to living on the other side of the world. We won't even have the luxury of being able to webcam or chat on the phone whenever we like."

"Satellite phones aren't the most reliable. But maybe Skeeter can hook you up on his computer when Maggie's in town."

"Still won't be enough. Honestly, I don't know how I'll be able to afford coming out here except maybe once every couple of years." Karla had been in Alaska only a week, and already she was dreading the thought of leaving her new family and Bryson to go back to her empty apartment. The long howl of a wolf from far off to their left pierced the quiet. An answering cry followed from their right, much closer. Karla shrank back against her chair, peering out into the black forest for signs of movement. "Every morning and every evening. Like clockwork. But it always unnerves me. I don't know as I'd ever get used to it."

"I love it," Bryson said. "Has to be the loneliest sound in the world, but somehow reassuring at the same time. Another creature reaching out, trying to make a connection that transcends distance. Makes me feel like I'm not so alone, somehow."

"I still don't know how you can deal with living by yourself so far from everything, especially in winter. I'd go nuts."

"Not for everyone. I have my moments, too, when it gets hard." Bryson paused as another howl echoed across the lake. "Living here is like sailing alone around the world on a tiny boat. Your life is stripped down to bare essentials, and your priorities really become clear. Food, shelter, family. All the trivial and insignificant things that most people worry about don't matter. It's freeing in many ways, but it does drive home the fact that you're all by yourself."

"Doesn't have to be that way," Lars interrupted from the doorway. "You get opportunities, Bryson. You just don't follow up on 'em."

Bryson squirmed and glanced at Karla. "I should have warned you to watch out for this one. He loves to play matchmaker."

"There are worse things than being someone who looks out for their friends."

"Well put, Karla." Lars leaned against the front rail and grinned down at Bryson. "Sometimes you need to push people a little to get them to fulfill their potential."

"I'm ready for a push." Karla said, getting to her feet to stretch. "I feel kind of rudderless at the moment, to use your boat analogy."

"You've had a lot to deal with all at once. It's understandable." Lars put an arm around her shoulder and squeezed. "But now you've got all of us to help steer you in the right direction. Right, Bryson?"

"Whatever we can do."

"Your first order of business will be to get me on that plane in the morning without hyperventilating." Karla fought back a yawn as she reached for her coffee mug. "I'll deal with everything else once we all get back, how's that?"

"Sounds like a plan. Looks like you're about ready to hit the sack," Lars observed.

"I am. It's these crazy short days. I know it's not that late, but I guess my body is programmed to fade when it gets dark."

"We do have an early start tomorrow. I'll join you. Coming, Bryson?"

"Be there in a while." As soon as they went inside, Bryson relaxed back against the chair and allowed herself to relive images from the evening. It had been wonderful seeing Maggie again, and she always had a relaxing, fun time with the Rasmussens. But she'd focused on their house guest tonight. Karla had almost caught her staring several times, but she couldn't stop herself. Whether she wanted to or not, her mind was determined to record every little detail about her: the almost imperceptible bump in her nose, the thin scar above her left eyebrow, the way she slightly pursed her lips a millisecond before she laughed and so gave herself away. It was foolish, she knew, pining after someone totally unavailable. She told herself it was just a crush that would pass in time. What else could she do?

CHAPTER FOURTEEN

November 2

"Breathe, Maggie. Nice deep breaths. Try to relax." Karla kept her voice calm as she adjusted the cuff to take another reading. Maggie's blood pressure had been rising steadily since they'd been in the air, and they were still several miles from Fairbanks.

"Should we be worried?" Lars turned in his seat beside Bryson and glanced back anxiously at Maggie as Karla fitted the stethoscope in her ears and inflated the cuff.

"I'm a bit concerned because your blood pressure's up," she told Maggie. "And your headache isn't good news. Has it gotten worse?"

"Yeah. Quite a lot, as a matter of fact." Maggie closed her eyes and leaned back against the seat. "How much longer, Bryson?"

"Fifteen minutes or so," she called back. "I've got the throttle wide open. Want me to have an ambulance waiting for us?"

"Oh, no, there's no need for that," Maggie said. "I'm sure I—"

"I think it's a good idea. Better to be careful."

"Do it, Bryson," Lars said immediately.

"You got it." Bryson relayed the request on her radio and asked the Fairbanks tower for priority clearance to land on one of the two water runways reserved for floatplanes.

Karla took Maggie's blood pressure again as they began to descend. Everyone's attention was on her, so she forced herself not to frown as she heard the *whoosh* that registered the systolic pressure. The number was too high. Too damn high.

❖

"You know more than you're saying, don't you?" Bryson kept her voice low. She was standing just behind Karla, both of them watching doctors and nurses go in and out of the ER cubicle down the hall where Maggie had been taken.

"They'll know something soon. She's in good hands."

"What do you think it is?" Bryson could tell from the look on Karla's face that she understood precisely why Maggie was getting such a bustle of attention. She'd seen her intercept the first doctor as he was going in, to brief him. "Please tell me."

Karla half turned and met her eyes. "It might be preeclampsia. Do you know what that is?"

Her body tensed and she made fists. "Not really. I've heard the term. Is it bad?"

"It's a condition pregnant women sometimes get, a narrowing of the blood vessels. Maggie has several of the common risk factors for it. Her age, for one. The fact it's her first pregnancy. And her normal blood pressure is on the high side anyway, which is why her doctor told her to rest in bed as much as possible the last few weeks."

Movement made Karla turn toward Maggie's cubicle. The curtain was pulled back, and a nurse emerged with a tray and headed off toward the lab. "It spiked during the flight, and her headache is a symptom. Blood and urine tests should tell the doctors more."

"Is it bad?" Bryson asked again. Her chest felt constricted. *Don't let anything happen to her.*

"It could be dangerous to both Maggie and the baby. If that's what it is, the doctors may want to induce labor or deliver by C-section right away, since she's so close to her due date." Karla met her eyes again. "It might be something else, though she doesn't seem to have any other symptoms."

"If they go ahead and take the baby, will both of them be okay?" She hadn't realized how tense she was, until Karla gently released her fists and took her hands in hers.

"They'll be all right. Have faith." Karla's smile and grip of reassurance were so convincing she relaxed a little.

❖

The doctors verified Karla's diagnosis and scheduled Maggie for a C-Section for later that day. She was moved to a prep room and put on a magnesium drip to keep her from developing eclampsia and having a seizure during the surgery. The drip made her sick and fuzzy-headed, and Bryson and Karla couldn't see her for a couple of hours.

Karla's trepidation grew when she entered the room. Maggie was visibly sweating and looked paler than she should.

"Where's Lars?" Bryson asked.

"I sent him to stretch his legs so I could talk to you." Maggie patted the bed on either side of her, and Karla and Bryson both edged carefully onto the mattress, facing her. Each took one of her hands. "I'm counting on you both," she said. "Now, I know everything's going to be fine. But I like to plan for every possibility. If something happens to me..." She'd been composed and calm until now, but Karla could see in her eyes that the doctors had explained all the risks and dangers. "Lars will need looking after."

She wanted to interrupt with reassurances, but neither she nor Bryson moved.

"He'll need both of you, as much as you're able, especially at first. Oh, he'll make a great dad, I know, but newborns are a handful." Maggie took a deep breath and looked from one to the other. "Promise?"

"Of course," Karla said.

"You know I will." Bryson nodded solemnly.

"Good. Now that's settled, let's talk about the way it's really going to be." Maggie glanced down at her stomach. "The doctors say I'll be here a while. At least several days. And the baby maybe longer." She looked up at Karla. "Lars plans to stay with me. They'll move a cot in for him."

"Great." Karla squeezed her hand. "I'll get a room at a hotel nearby."

"So will I," Bryson added.

Maggie shook her head. "Very nice of both of you to offer, but Lars will be here around the clock, watching me like a hawk." She looked up at Karla. "You can stay until I come home, right?"

"And for a while after. I'm sure it'll be no problem. I'll call and verify that while you're in surgery."

"Good. But I don't want you hanging around a hospital for the next week. Go home with Bryson and have some fun. See some of the area while the weather holds. We'll get freeze-up soon. If you're comfortable at our place, of course you're welcome there. Or I'm sure Grizz can put you up at the Den."

"Or she can stay with me." Bryson faced Karla. "We'll work it out, whatever you want." She returned her attention to Maggie. "I'll watch after her, don't you worry. Lars will call us when we can come, and I'll have us down here and bedside before you know it."

"I knew I could count on you both." Maggie sighed and extracted her hand from Bryson's to run it over her stomach. "Won't be long, now. You'll both have a little niece."

"I get to be an aunt, too?" Bryson's pleased expression told Karla this was unexpected news.

"Of course, idiot." Maggie slapped her lightly across the arm. "Since when did you cease being a member of my family?"

"Duh," Bryson teased. "No clues on a name yet, I suppose?"

"She'll let me know," Maggie said confidently.

"Believe me, Mag won't drop any hints until she's here," Lars said from the doorway. "I've tried everything." He was smiling, but his forehead was creased with worry. Karla knew they all felt the same. Putting on brave faces, but terrified inside.

The anesthesiologist appeared behind Lars. "It's time for her epidural. Lars, you can stay, but you ladies need to wait outside."

"Can't wait to meet my niece." Karla gave Maggie a quick kiss. "See you soon."

"We'll be in as soon as they'll let us." Bryson did the same.

Karla called her supervisor at Grady Hospital and confirmed her indefinite leave of absence. Not long after, they took Maggie to surgery, and she and Bryson accompanied Lars to the lounge to begin an agonizing wait.

❖

"The doctor said she'd be in the operating room an hour or so." Lars glanced up at the wall clock, though it had barely moved since the last time he'd looked. "Do you think we should be getting worried?"

Nearly ninety minutes had passed since they'd wheeled Maggie to the OR, and Lars had spent nearly the entire time pacing. Bryson and Karla had been through every magazine in the room and had alternated trips to the cafeteria for coffee, most of which went cold before it was consumed.

"We should be hearing something soon." But Karla was beginning to be concerned, too. The typical C-section only took a half hour or forty minutes, so she'd expected someone from the OR to update them by now. Almost unconsciously, she removed the tigereye necklace from her pocket and began to stroke the smooth stone with her thumb.

"What's that?" Bryson asked. "If you don't mind my asking. You were doing that earlier, in the ER."

She opened her palm so Bryson could see the necklace. "It was my mother's. She wore it all the time. I know it probably sounds silly, but it gives me strength. Makes me feel closer to her, somehow."

"I don't think that's silly at all. I feel the same way when I sit in Pop's chair." Just as the words left Bryson's mouth, a doctor in scrubs emerged from a door at the end of the hallway and headed toward them. He was smiling.

"Congratulation, Lars, you have a beautiful baby girl. Seven pounds, eight ounces. Because she was a little premature, she's been taken to the NICU—neonatal intensive care—but all the early signs look very good."

"Maggie?" Lars asked.

The surgeon put his hand on Lars's shoulder. "There was some bleeding, so it took a little longer than usual to close her up. She's running a fever, and her blood pressure's still high, so we're monitoring her closely. It'll be another hour or two before you can see her, but you can visit your daughter. The NICU's on the third floor."

As soon as he left them, Karla put her arm around Lars's waist. Concern was etched on his face. "Don't worry, Lars. These kinds of complications are to be expected. I'm sure Maggie and the baby will be fine. If you like, I'll talk to the charge nurse."

"I'm so glad you're here." He hugged her back. "I need a translator to understand what's going on."

Ten minutes later, the three of them stood outside the NICU window, admiring the fair-haired newborn.

"She looks so small and vulnerable." Lars's face was only inches from the glass, his expression a combination of awe and uncertainty.

Baby Girl Rasmussen was in a small bed enclosed by hard plastic, and leads ran from her chest and fingertip to a monitor.

Karla studied the numbers on the monitor. "Her breathing and heart rate are good, and so is her blood pressure. Blood-oxygen level is within normal range. She's in the isolette to keep her warm, which is common with preemies."

"When will I be able to hold her?"

"She's not on a ventilator, so I bet they'll let you in right now. Let me go talk to the charge nurse." Karla found the shift supervisor and was relieved to hear that her niece had had no complications and was being monitored only as a precaution. She passed the good news to Lars, who was led away to wash up and don a hospital gown.

She and Bryson watched through the window as he held his daughter for the first time, mindful of the various lines attaching her to the monitor.

"Should have brought my camera," Bryson remarked. "Sure never expected all this when we left this morning."

"They're lucky this happened so late in Maggie's pregnancy, and that she was headed here," Karla said. "I hate to think about the outcome if she'd worsened during a blizzard or something, and we hadn't been able to get them to a hospital. We might have lost them both."

"Damn good thing you're here. Makes it seem as though there was a reason all of this happened as it did. You coming here, I mean."

"Well, apparently I'll be hanging around a while longer than I expected. Maggie probably won't be out of here for a week or so, and it'll be another five or six before she's able to do much because of the C-section. Looks like I'll be here for the holidays."

"It'll sure make them both happy to hear that." Bryson smiled. "And me, too. I don't mind saying, I look forward to the chance to spend some more time with you."

The words themselves didn't surprise Karla because Bryson had already acknowledged she enjoyed her company. But now she noticed an expression in Bryson's eyes she hadn't seen before, or had perhaps been too preoccupied to recognize.

It was a subtle but unmistakable sign of *interest*. Romantic interest. Sexual interest. Even in her daydreams of late, she hadn't imagined that Bryson could be harboring any such attraction, and the realization she *might* both excited and terrified her.

❖

Bryson set the coffee cup on the table in front of the couch and eased quietly into the chair beside it. Karla was still out cold, though it was nearly eight a.m., but they'd been up late, visiting the NICU and getting updates from Lars on how Maggie was doing.

She adjusted Karla's jacket so it covered her, then hesitated as she withdrew her hand, the urge to caress Karla's hair away from her face so strong she could hardly repress it.

Something was different between them, though she couldn't put her finger on what or why. Ever since that moment outside the NICU the night before, Karla had been almost shy around her, rarely meeting her eyes. And when she did, she seemed curious in a way she hadn't before.

A nurse poked her head into the lounge. "Maggie's awake," she quietly informed Bryson. "You can go in to see her."

She rubbed Karla's shoulder and was rewarded with a low moan of protest. "Karla? You awake?"

"Half," Karla said groggily, rubbing her eyes as she sat up. "What's happened?"

"We can see Maggie."

"Oh, great." The news roused her from her semi-stupor, and she blinked several times. Her gaze focused on the full coffee cup in front of her. "Please tell me this hasn't been sitting here for hours."

"Still hot."

"You're an angel." Karla reached for the cup and downed half the contents in three quick sips. "Okay. Now I'm ready."

Karla fixed her attention on Maggie's monitor as they entered the room. Her blood pressure was still elevated—142 over 95—but that was an improvement over the night before, and it could take a few weeks for Maggie's BP to return to normal. Her color was good, and the empty food tray in front of her indicated she'd been able to start taking liquids on her own. "Hi, sis. How you feeling?"

"Weak. Sore." Maggie groaned when she reached for the bed control to raise her head a few inches. "And glad it's over. But it sure was worth it." She smiled. "Isn't she beautiful?"

"Sure is. And lucky. She's got your eyes." Bryson looked over at Karla and grinned. "Hazel, with tiny gold flecks."

Karla's cheeks warmed. Of course it was natural that Bryson knew the color of her eyes. She noticed everything in her environment, paid attention to the details. And they actually had spent a lot of time together, at least it sure felt that way. But it was how Bryson looked at her when she said it that unnerved her. Maggie wouldn't have interpreted it as flirtatious, but it seemed so, to her. Bryson had sounded quietly joyful, as though hazel eyes with tiny gold flecks were her idea of perfection.

She had to be imagining Bryson's interest. *Had* to be. Bryson hadn't said or done anything overt. Had she? Karla was out of practice when it came to reading clues that said a woman was interested in her.

"Her eyes were the first things I noticed, too." Maggie reached for Karla's hand. "Another tie that binds us."

"Mom would've liked that. Where's Lars?"

"I sent him to get some breakfast. Poor thing hasn't eaten since yesterday morning, and I know he was up all night. He looked like he was ready to drop."

"So, the big question. Do you have a name yet?" Bryson asked.

"Yes." Maggie's lips drew back in an enigmatic smile. She was obviously enjoying making them wait to hear the long-anticipated decision. "We've named her after the two women who kept both of us safe. We're calling her Karson, with a K."

"Karson? Hey, how cool is that? I'm honored." Bryson looked over at Karla, who felt the same joy she saw on Bryson's face.

"So am I. Thanks, Maggie."

"Suits her," Maggie said. "She's a survivor, just like you two."

"I'm so glad you and little Karson are okay," Bryson said. "Has the doctor said anything about when you can both go home?"

Maggie shook her head. "He said five days at least, probably more. He wants to see how we do, and how fast I heal. And I'll have to stay in bed a lot when I first get there."

"Then lucky for you, you have a live-in nanny, cook, and health-care professional. I'm here as long as you need me," Karla said. "I talked to the hospital and told them I probably won't be back until after the first of the year."

"You're spending the holidays with us?" Maggie sat up so abruptly that she winced. "Damn."

"Hey, there. Watch it." Karla helped her lie back. "Be careful with that incision. Slow movements. And yes, you have me for Christmas.

Please tell me you're the deck-the-halls, singing-carols-nonstop types."

"Hell, we live in Santa's backyard. What do you think?" Maggie laughed. "You won't find a house up here without mistletoe, spiked eggnog, the works. Hey, Bryson, you should get Chaz to loan you a team to take her up to Arrigetch Peaks."

"Already thought of that. Just wasn't sure Karla would be around long enough to get the snow for it."

"What are you two talking about?"

"The Arrigetch Peaks are at the entrance to the Gates of the Arctic," Maggie explained. "Unbelievably beautiful. Best way to get there is by dogsled."

"Dogsled?" Much as she hated being cold, that did sound exciting, mushing up into the wilderness with Bryson. "I take it you've done that before?"

Bryson grinned. "Many, many times. I'm an alternate guide, if someone gets sick at the last minute."

"No one better to take you into the backcountry," Lars added from behind her. "You know, you two look worse than I do. Why don't you head on home and get some rest? I'll call with updates, and you can come back if there's a need. Otherwise we'll see you when Mags can go home."

"Lars is right." Maggie glared at them with playful sternness. "Go get some rest and have some fun. I don't have the energy to deal with three hovering mother hens."

"You're sure?" Bryson asked.

"No arguments. Don't make me mad." Maggie was grinning when she said it, and she reached out for farewell hugs from them.

"Think you'll be going back to the cabin?" Lars dug into the pocket of his jeans and extracted a key ring.

"I don't know. I hadn't really given it much thought," Karla admitted.

"Take this in case you do." Lars held out the keys. "The cabin isn't locked, but the shed is, and there are keys for the skiff, ATV, and snowmachine. You know where everything else is."

"Okay." Karla zipped the keys into the pocket of her coat. "Hopefully it'll only be for a few days."

CHAPTER FIFTEEN

Better view sitting up here, don't you think?" Bryson said as they strapped themselves into Skeeter's Cessna, Karla beside her in the copilot's seat. "Is it getting any easier for you?"

"I wouldn't say that." Karla was careful to keep her hands clear of the dual steering wheel and control panel, afraid she might accidentally hit something that would create problems for them in the air.

"Wish I could do or say something to help you enjoy this as much as I do."

"It would take an awful lot for that to happen." Karla fell silent as Bryson got on the radio and readied for takeoff. A few minutes later, the floatplane was skimming along the water runway. She was grateful for the Cessna's powerful cabin heater because the weather had turned noticeably colder during their day in the hospital. The sun was out, but the temperature was still well below freezing.

"I meant it when I said you could stay with me. I'd be more than happy to have your company until Maggie gets home."

Karla glanced over at Bryson. She probably would have readily accepted her offer just twenty-four hours ago. But realizing that Bryson might be interested in her had thrown her off-kilter, and she wanted some time alone to think. Had she imagined it? Was she so adrift because of recent events—especially Abby's leaving—that she was merely longing for some kind of meaningful connection with another woman?

"I think I'll go back to Lars and Maggie's. At least for now." She gazed out over the landscape below, struck yet again by the desolate endlessness of the Alaskan wilderness. She could see why so many who came here found themselves re-evaluating the choices they'd made. "I've spent so much time lately grieving or grasping for anything to keep me from thinking too hard about the future. I'm finally ready to face things. Try to figure out what I'm going to do next with my life." The prospect scared the hell out of her, but the birth of her niece had inspired her to begin looking forward, not back.

"Sounds like quite a challenge. If you need someone to listen, you have my number. Hope you won't hesitate to use it."

"I appreciate the offer, Bryson."

"Well, I promised Maggie and Lars I'd look after you. And I know what it feels like to lose a parent and find yourself at a crossroad."

"Thanks. I'll keep that in mind."

The rest of the trip they talked about more innocuous matters. The baby, Christmas in Alaska, the sorts of mundane things that Karla should remember since she was staying alone at the cabin. Karla knew that Bryson was being unusually chatty to keep her mind off the flight, and she was grateful. Before she realized it, they were descending toward Wild Lake.

"Should take right off again pretty quick, so I can get Skeeter's plane back and still make it home before dark," Bryson said as they splashed down. "Need anything before I go?"

"I'll be fine."

The plane drifted to a stop and Bryson cut the engine, then came around to help Karla out. They faced each other for a few seconds, the sudden tension between them so palpable Karla could feel herself beginning to blush. "Sure you don't mind if I call you to come get me if being alone turns out to be a bad idea?"

Bryson grinned with that same sweet look of joy that gave her butterflies in Maggie's room, and her voice was velvet soft when she replied. "I'd like nothing better. I very much hope you will."

❖

The next three days gave Karla a powerful demonstration of how quickly the weather in Alaska could change, and a glimpse of how the isolation of a long winter in the bush could do quite a number on someone's psyche. The weather had kept her indoors and forced her to keep her promise to use the time to sort out things. Her life. Past, present, and future. What she'd done with it so far, and what dreams she had yet to fulfill.

Bryson had barely left when the snow began to fall, and it had been coming down steadily ever since. The thermometer now dipped into the single digits at night and rose to just below freezing during the short days, so the ground was frozen solid. Ice had begun to form at the shore of the lake, and every bit of snow that fell clung tenaciously to every surface, painting the world around the cabin a solid landscape of white.

The warm embrace she'd received into the Rasmussen household and sharing the best of her childhood memories with her sister had tempered her grief over her mother's death. Other, happier recollections had begun to replace the haunting image of her mom in the coffin. And though the loss still overwhelmed her often, such moments were less frequent now and briefer.

And she'd begun to be able to think of Abby with a greater degree of detachment. Hours of picking their life apart, seeking answers to how she could have been so blindsided, had given her some insights on why their relationship had not been the unbreakable connection she'd considered it to be.

She accepted that they needed to share the responsibility for the breakup. It might have been Abby's decision, but Karla had failed to see the warning signs, had become too complacent about the way they were living. Their life together had become so predictable that she assumed Abby would have no problem with the uncommon demands of her nursing job: her long hours, her frequent exhaustion, her preoccupation when she lost a patient.

Not that Abby had been blameless. She should have spoken up if she'd considered their communication lacking and their love life less than satisfying. Karla couldn't read her mind. And from her viewpoint, it was unconscionable to begin an affair when they were living together and partnered in what they'd both agreed was a monogamous, long-term commitment. She was aware that couples sometimes drifted apart. She might have accepted that fact if Abby had been honest with her when she'd first felt the distance and inclination to stray.

But finding out that Abby kept pretending to love her even while she was sharing someone else's bed was the part she couldn't understand or bring herself to forgive.

Often when she'd been thinking about Abby, images of Bryson intruded, inviting comparisons between the two, and Abby always fell short. Bryson was generous and caring, while Abby was not only a liar but a manipulator. From the beginning, she'd used tears, charm, or anger to maneuver Karla into getting what she wanted, whether it was which movie they watched, their next vacation spot, or the type of dishes they would buy for their kitchen. And like a sheep, she had always demurred to Abby's desires.

Abby had been all about herself and her own needs. She'd have hated Alaska with its lack of conveniences and isolation. And she cared nothing at all about wildlife or the out-of-doors, while it was clear that preserving and appreciating the environment was at Bryson's core.

As the days passed, Bryson dominated her introspections more, but Karla couldn't decide what she might do if Bryson was indeed as interested in her as she was in Bryson. What then? It was one thing to engage in some harmless fantasizing, and another thing altogether to contemplate acting on those desires. Could she trust someone enough again to open her heart? Especially someone she knew she'd be thousands of miles away from in just another few weeks?

The only way to find out was to take a leap of faith. Not something she would ordinarily do, but the one she'd made coming to Alaska had certainly been worth it.

A raging blizzard that morning, with high winds and snow so dense she could see only a few feet outside the window, had tapered off to flurries by early afternoon. Deciding to take advantage of the slight break in the weather, she went to the satellite phone to dial Bryson's number. To her relief, the connection went through.

"Hello?"

"Hi, Bryson. It's Karla."

"Hey there! I was just about to call you. Everything okay?"

"Yes, everything's fine." Except perhaps the fact that she couldn't stop thinking about Bryson. "Why were you going to call me?"

"I just heard from Lars. The baby's been moved into their room. But Maggie's blood pressure is still high, and she's had some problems keeping down food, so they're not releasing her for at least another few days."

"That's not uncommon."

"Yeah, that's what they told her and Lars. So what were you calling me about?"

"I…uh…" She gripped the phone tighter. Her mouth had suddenly gone dry. "I wondered whether the offer's still open to come spend some time at your place. I'm getting a little tired of my own company." And she wanted to find out what the hell was going on between them, if anything, but she wasn't ready to admit that part.

"Sure." The enthusiasm in Bryson's voice reassured her. "Do you want me to try to borrow Skeeter's plane again to come get you, or can you manage in the skiff?"

"I think I can get there fine. I've handled small boats before, and I watched Lars pretty closely."

"If you're sure. When do you think you'll be heading out?"

"Oh, a half hour or so. I just need to do the dishes and throw a few things into a bag."

"I'll expect you here in an hour or so, then. Be sure to wear a life vest, and take it slow and easy. Visibility isn't great, watch out for logs and rocks."

"Don't worry. I'll be fine. See you soon."

❖

Karla began to have second thoughts not long after the skiff was under way. The flurries had thickened by the minute to another blowing blanket of thick, heavy snow, and in the dark of the overcast sky she couldn't see more than a few yards in any direction. The lake was a breeze, but once she got to the river, danger was everywhere—logs, rocks, gravel bars, and fallen trees to avoid.

"It's not that far," she said aloud to reassure herself. *Just keep calm and go slow.*

The words were scarcely out of her mouth when the boat slammed against a rock, mostly submerged in the river. A loud crunch of metal sounded as she lost her footing and hit the deck, hard. The engine died, and the boat began to slip sideways to the current.

"Damn it." She grabbed the nearest bench and hauled herself up. The boat was spinning out of control, just a few feet from the shore. She dove for the controls, but before she could restart the engine, the skiff bounced off another rock and tossed her back onto the deck. She tried to catch herself but took the brunt of the impact in her right wrist. Momentarily stunned by the pain, she gritted her teeth and clutched her wrist as the boat whirled around, caught in the current, and grounded itself on the next gravel bar.

"Great. Just great." As the pain began to subside, she wiggled her fingers, relieved to discover it was a bad sprain and not a break. Her circumstances, however, were less than ideal. The boat wouldn't start, and the gravel bar she was stranded on was in the middle of the river, the temperature below freezing. She'd have to get wet to hike out, and she was probably about midway between the two cabins.

She climbed out and inspected the boat. Though the bow was dented, it seemed watertight. She secured the vessel to a large rock so it wouldn't drift away if the water rose, then slung her duffel bag over her shoulder and peered through the snow at the distance between her and the nearest shore. It seemed only fifteen feet or so, but she couldn't judge the water's depth. As tempted as she was to cross as quickly as possible, she had to keep her footing, so she resigned herself to take it slow and easy.

The icy water flooded her boots on her second step, piercing her wool socks like a thousand tiny needles. She continued, cautiously, the water soon up to her calves, numbing her. Turning slightly upstream against the current, she fought every inch to keep from being swept away. Halfway there, the water was up to mid-thigh, the current exerting its full force and Karla more powerless by the moment. She almost succumbed to the rapidly rising panic that had sucked all the air out of her lungs and started her heart hammering.

By the time she reached the shore, she was gasping from the cold and had lost nearly all feeling in her legs. With trembling hands and chattering teeth, she stripped off her boots and her clothing from the waist down and pulled on long underwear, dry jeans, and fresh wool socks from her bag. She rubbed her feet vigorously to try to warm them, wincing at the pain in her wrist when she did, but her boots were the only footwear she'd packed, so when she put them on again, her new socks were almost immediately saturated as well.

She had at least three or four miles to go to get anywhere, but she was determined to tough it out. Rising to survey the shoreline in either direction, she decided to head to Bryson's rather than return to the Rasmussen cabin. She'd doused the fire in the woodstove before she'd left, and Bryson's home would provide the immediate warmth her feet desperately needed.

She stayed near the river for the first several hundred yards, but the snow completely covered the rocky bank, which made for treacherously slow going. Her feet felt half frozen and she had difficulty maintaining her balance. A twisted ankle was something she couldn't afford.

Hoping for smoother footing, she entered the woods and paralleled the river, threading through the dense spruce trees. The wind began to pick up, and the snow showed no sign of diminishing. Now and then, a whiteout would temporarily obscure her view of the water, but she wasn't afraid of getting lost. The river was on one side of her, and the mountains on the other, some half mile or more distant. As long as she kept moving downstream along the shoreline, she should find Bryson's cabin.

❖

Bryson peered north, listening for the skiff's engine, cursing the fact that the thick snow muffled all sound. It was a little after three. Only an hour of daylight left, and Karla was so overdue she was edgy with worry. She debated whether to strike out on foot or take to the air. Hiking would be slower, but conditions were awful for flying. Even keeping the Cub low, she might miss seeing the skiff in the blizzard.

Frustrated, she hurried back to the cabin and threw a few essentials into a backpack, pulled on an extra layer of clothes, and set off to find Karla, working her way slowly upstream along the rocky bank of the river. She'd brought along a rescue whistle, which carried farther than her voice, and every quarter mile or so she would pause and blow it, then strain for an answer, but none came.

Something had happened. Something bad. She could feel it in her gut. It had been a mistake to let Karla set out by herself, after promising Lars and Maggie she'd take care of her. She'd covered less than two miles when dusk fell. She clicked on her flashlight and kept moving forward, sweeping the terrain ahead and the river to her right. The only answer to her repeated whistle blows was a lone wolf howl, far off in the woods to her left.

❖

She was lost. Karla had been trying to deceive herself, but she accepted now that she had no idea where she was in relation to Bryson's cabin. Not that it mattered, because it was pitch-black, and her feet were almost incapable of supporting her.

She felt like she had walked a great distance, but only because each step was so difficult. From the start, her feet were so numb from the river she had difficulty maintaining her balance. She'd fallen several times, twice on her sprained wrist. And the heavily laden trees around her had dumped their cargo of snow directly onto her head, sending icy pellets deep into the collar of her jacket. She was miserably cold. The biting wind had penetrated every available orifice and frozen the top of her wet socks into ice.

At some point, she realized she hadn't spotted the river through the trees for quite some time. She headed in the direction she thought was right, but the shoreline wasn't where she thought it was, and the forest and blowing snow were too thick for her to see the mountains to get her bearings.

She panicked and wanted to run. But she decided she better try to warm her feet. She sat on a downed tree and stripped off her boots, then her ice-crusted socks, with difficulty. She had two dry wool pairs left in her duffel and put them both on, then wrapped her feet in two thick sweaters and prayed for a letup in the blizzard so she could see.

She couldn't have passed the cabin, she tried to reassure herself. It had to be just a short distance ahead. But her sense of direction was too unreliable to give her any confidence. The river valley was very wide at Bryson's cabin. If she'd been traveling close to the mountains instead of the river, she might have passed by without seeing it.

And if she had, thirty miles of wilderness stretched between her and Bettles.

Indecisive, she froze, and soon it was getting dark. No flashlight. No matches. No weapon. Nothing but a few extra clothes, which didn't seem to be doing much to warm her feet.

She tried not to be afraid, but she'd heard the wolves howl too often. Most of the time, they came from the right of the Rasmussen cabin and were a long way off. *A few miles downriver*, Lars often estimated. In other words, right about where she was sitting.

She pulled out the tigereye necklace and shoved it into her right glove, comforted by the smooth stone against her palm. She didn't have many options. Try to keep walking, risking further injury and possibly getting even more lost. Or she could sit tight and hope someone found her before she froze or some predator got too interested. She was long overdue, so Bryson would already be out looking for her. She was that kind of woman.

But if Karla had already passed Bryson's cabin in the storm before she started searching…or if they had been too far apart to see each other when they passed…then Bryson was heading away from her.

CHAPTER SIXTEEN

Karla couldn't erase the image from her mind. A homeless man who refused to give his name had been admitted to the ER one bitterly cold February night, suffering from hypothermia and severe frostbite. Thousands of homeless lived in the city, many in the downtown area, and Grady Memorial got the bulk of them when they required care. So she had seen her share of cases like this, but they'd never been bad enough to warrant amputation.

When the man regained consciousness after the surgery and saw that both his feet and several of his fingers were gone, shock and horror, then tears, then anger crossed his face. "Why did you do this? Why not just let me die? I can't survive like this!"

Karla had lost all feeling in her feet and couldn't stand. And though she'd pulled her hands inside her sleeves to warm them beneath her armpits, she only felt colder. Worse, she yearned to close her eyes and sleep. But if she did, she would probably never wake up again.

❖

Bryson gave herself another hour to find Karla. If she didn't succeed by then, she would go home and call in reinforcements from Bettles to expand the search. The conditions couldn't have been worse: full dark and sub-freezing temperatures. The strong winds and heavy snowfall were muting her whistles, and it would be even more difficult to hear shouts. Unless she was relatively close to Karla, they might miss each other.

She swept the flashlight back and forth, from the woods to the river, hoping Karla might spot the beacon. And she paused frequently to listen, but so far all she'd heard were wolves and the howl of the wind in the trees. She prayed that Karla was all right.

Of all the search-and-rescue operations she'd participated in, none but the search for her father had ever affected her so personally. And it wasn't because of her sense of responsibility to Lars and Maggie. She'd come to care about Karla, too, more than she'd allowed herself to admit.

She blew her whistle long and loud, turned ninety degrees and did it again, then froze to listen.

Her heart raced when she thought she heard an answering call, too indistinct to be sure. Had it been just the wind? She blew the whistle again and followed up with a shout. "Kaaaaarlaaaaaaaa!"

She listened again and caught that same distant hint of reply. More certain now that she was not imagining it, she hurried in the direction she thought the sound had originated from as fast as possible, skirting trees and sweeping the ground in front of her with her flashlight to avoid logs and rocks. It seemed to come from deep in the woods. "I'm coming, Karla! Hang on," she hollered as she crashed through a thicket of willows.

When she'd gone a few hundred yards, she paused to shout again and this time clearly heard the reply. "Bryson! Over here. To your left."

She followed the voice and found Karla sitting on a downed tree, her expression in the glare of her flashlight a mixture of worry and relief.

"I've never been happier to see anyone in my life," Karla said as Bryson hunched down in front of her.

"Are you all right?"

"Freezing." Her teeth chattered. "I crashed the boat and got my boots wet getting to shore. I think my feet are frostbitten, which means I can't and shouldn't walk."

"Shit." Bryson's mind raced, trying to think of the best way to move Karla. There might be enough snow on the ground to use the snowmobile, but she'd waste a lot of time getting back home to retrieve it, and it would be difficult to negotiate the machine over the uneven, densely forested terrain.

"How far is it to your place?" Karla asked.

"Three or four miles." Bryson took off her backpack and set her flashlight beside Karla so she could see what she was doing. "I have some disposable hand warmers with me, and a survival blanket. Let's see if we can get you warmed up some." She opened four of the packets, which began to heat up as soon as they were exposed to air.

She could see that Karla had her hands inside her clothing. "Gonna open your coat for a second to give these to you." Bryson unzipped the jacket halfway. Karla wore a crew-neck navy sweater beneath it.

Karla reached one hand up shakily through the neck of the sweater to retrieve the packets. "Thanks."

She zipped her jacket back up and shone the flashlight down Karla's legs. Her feet were encased in the duffel bag. Beside the bag, covered with snow, were her boots and gloves.

"I guess you don't want me to put any warmers on your feet? You want to wait for warm water?"

"Right. I might be bad enough that those would damage the tissue." Karla wasn't surprised Bryson knew a lot about frostbite. What Alaskan wouldn't? Especially one with search-and-rescue experience. "Any idea how you might get me out of here? And how quickly?"

Bryson unfolded the thin reflective survival blanket and wrapped it around Karla like a cocoon. "Working on that. Is the skiff out of commission?"

"Not structurally, but I couldn't get the engine to start, and it's grounded on a gravel bar. It's quite a way upstream. Hit a rock I didn't see."

"Easy to do, especially in these conditions. I shouldn't have let you try it alone."

"Don't blame yourself. This is totally my doing," Karla said. "These packs are really helping. My hands are tingling and burning like crazy. A good sign."

"Okay, here's the plan." Bryson shook off Karla's boots and put them in her backpack. "I'll take you as far as I can, moving along the river." She was strong, but four miles, especially in the dark in this terrain, was quite a distance. "A fireman's carry is the best way to keep from jostling your feet. Ground's too uneven and rocky to try to drag you out. If I can't carry you any farther, I have a plan B ready." She hoped it wouldn't come to that, but she could always hoof it back and retrieve her fishing raft. Built for one, it could hold them both and get them the rest of the way fairly quickly.

But she hated the time she'd eat up making the round trip on foot and the fifteen minutes wasted inflating the raft. And she didn't want to leave Karla alone. In addition to the worry about being lost and getting frostbite, Karla had looked tremendously relieved when she found her. She must have been terribly afraid. Lost in the wilderness, all alone in the dark, unable to move, and freezing to death.

"You sure you can carry me?"

"You're talking to a woman who chops enough firewood to keep her cabin nice and toasty all winter." She used her most reassuring smile as she took off her belt. She threaded it through the top loop of her backpack and then put it back on, so the pack would hang from her left hip. "I'll need one of your arms out in your sleeve, preferably your right. You warm enough for that yet?"

Karla nodded and slid her right arm into position. Bryson shook the snow from Karla's gloves and inserted another warming pack inside the right one before she pulled it over her hand. She stuck the other glove in her pocket.

Then she crouched in front of Karla, facing away from her. She glanced back as she reached for Karla's right arm to put it over her left shoulder. "I take it you know the fireman's carry?"

"I do."

"Good." She bent sideways and inserted her right hand between Karla's parted thighs. Karla helped position herself by raising her right thigh as high as she could so Bryson could wrap her arm around it. She draped Karla's body over her upper back and shoulders, took the flashlight in her left hand, and slowly stood, taking the weight. "That'll work. You don't weigh a thing." Bryson had guessed her weight at 115 or 120, at most; Karla was at least two or three inches shorter than she was, and slender. And she felt even lighter, probably because of all the adrenaline pumping through her system. "Hang on. Here we go."

Sweeping the flashlight in front of her, Bryson angled north toward the river as fast as she could safely travel, keeping well away from trees on either side. She made good time, considering her burden and the uneven ground, and her back and legs and lungs didn't begin to protest until after she covered the first mile.

"How're you doing?" Karla asked, when Bryson paused a moment to catch her breath.

"About to ask you the same," she managed, between big gulps for air.

"Why don't you set me down for a minute and rest, huh?"

"Will when I need to." She set off again at a slightly slower pace, trying to push away the pain and find a second wind.

Karla kept quiet during their traverse back to her cabin. Bryson hoped it was out of consideration, not pain.

She struggled another mile. Her lungs were burning and her shoulders, back, and knees were in agony. "Rest," she wheezed, as she eased Karla down into a sitting position on a fallen tree.

"You can't go farther. You're killing yourself. I don't know how you're doing this."

She held up a hand to forestall further protest while she eased onto the log beside Karla and took in deep lungfuls of air. Moving slowly, she raised her arms above her head and stretched. Her muscles screamed in relief, but she knew she wouldn't be able to move tomorrow. "Not much more," she said, once her breathing had returned to normal. "Only another mile or so."

"Think you can make it?"

"Might have to stop again. We'll get there." In truth, she wasn't certain her body could endure much more of this punishment. But she wanted to keep Karla as calm and reassured as possible. She already had plenty to worry about.

After a few more minutes of rest they pushed on, Bryson's body screaming in agony with every step. She made it only another quarter mile before her back and shoulders and legs gave way. Her arms were shaking and her calves were cramping painfully as she struggled to set Karla down on a large boulder. Even with rest, she couldn't carry her any farther.

"Can't." She gasped as she collapsed beside the rock. Her heart was booming in her chest, and sweat soaked the inner layer of her clothing.

"Jesus, Bryson. I'm surprised you made it this far. I'm afraid you'll give yourself a heart attack."

"Gotta…" A maddeningly short distance remained, less than a mile. "Gotta leave you here for a while," she wheezed. "Sorry."

"Leave me?"

"Not long." She spoke in short bursts as she tried to catch her breath. "Back soon. Soon as I can." Gripping the edge of the boulder, she hoisted herself to her feet. "Don't fall asleep."

"I won't."

Bryson took off her whistle and put it around Karla's neck. "Wish I could leave this, too," she said as she picked up the flashlight. "But I'll need it to move fast."

"I understand. I'll be fine."

Bryson tucked the survival blanket tight around Karla, then leaned over so their faces were close together. The flashlight cast deep shadows around their features. "You'll be warm soon, I promise. Hang in there, and trust me."

"I do, Bryson. Be careful."

She ached at the worry and fear in Karla's eyes, though she was putting on a brave front. Leaving her alone in the dark was one of the most difficult things she'd ever had to do.

"See you soon." She forced herself forward on rubbery legs, surveying the ground with a critical eye as she headed toward the cabin. Snowmobile or raft? They were her only options, and neither was ideal. The raft would take more time, and they risked getting wet, something neither of them could afford. Her sweat-soaked clothing was making her miserably cold, and Karla's feet could be further damaged. But the snowmachine was an iffy bet as well. The snow wasn't deep enough for it to glide smoothly over the rocky, log-littered shoreline. It could easily get hung up on something and founder.

When the path to her cabin appeared, her spirits lifted slightly. She turned on the generator and went inside to flick on lights, grab her keys and a pair of down booties, and throw a couple of logs into the woodstove to get the heat cranked up.

"Be nice," she urged the snowmobile as she checked the kill switch and turned the key to *on*. The Polaris was an older model, and it usually balked at the first effort every season to get it going. Last year, she'd had to replace the spark plugs and oil to start it. The year before, it needed new valves. She'd always managed to get it running, but often only after hours of labor and a trip to Bettles or beyond for parts.

She pulled the start cord and heard a muffled *pop*, but the engine failed to turn over. She tried twice more, with the same result. "Start, damn you," she said through gritted teeth as she pulled the choke out halfway and tried again. This time, the engine fired, but quickly died again. A bit more choke, then another pull on the cord, and the Polaris roared to life.

Breathing a little better, she gradually reduced the choke until the engine was warming smoothly. A glance at the gas tank and a brief diversion to stuff her raft into a large backpack—just in case—and she was ready to go. She checked her watch. Forty minutes had passed since they'd parted. The time had flown for her, but every second probably seemed an eternity for Karla.

Chapter Seventeen

Karla scarcely felt the bitter chill except when the wind gusted, blasting icy pellets of snow against her face and down her collar. She moved the heat packets around on her body, and they did a good job warming her torso. Unfortunately her feet weren't bothering her because they were completely numb from the ankles down, like wood blocks attached to her legs. She was careful not to move around too much.

As the minutes ticked by, she tried not to think about how her headlong foray into an arctic wilderness she didn't understand and was unprepared for might change her life forever. If she'd only taken matches, she could have built a fire. Or a second pair of boots, and she'd have made it to Bryson's without assistance. How stupid she'd been.

She might forgive herself more readily if this had happened during her first night in Alaska, before Bryson and Lars and even Maggie had all found ways to tell or show her how important it was to be prepared for any eventuality. To never underestimate the awesome and unpredictable power of the weather here.

Instead, she was desperately fighting fear and despair. When the darkness had swallowed Bryson's flashlight beam, she'd had to force herself not to call out for her to come back.

She wished she had even a fraction of Bryson's courage. To live by herself out here, facing down every challenge. To take to the skies every day, knowing a storm or freak wind could arise out of nowhere and slap her to the ground. Bryson hadn't hesitated to risk her own safety to search for her, a virtual stranger. Yet another example of her selflessness and strong character. Would Karla do the same?

When she heard the distant roar of the snowmobile and glimpsed its lights through the trees, the sense of calm that seemed to settle on her whenever Bryson was around returned.

The machine slowed to a stop a few feet away, and Bryson dismounted but kept the engine running. She crouched down in front of her so they were face-to-face, but she still had to speak loudly to be heard. "You all right?"

"Ready to get out of here."

Bryson pulled two down booties from the pocket of her coat. "Better for the trip back." She carefully lifted Karla's feet from the duffel, unwrapped the sweaters that surrounded them, and eased on the booties. Then she put one arm beneath Karla's legs, the other around her back, and lifted her, cradling her against her chest. "Careful of your feet," she warned as she carried her to the snowmobile and slowly lowered her onto the seat. "And I need your arms out. You'll have to hold on to me, it's kind of rough going." She helped Karla with her gloves, then slipped into the seat in front of her. She'd put her large backpack on her chest so Karla could snuggle up against her back.

Karla wrapped her arms around Bryson's waist and bent her legs to keep her feet up.

"All set?" Bryson yelled over her shoulder.

"Yes," she shouted back.

It was very slow going. The blowing snow reduced visibility to only a few feet, so Bryson frequently rose out of the seat to peer over the windscreen for a better look at the trail they were backtracking. Now and then, the machine would slow to a crawl as she negotiated around a fallen log or stump. Finally, in the distance, Karla could see the lights of the cabin through the blowing streaks of snow.

Bryson pulled the snowmachine into her outbuilding and cut the engine, then tossed her backpack beside the sled. "Let's get those feet warmed up." Gently lifting her as she did before, Bryson carried Karla inside and lowered her onto the couch. The logs she'd tossed into the woodstove had done a fine job of heating up the cabin.

"I'll get some water on and warm up my big tub," she said as she helped Karla out of her gloves and coat.

"Great. I'd like to take some ibuprofen when you get done with that. My feet will hurt like a bitch when I start to get some feeling back."

"You got it." Bryson set water to boiling in several large pots and tipped her galvanized tub next to the woodstove. "You need something hot to drink. Coffee? Tea? Cocoa?"

"Cocoa, please."

When the water was ready, Karla downed four ibuprofen from the bottle Bryson gave her and warmed her hands on the mug while Bryson filled the tub.

"The weather's too bad to fly out right now," Bryson said. "But I can try to raise the hospital in Fairbanks for you on the sat phone, if you want to talk to a doctor."

"I'll keep that option open." Karla lifted her legs and glanced at the down booties on her feet. She couldn't see them when Bryson had put them on, and she hadn't noticed them until now. She couldn't help smiling. The booties were brown, covered in short faux fur, and shaped like grizzly-bear feet. They reminded her of the whimsical orange tabby-paw slippers she'd bought Abby for Christmas one year. Abby had called them ridiculous and returned them the next day. What had she been thinking? Abby had no sense of humor. Karla wondered how it was possible to be with someone for years and never really see her clearly until they had some distance between them.

Had someone given the bear-feet slippers to Bryson? For some reason, she hoped Bryson had picked them out herself.

"I think we're ready." Bryson swirled her hand through the water to test the temperature. "Lukewarm."

"Okay. Want to do the honors? Let's see what we've got."

Bryson's hands were sure, but tender. She eased off the booties, then, very slowly and carefully, cut away the socks.

Karla assessed her feet with a practiced clinical eye. They were a very pale white, with a bluish-purple tinge, but she'd seen much worse. "Easy," she told herself as she lowered them into the tub, scooting forward just enough so they were completely immersed but did not touch the bottom.

Bryson sat crossed-legged on the floor on the other side of the tub and began to swirl one hand in the water.

"Something tells me you've done this before."

"Unfortunately, a few times too often. But most of the time, things come out fine when someone's been out only a few hours. You kept them wrapped up well."

"We'll know pretty soon." Karla sipped her cocoa and told herself to be patient. Not being able to feel anything immediately told her nothing. She reached into her pocket for the tigereye necklace and, when she came up empty, only then remembered that she'd shoved it into her glove the night before. "Shit!"

"What's wrong?"

"I put my Mom's necklace into my right glove last night." She glanced frantically around. "Do you know where it is?"

Bryson hurried to retrieve the gloves from the pile of hats and mittens by the door. She frowned as she returned them to Karla. "Nothing in there but a warming pack. My fault. I remember shaking the snow off them when I found you."

Tears sprang to Karla's eyes. "It's gone, then." She exhaled a long breath as the loss fully registered. Only a piece of jewelry, she tried to tell herself. But she felt almost like she'd lost her mother all over again.

"I'm sorry." Bryson put a hand on Karla's shoulder. "I know how much that meant to you."

"Not your fault, Bryson. My own carelessness."

"No. It was foolish of me to suggest you try to get here on your own in this weather." Bryson sat back beside the tub to slowly agitate the warming water, adding a little from the teakettle now and then to keep the temperature consistent.

"Stop blaming yourself. I mean it. It was my decision." Bryson's expression, however, showed that she was determined to accept responsibility for what had happened. "You saved me. Yet again, I might add. You're turning out to be my guardian angel."

Bryson gave a reluctant but genuine smile. "Glad I seem to have developed a habit of being in the right place at the right time with you."

That was certainly the truth. "Do you mind if I ask you a personal question?"

"No. Shoot."

"Don't take this the wrong way, but…what's *wrong* with you?"

Bryson looked at her curiously. "I beg your pardon?"

"I mean…you're gorgeous, and incredibly sweet. Brave. Selfless.

Loyal to your friends. Why the hell hasn't someone snapped you up long ago? Do you have an aversion to commitment or something?"

Scarlet rose in Bryson's cheeks as she looked away, and a sudden shyness softened her features. "Thanks for the compliments, but I'm sure not perfect." She poured more hot water into the tub. "It's not a matter of fear of commitment. Just haven't met the right person."

"I thought you might have something going with the waitress at the Den. And it looked as though that pretty gate attendant in Fairbanks was interested, too."

The blush deepened. "I've dated them," she said, without meeting Karla's eyes. "And they're both great women. Just not long-term material, for me."

"Why not? If you don't mind my asking."

Bryson shrugged. "Don't know if I can really explain. Maybe it sounds naïve, but I just feel in my gut that I'll *know* when it's really *right*."

"I used to think that way." And look where it had gotten her.

"You don't anymore?" Bryson's voice had an edge to it that almost sounded like disappointment.

"Let's just say I don't think *my* gut is very reliable. I was sure I'd found *the one*, but now I think I was just too anxious to settle down."

Bryson was watching her intently, waiting for her to continue.

"I dreamed all my life of falling in love, so when I experienced that real first flush of…oh, I don't know. Physical chemistry, joy of companionship, feeling like I was needed and appreciated, I mistook it all for more than it was. I see now we didn't have the foundation to make it work long-term—the same goals, the same dreams. The same level of mutual support and commitment to staying together and working through problems, no matter what. You want to talk naïve, I was the definition of the term."

"Sounds like it didn't end well," Bryson said sympathetically. "Were you married?"

"Not technically, no. But I felt like I was." A sigh escaped her. "Apparently I was the only one who felt that way."

"I'm sorry. It sounds like you really got hurt."

"Well, I didn't see it coming. That's what hurt the most. And it happened just two weeks before my mom died."

"That recently?" Bryson said. "You've really had a hell of a lot to deal with, then. No wonder you seemed so…well, kind of preoccupied and troubled when you came here."

"Basket case is more like it. The trifecta of startling surprises—divorce, death, and finding out I had a long-lost sister, all within the space of a month."

Bryson's voice got quiet. "Tonight aside, has it helped? Being here?"

"Yes, it has. Much more than I even dared hope for, as a matter of fact. The distance, all the hours of thinking time…" She waited for Bryson to look at her before she continued. "And especially the new friends and family who've helped me see things with a fresh outlook. I'm very glad I came."

"I am, too." Bryson smiled, but her eyes clouded with regret. "Won't be easy to see you leave. I hope you'll keep in touch once you get home."

"For sure, I—" Her feet tingled slightly. She bent over at the waist to get a better look at them, and as she did, Bryson stopped agitating the water.

"What is it?"

"Getting some feeling back." Her feet were pinking up again, a good sign.

"That's great!"

"Yeah." But even as she acknowledged the positive development, the slight tingling escalated into excruciating pain as circulation returned. It felt like someone was carving her feet up like a Thanksgiving turkey. She slumped back against the couch, wincing. "Christ, that hurts."

"The ibuprofen isn't helping?"

"Not much," she said through tightly clenched teeth. "Oh, what I wouldn't give for a morphine drip right now."

She spent the next hour in agony, her body so rigidly tensed against the pain that the muscles in her shoulders and back began to spasm. Bryson continued her warming duties, keeping the water agitated and boiling more as needed so the temperature would be consistent. For a while, she tried to make small talk to keep Karla's mind off her feet, but no amount of distraction helped.

Finally the suffering ebbed to a dull throb. Her feet were red and swollen, but she could feel them again, all too well, and detected no immediate sign of tissue damage. She'd have to keep her weight off them and monitor the skin closely during the next few days for signs of blistering and other complications, but she'd evidently escaped permanent damage. "I think that's done the trick. Need to bandage them though," she told Bryson as she lifted her feet from the water. "How are you set for gauze and tape?"

"Plenty. Let me." Bryson got her first-aid supplies out and did a more-than-credible job of carefully drying and bandaging her feet. "You've got to be exhausted," she said when she'd finished. "Think you can get some shut-eye?"

Karla stretched, trying to work out the huge knot of tension that had taken up residence between her shoulder blades. "Feel like I've been run over by a convoy of tanks. But, yeah, worth a shot."

"Wish I could give you my bed, it's more comfortable than the futon," Bryson said as she got to her feet. "But I don't think it's wise to try to haul you up that ladder."

"Hey, this will be fine. Just toss me a pillow and blanket and I'm golden."

"I can do a little better than that." Bryson came over and stood before her. "But I'm gonna have to move you a minute," she said as she reached down to hoist Karla into her arms. She started to set her down on the futon chair, but changed her mind halfway there and straightened again.

Their faces were close together, and Karla was acutely aware of every place where their bodies touched. Her arm was draped across the top of Bryson's back, palm resting on the exquisitely rounded deltoid muscle of her right shoulder. Bryson's arms securely cradled her lower thighs and back. Most disquieting of all, her breast was only a few inches from Bryson's full, moist lips.

"You obviously won't be able to walk for at least a few days. I just wanted to say don't hesitate to ask me to help you." Bryson appeared to be not at all as affected as she was by their rather intimate position. "I just realized, you probably need a pit stop before I get you settled in for the night."

"A good idea. That cocoa's beginning to catch up with me."

Bryson carried her over to the corner and set her down on the portable honeypot toilet set up behind a small screen. "I'll bring more wood in and shut off the generator," she said, withdrawing to give her some privacy.

Karla wrestled off her jeans, careful not to put weight on her feet. Pulling the snug denim up again was so tough she vowed to live in sweatpants until she could walk again. Her exertions amplified the throbbing in her feet. The healing process wouldn't be fun, though having to be reliant on Bryson for a while certainly wasn't *all* bad.

The lights in the cabin went out as the loud hum of the outside generator halted abruptly. Bryson came back in, stomped the snow from her boots, and called, "Be just a minute."

A welcoming sight awaited her when she emerged from behind the screen, once again nestled in Bryson's arms. Bryson had converted the couch into a bed and covered it with flannel bedding, a thick down comforter, and three fluffy pillows. On the table beside it, a pair of thick round candles cast a soft amber light.

"Nice." Though she didn't know which was nicer, the fuss Bryson had made or how it felt to be wrapped in her secure embrace. Karla had an urge to run her hand through Bryson's hair to see what it felt like. "You didn't have to go to all this trouble."

Bryson's arms tightened around her, ever so slightly. "No trouble." As she eased Karla onto the futon, she added, "Anything else I can do for you tonight?"

Her mind leapt to all sorts of answers, none of which she could volunteer and all of which surprised her. *You can stay with me until I fall asleep. You can lie here with me and hold me in your arms. You can kiss me senseless and make me feel alive again.* "I'm fine. Thanks for everything."

"Good night, then. Sleep tight."

"You too, Bryson."

As Karla wrestled out of her clothes, Bryson lit a small kerosene lamp and took it with her up the ladder to the loft. Not long after, the light was extinguished.

Karla blew out her candles but lay awake for a long time, staring at the flames dancing in the woodstove. Her life was chaotic enough already. She shouldn't even be *thinking* about getting involved with anyone right now, let alone someone who lived on the other side of the world.

She had become involved with Abby because she let her hormones and heart blind her to reality, and she was determined not to make the same mistake twice. There didn't seem any way to make this work.

But every moment she spent with Bryson made it harder for her to keep her distance. No amount of rationalization or will power could stop her heart from pounding when Bryson got near, or calm the raging butterflies that invaded her stomach every time she caught Bryson watching her. It already seemed unthinkable to return to Atlanta without ever knowing what Bryson's soft lips tasted like. How would she feel after a lot more time alone together?

Chapter Eighteen

Bryson's body was screaming for rest because of her grueling ordeal, but her mind would not allow it.

You sure had to be careful what you wished for. She was about to have exactly what she'd been fantasizing about—time alone with Karla so she could get to know her better. In fact, because of her temporary disability, they wouldn't have much to do *but* get better acquainted.

But she hadn't imagined this at all. They would be spending several *days* alone together, for one thing, not just a few hours. And though she'd be holding Karla in her arms frequently, she didn't really want it to be like this.

Touching her this way, being close enough to kiss her without being able to, would definitely drive her crazy. Every time she picked her up, she became hyperaware of their proximity. Every nerve ending bolted to alert, her heart raced, and her sense of smell became acutely attuned to the subtle fragrance of Karla's shampoo. She ached to study, close up, the soft skin of Karla's cheek, the extraordinary length of her gold-blond eyelashes, and the full, lush lips that invited her own. But if she did, Karla would be able to see how much she wanted her, so she forced herself to look away.

Sooner or later, however, no matter how hard she worked to appear nonchalant, Karla would realize the effect she was having on her. And then what? If that happened she hoped Karla would feel flattered and laugh it off. It'd make for an uncomfortable arrangement if she reacted poorly to the news.

She held her breath when a sound from below broke the quiet. Karla was shifting in bed, trying to get comfortable; a soft groan of discomfort followed the creak of the futon. *What would you say if you knew how much I want to crawl in next to you right now? Wrap my body around yours and hold you until you fall asleep?* The cabin went silent again, and she relaxed back against her pillow.

It was ludicrous to even consider getting involved with Karla. They didn't have a future, even if Karla *was* interested in being more than just a friend. And she wouldn't be able to detach from a brief affair with her as readily as she disengaged from all the other women she'd been with. Why was that? What made her so different?

She lay awake for another hour trying to find the answer and finally concluded that something about Karla *spoke* to her, connected with a part of her that had been dormant all her life. Chemistry, that's what it was. It just felt right to be around her.

❖

The cabin was still dark and quiet when Karla roused, though she sensed it wasn't too early because she felt well rested. Her feet throbbed dully, but mostly her bladder was extremely full. As much as she hated to disturb Bryson, she didn't have an alternative. "Bryson? Hey, you awake? Bryson?"

"Yeah," came the sleepy reply from the loft. "Yeah, I'm here. You okay?"

"Sorry to get you up, but I need your help. I have to pee like there's no tomorrow."

"Oh, sure. Be right down."

Bryson's feet hit the floorboards of the loft, followed by a muffled groan. Karla craned her neck and saw a soft light flickering from above. Bryson appeared with the kerosene lamp and slowly descended the ladder.

"I bet you're sore as hell, aren't you?" she asked as Bryson came over to her with the light.

"I'll live." She smiled down at her. "Can you wait long enough for me to turn on some lights and throw a couple of logs on the fire?"

"If you're Speedy Gonzalez about it, yes."

Bryson hurried outside to crank on the generator, then bustled about turning on lights and stoking up the woodstove. She was wearing a pair of old navy sweatpants and a thick fleece turtleneck the same color, and her dark hair was so full of static from the dry crisp air it was sticking up in all directions.

"Do you have another pair of sweats I could borrow?" Karla asked. "I didn't pack any, and they'd be a lot easier to get on and off than my jeans."

"Sure." Bryson headed back up the ladder and returned with a thick pair of emerald-green sweatpants. While Karla pulled them gingerly over her swollen feet, Bryson put water on to boil.

"Ready." She turned to dangle her feet over the side of the bed. The sweatpants were a pretty good fit at the waist, but the excess length pooled around her ankles and over the bandages.

Bryson came over and smiled at the fit before picking her up. Karla put her arms around Bryson's neck, and as she did, Bryson stiffened.

"You all right? Your back okay to do this?" She tried to see if Bryson was in pain, but she averted her gaze.

"No, I'm fine." Bryson strode off in the direction of the screen, carrying her as though nothing was wrong. But her voice was strained and she responded almost too quickly. Something was going on. She set Karla down on the honeypot and withdrew. The pottery mugs clinked as she set about making coffee.

"Ready for a ride back," she called, and Bryson materialized almost at once.

"What would you like for breakfast?" Bryson asked as she set her back on the futon bed. "I've got cereal, pancakes, or eggs with some reindeer sausage and toast."

"A full-service establishment, I see." Bryson smiled. "Cereal is fine, don't go to any bother. And I'm good to wait a while until my stomach wakes up, but coffee sounds heavenly."

"Coming right up." Bryson poured two mugs and handed one to Karla, then took hers to the futon chair beside the bed so they could chat.

"Tell me the truth," Karla insisted.

Bryson nearly choked on her coffee, and a look of surprised panic crossed her features. "Say what?" she asked, wiping at her chin.

"Tell me the truth. You're so sore you can barely move, though you're doing your best to hide it. Am I right?"

The corners of Bryson's mouth twitched upward in a smile. "Maybe a little." The look of relief that crossed her face was unmistakable, and

Karla wondered what Bryson wasn't saying. What did she think she was referring to?

"Looks like we both need to just relax and heal. You know, you can stretch out here with me. You'd be more comfortable, I'm sure." She patted the pillow beside her invitingly. Maybe she couldn't snuggle up to Bryson the way she wanted to, but having the object of her fascination within reach would sure distract her. "We can read, play a game, whatever you like." Bryson's expression was unreadable, but the fierce reddening of her face and cheeks was obvious. She'd struck a nerve. Her heart began to beat wildly. Was Bryson thinking, hoping for, the same thing she was? Maybe she wasn't misreading her interest at all.

"I'm okay," Bryson finally replied, and got to her feet to fetch them more coffee. "But thanks. You just stretch out and be comfy. Can I get you something to read? What type of book do you like?"

What a perfect opening, she thought. "As a matter of fact, I had a good look at your library the last time I was here and noticed we like a lot of the same authors."

"Oh?" Bryson set down their mugs and walked over to her bookshelves.

"That's what I was referring to that day when I said we had a lot in common."

"I remember. Lars came in just then. I kept meaning to ask you about that. Yeah, I'm a pretty voracious reader. So, what'll it be? Mystery? Sci-fi?"

Karla couldn't keep from smiling, but she was nervous, too, about how Bryson would react. "Anything on one of those eight shelves to your far right is fine. Though I've already read most of Radclyffe's books, and Ann Bannon's."

Bryson froze. The quick succession of emotions that crossed her face in that unguarded moment was almost comical. Surprise and disbelief, then pleased realization hit home. "Oh?" It came out as a squeak, confirming Karla's suspicions.

"That surprise you?"

"Uh, yeah, have to admit it does. I had no idea." Bryson started to jam her hands in her pockets and seemed chagrined to discover her sweatpants didn't have any. Instead, she folded her arms over her chest in a transparent effort to appear unaffected.

Karla laughed. This awkward and shy Bryson, with her wayward hair and disheveled sweats, was adorable. "I kind of gathered that, from your reaction."

"Reaction?" Bryson repeated, as a new flush of scarlet rose to her cheeks.

"Come over here, will you?"

Bryson looked uncertain, as though she'd just been asked to walk through a room full of snakes. But she shook off her inertia and slowly crossed to stand beside the futon bed, biting her lip.

"Can I ask you something?"

"What do you want to know?" Her voice was soft and husky, like she knew exactly what was coming next.

"Are you...*interested* in me? And don't pretend you don't know what I'm asking."

Bryson stared deeply into her eyes for a long moment before she answered, as though wanting to know if Karla would welcome a *yes*.

"And if I am?"

Excitement fluttered low in Karla's abdomen. "If you are, then I suspect we'll get a lot closer in the next few days."

Bryson's face lit up with a huge smile and she visibly relaxed. She stepped closer and placed her hand against Karla's cheek, then slowly bent to kiss her. It wasn't a *real* kiss, not the long, lingering heat she'd been imagining their first kiss might be. Bryson's lips touched hers firmly but briefly, a kiss that said *oh, yeah, I'm most definitely interested.* A tease of things to come.

Then she withdrew a step, but her face lost none of the joy and longing that had flared when Karla confirmed their mutual attraction. "I better break out the ibuprofen and a good hot breakfast, then," Bryson said playfully. "And hope for some fast healing. Because neither of us is in any shape right now to..." She let her gaze travel the length of Karla's body, outlined beneath the comforter, with open admiration. "Let's just say I don't want to be too hampered by frostbitten feet, aching backs, and growling stomachs."

They grinned at each other for several more seconds before Bryson retreated to the kitchen to cook breakfast, humming to herself.

The prospect of living out some of her recent daydreams about Bryson was thrilling, but daunting. It had been more than four years since she'd slept with anyone besides Abby, and until this moment being intimate with Bryson had been abstract. A twitch of doubt threatened to deflate her euphoria. Bryson had apparently been with a lot of women. She didn't want to disappoint her.

But as quickly as the thoughts arose, she pushed them aside. Seize the moment and enjoy it while you can, she told herself. No more looking into the future, and no more living in the past.

CHAPTER NINETEEN

Bryson wanted to give Karla the most romantic day of her life, one she would look back on often with longing and joy. When she was seeing a woman, she usually took flowers on a first date and planned a nice evening. And she especially wanted to favorably impress Karla.

Amazing how a few words made her walk on air. Her body hadn't ached this badly since she'd wrenched it building her cabin. It hurt just to straighten completely. But she felt absolutely *fabulous*, knowing Karla was as interested as she was in *them*.

She'd gone a little overboard with breakfast, using her most precious stores with abandon and cooking enough for three or four people. Fresh scrambled eggs accompanied reindeer sausage, homemade sourdough toast, and blueberry preserves. An elderly client who flew often from her Fairbanks retirement center to Bettles to visit her grandchildren had given her the bread and jam.

"Not ideal conditions for a first date," Bryson said as she carried the plates to the futon. "I'd like to take you to a nice restaurant, maybe go dancing."

Karla smiled and patted the space next to her on the bed. "Aside from our disabilities, I can't imagine a more perfect way to spend some time with you. No distractions. No interruptions. Beautiful setting."

Bryson sat beside her on the bed, her back cushioned with pillows. "I'm so glad you're here. How are the feet?"

"Ibuprofen and giddy delight make for a potent pain-killing combination."

"Giddy delight?" The description warmed her from within, because it was exactly the way she felt, too.

"I've had so much on my mind it took me a while to realize what was going on," Karla said. "How attracted I am to you, and how much I want to get to know you better."

"I have to admit I didn't get the best first impression of you, not that I was so charming myself," Bryson admitted with a smile, and they both laughed at the memory. "But once I got to know you, that changed pretty fast. And boy, especially these last few days since our walk up the mountain, I've been thinking about you a *lot*. But I don't think I'd have ever volunteered that info."

"Why not?"

"I didn't suspect you're gay. And you were dealing with so much else in your life." She didn't mention the other reason. Karla was a woman she could fall head-over-heels for and have a hard time forgetting. But as much as she feared a broken heart, she dreaded more that they might never know where their feelings might take them.

"I've been thinking a lot about you since our hike, too. Bryson, you've been more help to me with everything than I could ever begin to tell you. Getting away and meeting you and Maggie have been exactly what I needed to sort things out." Karla finished her toast and set her plate aside with a contented sigh. "Great breakfast. You know, I could get used to being spoiled like this."

"You deserve to be, especially after all you've done for Maggie and Lars." Bryson carried their plates to the kitchen and returned with a carafe of coffee.

Karla frowned. "I hope I'm ambulatory before Maggie's released. She'll need a few weeks to heal completely from the C-section."

"Well, if you're still not fully recovered by the time she brings the baby home, I'll just have to move in, too, and take care of both of you, since Lars is worthless in the kitchen."

"Hmm. That offer is almost enough to make me *not* want to get back on my feet." Karla lay gingerly down on her side facing Bryson, propped up on one elbow.

Bryson moved just as slowly in mirroring her actions. As she shifted her weight, a muscle spasm in her back made her wince.

"Quite a pair, the two of us." Karla laughed. "Gimpy and Gimpier."

She laughed, too. “I know, right? Right now I’m completely incapable of doing just about everything I’ve imagined doing with you. The spirit is sooo willing, as they say, but the flesh has definitely seen better days.”

“Oh?” Karla’s tone turned flirty. “I want to hear all about these things you’ve imagined. Let me know what I’m in for.”

“Much rather play that by ear.” She trailed her fingers over Karla’s shoulder and down her arm. “Although I can tell you that stripping off your clothes—very slowly—and exploring every inch of your body is definitely at the top of my list.”

“Mmm, I like the sound of that.”

“And you’ll notice I said *just* about everything is impossible.” She inched closer until their bodies were nearly touching, slipped her fingertips into Karla’s palm, and Karla’s fingers closed around them. “If I don’t kiss you right now,” Bryson said, “I won’t be able to think straight.”

“Thinking is the last thing I want you to do.” Karla moistened her lips in invitation.

They met halfway in a soft brush of lips, a glancing, tentative joining. Then again, they pressed their mouths against each other just as sweetly. Karla was as patient as Bryson, and apparently equally determined to make every moment of this kiss last.

The tip of Karla’s tongue emerged to stroke Bryson’s lower lip, then she playfully nipped the same spot. The slow seduction was stoking a fire of arousal within her, and each pass of Karla’s tongue fanned the flames higher.

She returned the provocative caresses, skimming her tongue along the curve of Karla’s mouth and sucking lightly, until Karla’s lips parted wider to welcome her into a deep-tongue kiss. They stroked hotly, wetly, and desire poured through her, sending her higher still, until the need for more became almost unbearable.

“Jesus, Bryson,” Karla rasped when they pulled away from each other a few inches to catch their breath. Her lips were rosy red and slightly swollen. “I…I can’t begin to describe how you make me feel when you kiss me like that.”

“Definitely mutual.” The open, unbridled yearning in Karla’s eyes captivated Bryson. She’d seen it before in women, certainly, but it had never touched her this way. "But dangerous right now, since we can't carry this further. I'm kind of wound up, if you know what I mean."

Karla squeezed her hand. "You'd barely have to touch me right now and I'd come."

The words resonated through her body and settled like a hot fist in the pit of her stomach. "Oh, God, don't say that. That's definitely not helping."

"No?" Karla teased. "How about if I tell you where I'd most like to put my tongue?"

"Cruel. That's just plain cruel." Bryson sat up abruptly, grimacing at another spasm in her back, and put her fingers in her ears. "La la la la. I can't hear you. La la la."

Karla sat up, too, and grabbed for the nearer hand to pull it away. She was laughing. "Okay, okay. I'll stop. Not doing me any good either, to have those pictures in my head."

"Maybe we'd better, um, better…" That haze of lust was still radiating from Karla's eyes, and she was drawn to it like a moth to light. "Will you stop looking at me like that? It turns my brain to mush."

"Can't help it," Karla replied, all innocence.

"In that case, I'll have to be the strong one." Bryson forced herself painfully off the bed and stood beside it. "Maybe we should turn this back into a couch for a while?"

"Spoilsport." Karla poked out her lower lip in a pretend pout.

No matter how much Bryson's body was hurting, it was still impossibly difficult not to ravage Karla when she looked so damn irresistible. "I should take a look at your feet. Put some more wood on the fire. See about the skiff." Something, anything to get her mind off how turned on she was. She'd take a cold shower, if she had one.

Karla frowned. "The first two I can agree with. But surely you don't mean to go back out there, as sore as you are, to look for the boat. It's a long way, Bryson. I'd hiked a while before you found me."

Bryson glanced toward the front window. The sun was up, and for the moment, anyway, it wasn't snowing. "Grant you, I'm not looking forward to it, either. But freeze-up is a tenuous time. The water level can rise a lot from ice jams, and all kinds of debris comes floating downriver. Even if the skiff was grounded and you anchored it, it might come loose. It'd be a big loss for Lars and Maggie."

"It wouldn't start," Karla reminded her.

"I'm pretty mechanically inclined and Lars has tools on board. I can probably get it running again."

Karla didn't look happy. "You sound determined. I can't talk you out of it?"

Bryson sat on the edge of the bed and stroked Karla's cheek. "I'll be fine. I'll take it slow and easy, and won't overexert myself. I promise."

"How long will you be gone?"

"Two or three hours, at least. I should probably go while the weather holds." She threw a trio of thick logs into the woodstove. "Think we can wait until I get back to look at your feet?"

"Yes, they'll be fine. But I'd like to get rid of some of this coffee before you go."

"Oh, right." As Bryson returned to the bed, Karla put her arms out in anticipation. She had a glint of mischief in her eyes. "No funny stuff, now," Bryson warned as she bent to pick her up.

Karla's arms circled her neck again, and this time she twined her fingers playfully in the hair at the back of her neck. Halfway to the screen, she traced her tongue wetly along Bryson's ear before whispering, "I want you so much."

Bryson went weak in the knees. "I won't be held responsible for dropping you if you keep that up." She struggled the rest of the way and set Karla down, suppressing a moan as another shooting pain ripped up her spine.

Karla sensed her stiffening and grew serious. "You really shouldn't go out again, Bryson."

"Have to. And stop worrying, I'll be home before you know it. I'm gonna throw on some warm clothes. Be right back." She took a couple more ibuprofen and returned the futon to a couch before she headed into the loft to layer up for her trek. To her pack of survival gear she added neoprene wetsuit pants, neoprene socks, and a spare pair of boots, since the crossing to the boat was evidently a deep one.

"All set?" she called from outside the screen.

"Come and *get* me," Karla replied breathily, in her most provocative tone.

Bryson rounded the barrier and shook her finger at Karla. "Cruel. That is definitely the word for you. Do you plan to taunt me the entire time you're here?"

Karla grinned. "That's the plan. Can I help it if I like to make you squirm?"

Steeling herself, Bryson picked up Karla without further comment and headed back to the futon, trying hard not to succumb to the caresses along the back of her neck. She didn't look at Karla until she got in position to set her down. "Play with fire, and you'll get burned," she warned, before kissing Karla again. She tortured them both, putting everything into the kiss, all the pent-up desire that had been building for days.

The frustrated arousal on Karla's face when she left was priceless.

Chapter Twenty

Bandit dive-bombed Bryson as soon as she emerged from the cabin, and because she didn't offer him breakfast, the raven accompanied her down the trail to the water, squawking as he darted from spruce to spruce just ahead of her.

"Yeah, yeah. Such a rough life. Look at you. If I feed you any more you won't be able to fly."

As though he understood, Bandit buzzed her with a flutter of wings and a loud croak, then vanished into the woods, leaving her alone with her thoughts.

She stopped when she reached the river. The water level was up several inches, and the freeze-up along the bank had advanced another foot since the night before, not surprising since the temperature was in the teens now. Her Super Cub would soon be grounded until everything froze solid; she hoped the lake stayed open until Maggie was discharged so she could get them home in Skeeter's floatplane. On the other hand, she wouldn't mind if they were delayed and Karla was forced to stay longer with her, though their inevitable parting would be all the more difficult.

The snow must have tapered off just after they'd arrived at her cabin, because Bryson could still make out the slight indentation of her snowmobile track from the night before. As she followed it upstream along the bank, she considered the impossible. What if Karla didn't leave? She'd lived a solitary existence for so long it was difficult to imagine things any other way, unless she pictured Karla sharing her bed and her life. Then it was remarkably easy. She could see them in the morning, Karla snuggled deep in the covers after they'd made love, refusing to emerge until she'd made coffee and stoked up the woodstove. The two of them curled up on the couch together reading, stealing kisses between chapters. Hiking into the backcountry in the spring, when all the baby animals were out exploring with their mothers. Sitting on the porch, sipping wine and watching the sun paint the mountains gold-orange as it dipped toward the horizon. All the things she most enjoyed would be twice as special shared with Karla.

It was folly. Sure, Karla seemed to like it here. She'd raved about their hike up Mathews Dome, and she clearly appreciated the wilderness. But Karla had a well-established life elsewhere. A job, an apartment, and probably lots of friends. And she'd grown up with the modern amenities all outsiders had and were always reluctant to give up.

Also, Karla had been in a long-term relationship until only a month or two ago. She hadn't seen the end coming and had been deeply hurt. Karla probably wouldn't be able to fully trust anyone again enough to commit to them for a long time. She knew as well as Bryson did that what was happening between them would end in a few weeks. Maybe that was one reason she found it appealing. Maybe Bryson was just a way for her to move on and feel better about herself and her situation.

The thought depressed her. She wanted to mean more to Karla than that. But she would happily take what she could get, regardless of Karla's motivations. For many years, she had followed her pop's advice to live life in the moment and seize happiness wherever possible. She'd continue to do so.

The vague snowmobile track she'd been following ended at the large boulder where she'd left Karla. The remnants of her footprints beyond were much less distinct, disappearing entirely in the open places and visible only as faint impressions where she'd passed beneath thick clusters of trees. But she had a keen sense of direction and well-developed tracking skills, and was able to follow the footprints along the riverbank to the entrance into the deeper woods, where she'd found Karla.

It was a long shot, but she had to try to find the necklace. Carefully and patiently she picked her way along, circling when she lost the tracks until she found them again, until at last she came upon the downed tree where she'd first discovered Karla. She said a prayer as she got on her hands and knees to sweep the snow aside, and soon the sight of a gold chain peeking out of the white powder rewarded her.

Elated, she angled back toward the river and continued upstream, barely noticing the ache in her legs and back from carrying Karla the night before. But her brief euphoria dissipated when she spotted the skiff and realized what she was up against.

The rise in the water level would help her get the skiff off the gravel bar and back down the river. But crossing to it would be a bitch, even with neoprene on. She'd be punching through ice for the first and last few steps, and she'd have to go slow over the rocky bottom when she reached the fast, deep current in the middle or it would sweep her away.

Karla had been damn lucky. Just thinking of what could have happened chilled her, but she admired Karla even more. It had taken a lot of courage to face that crossing and make it as far as she had.

Bryson quickly shed her jeans and pulled her neoprene kayak pants on over her lightweight long underwear, then her neoprene socks and waterproof boots, laced as tight as they would go. Shortening her backpack so it rode high on her shoulders, she took a few deep breaths and stomped through the thick ice at the edge. She moved as quickly as she dared, but had to slow when she got in over her knees and began to feel the impact of the current. The middle was wicked deep, up to the top of her thighs, and she struggled to keep her footing.

The thought that Karla was depending on her to get back in one piece kept her from making stupid mistakes out of haste. She reached the other side and darted into the cabin of the skiff, out of the wind, and quickly changed back into her jeans and warm, dry footwear.

The clouds above her were thickening, and the wind began to pick up as she checked the exterior of the skiff for damage. The dent in the bow that Karla warned her about wasn't too bad; the boat was still watertight. The engine was balky but she managed to get it going on the fourth try. Things had probably happened so fast that Karla had flooded it.

Her final obstacle was getting the boat back in the water and to her place without further problems. The water already lapped against the bow and was only a few inches from the starboard side, so she didn't have to move the skiff much to get it afloat. Fortunately, Lars had a winch on board that should do the job nicely. She hooked it up and was headed downriver a half hour later.

❖

"Miss me?"

The nearly four hours Bryson was gone had seemed an eternity. "Talk about understatement," Karla replied. "Any problems? Did you get the skiff? How do you feel?" Everything rushed out.

Bryson laughed as she hung her coat and backpack on the pegs by the door and shed her boots. "No, yes, and don't take it personally if I suddenly fall asleep on you mid-sentence. Kinda beat."

"I'm amazed you're still standing. I was getting worried. I expected you a lot sooner."

"Took a little detour." Bryson's eyes twinkled as she approached the couch. "Close your eyes and hold out your hand."

Puzzled, Karla complied. Her heart filled with joy as she closed her palm over the familiar cold metal and smooth stone. But she still couldn't quite believe it until she opened her eyes and saw it was true. "Oh, my God! You found it! How in the world—"

"I knew how much it meant to you. I was lucky."

"Oh, Bryson!" She clutched the necklace to her heart. "I'd given up hope of ever seeing it again. I don't know how to thank you."

"Not necessary." Bryson looked down at her with a very pleased expression, but had dark circles under her eyes. "Seeing your face right now is ample reward."

"Come sit and relax. You look like you're ready to collapse."

Bryson nodded wearily but headed toward the kitchen. "Soon as I get some cocoa poured, you're on. Join me?"

"Please."

"How're you doing? Feet hurting much?"

"Just took a couple more ibuprofen. They're doing okay."

"Don't think there's much Lars will need to do to the boat," Bryson informed her. "Seems to run fine. The engine was probably flooded."

"That's good news. I want to pay for the repairs."

"Lars may fight you on that. And he's got a friend who'll probably do the work in exchange for a favor. Bartering is really popular up here." Bryson carried their cocoa over and sank onto the futon next to her. "Oh, yeah. Feels good to sit." She laid her head back and closed her eyes with a sigh. "In a minute, we'll see to those feet."

When she didn't move or speak for another couple of minutes, Karla reached over and gently urged Bryson's head into her lap. Bryson never opened her eyes and was quickly sound asleep.

Karla lightly stroked Bryson's hair and listened to her soft, steady breathing. *It's so easy to be with you.*

❖

"You sure about this?" Bryson sounded skeptical. She'd had urged her not to rush things, but after four days of depending on Bryson for absolutely everything, Karla was more than ready to get back on her feet. Not that she minded being carried around, nestled against Bryson's chest, but her swelling had disappeared long ago, and she had only a few blisters around her toes that were responding well to antibiotic ointment. It was time. The sooner she convinced Bryson she was back to normal, the sooner they might take their budding relationship to the next level. Bryson's soreness had faded, but she'd refused to consider being intimate with Karla until she was healed, too.

They'd spent their days and evenings getting to know each other, sharing stories of their lives and exchanging likes and dislikes. Bryson made her laugh until her sides hurt, and they had ample opportunities for long, lingering kisses that left her anxious for more.

"Stop being so protective. I'm a nurse, remember?" She eased off the futon and gingerly put her weight on her feet. "Feels okay." Bryson was standing beside her uncertainly, ready to support her if needed. "Just a little sore."

"Guess you know best. But I'm happy to keep toting you around."

Karla put her arms around Bryson's neck. "I know. But I hate being an invalid. I love how you've pampered me, but I don't need you to be my nursemaid any more." She pulled Bryson's head down and kissed her passionately. "I have other plans for your seemingly endless energy."

Bryson's arms encircled her waist. "That so?" she asked with a smile.

"Yup. And if you insist on sleeping in the loft again, I'm going to crawl up there with you. I'm tired of sleeping alone."

"Told you, I toss and turn a lot. I thought you'd be more comfortable—"

"That's not the real reason. You didn't want to succumb to temptation, that's all. You're not fooling me." She poked Bryson playfully in the chest. "No more delays, huh? If I don't get my hands on you soon, I'll spontaneously combust."

"Hmm. Well, we can't have that." Bryson initiated the next kiss, another heated exchange that left them both breathless. "I want you too, Karla. So much. So damn much."

"Hold that thought." If Bryson kept looking at her like that she wouldn't be able to keep to her plan. "First things first. Can you do something for me?"

"Anything."

"Mind drawing me a bath?"

Bryson grinned wickedly. "Definitely my pleasure. Damn shame the tub isn't big enough for two."

"I had the same thought. But we can take turns soaping each other."

"Mmm. Sounds like a very nice alternative." Bryson kissed her on the forehead and moved out of their embrace. "I'll put some water on and get things set up."

Karla sat back on the futon and removed the bandages from her feet while Bryson set the oval galvanized tub in front of the woodstove. It took a while to heat the water and fill it, and all the while, Bryson kept glancing her way with a goofy grin on her face. As a finishing touch, Bryson poured fragrant bath salts into the tub and stirred the water, then hung a couple of large towels and a terry-cloth robe from a chair near the stove.

"Ready for me?"

Bryson chuckled. "That's a loaded question. But, yes."

As Karla walked slowly toward the tub, she reached with trembling hands to undo the buttons on her emerald cardigan. Nervous excitement jangled her nerves and sent her pulse racing.

"Oh, no, you don't." Bryson quickly closed the distance and took Karla's hands in hers. "I've been undressing you in my mind too long to miss out on the real thing." She led Karla the rest of the way and stood facing her. "I'd like to take all day doing this," she added as she slowly unbuttoned Karla's sweater, "but I don't want you to get cold." She kissed the hollow at the base of Karla's throat while she slipped the cardigan off her shoulders.

"The way you get my blood boiling, that seems like a long shot."

Bryson's hands slipped beneath her turtleneck and paused there, cool fingertips grazing the warm flesh of Karla's rib cage. Her skin was so hypersensitive the light caress was electrifying, the unvarnished desire in Bryson's eyes amplifying the sensation.

"Trying to drive me crazy, aren't you?" she asked, when Bryson's hands skimmed over her sides to her back, then dipped beneath the waistband of her sweats.

"Can't help myself." Bryson's voice was husky as she squeezed Karla's ass.

"You know, the sooner you get me into this water, the sooner I can get out of it and into a bed."

"There is that," Bryson readily agreed. She pulled the turtleneck over Karla's head, then slowly removed the sweatpants, her fingernails etching light trails down her thighs and calves as she stooped to slip them down and off. Beneath, Karla wore only a sheer beige bra and panties, so transparent they left nothing to the imagination.

As Bryson's gaze drifted over her body, Karla heard her soft gasp of appreciation and noted the swift rise and fall of her chest. "Beautiful," Bryson murmured, as she reached behind Karla to unhook the clasp of her bra. The panties soon followed, and Bryson's pupils dilated as she withdrew a step to admire Karla's naked body. "You take my breath away."

"I'm awfully glad you approve." She shuddered, uncertain whether the cool air or the almost predatory look in Bryson's eyes caused her reaction. Bryson started to reach for her, but she tapped the outstretched hand and stepped into the tub. It was so small she had to bend her knees to fit, and the water barely covered her breasts, but it was gloriously warm, and the enticing aroma of the bath salts made the experience almost luxurious.

Bryson knelt beside the tub and rolled up her sleeves. "Where would you like me to start?" she asked mischievously as she dipped a washcloth into the water and lathered it with scented gel.

"Here." Karla stretched out her legs and rested them on the edge of the tub. Bryson ran the washcloth over them in circles, but kept her gaze fixed hungrily on Karla's breasts. Karla looked down, not surprised to find her nipples erect. "Guess I don't have to tell you what your touch is doing to me."

"Very hot." Bryson directed the washcloth up Karla's thigh, over her stomach, and then into the valley between her breasts. She leaned forward to kiss Karla, and as her tongue pushed insistently into her mouth, she played the washcloth over Karla's breasts, then descended between her legs.

When it skimmed over her clit, Karla's pelvis rose involuntarily to meet it. A moan escaped into their enjoined mouths, and Bryson answered it with another teasing pass across her sex. Karla broke the kiss and wrestled the cloth from Bryson's hand. "Dangerous," she gasped. "Maybe I better finish this. Will you do my hair?"

A flicker of disappointment crossed Bryson's face, but she smiled knowingly and nodded. "Of course." While she wet Karla's hair from a pitcher of warm water and rubbed shampoo into her scalp, Karla shakily ran the washcloth over the rest of her body, avoiding further stimulation to her already oversensitized breasts and groin.

"Is this torturing you as much as it is me?" Bryson asked as she rinsed Karla's hair with more warm water.

"Torture is sure the word for it. And now it's your turn, I believe." As she boosted herself from the tub, Bryson enveloped her in a warm towel, drying her thoroughly before wrapping the towel around her head like a turban. Then she helped her into the robe, kissing her lightly on the forehead as she tied the sash.

"Drawing a fresh bath for me will take a few minutes," Bryson said, looking down at her. "You may get chilled. Sure you don't want to warm up the bed while I bathe? I'll be very fast."

Much as she'd looked forward to giving Bryson a little payback, her bare legs were already raising gooseflesh, and the idea of watching Bryson bathe from beneath the thick down comforter held even greater appeal at the moment. They would have ample time for touching soon. "Maybe you're right."

While she converted the couch back into a bed, Bryson emptied the tub with a large bucket, ferrying the tepid water outdoors in several trips. By the time she had the tub refilled, Karla was ensconced comfortably between the sheets, pillows propped up so she could get an unobstructed view of Bryson stripping for her bath.

Bryson ran a hand through the water to test the temperature. Satisfied, she hurriedly pulled off her socks and her sweatshirt, then reached for the fly on her jeans. She'd been so busy with her preparations that she hadn't looked directly at Karla until that instant. From the way Bryson suddenly froze, it was clear she could see in Karla's eyes how stirred up she was.

Bryson returned the intense stare as she resumed undressing, sliding the jeans down her legs and shedding her long-sleeved T-shirt to reveal black panties and a matching bra. Bryson also quickly tossed these aside, but hesitated before she stepped into the tub, her wide grin acknowledging how much she was enjoying the way she'd mesmerized her audience.

Karla realized her mouth was hanging open and quickly closed it as a blush warmed her cheeks. She was awestruck at the perfection of Bryson's naked body. Though well aware that Bryson was in superior shape—no other woman she knew could have carried her like that—she was still not fully prepared for the exquisitely toned lean physique. Not an ounce of fat anywhere. Her thighs looked hard as rocks, the muscles of her shoulders and upper arms were finely sculpted, and the flat plain of her stomach provided the perfect contrast to the curves of her high, round breasts. The neatly trimmed triangle of dark hair at the apex of her thighs made Karla's mouth water. "Hurry," she urged, when she regained her wits enough to speak.

Bryson chuckled as she lowered herself into the water, but Karla could tell she was just as eager as she was. She washed up and dried herself in record time, then jogged toward the bed.

Karla pulled the comforter back in anticipation, but before Bryson could dive in next to her, the shrill ring of Bryson's satellite phone broke the quiet.

Chapter Twenty-one

"*Now?*" Bryson glared at the phone as it continued to ring. She snatched up her robe and shrugged it on, glancing at Karla, whose face registered the same frustration at the interruption that she felt. "This can't be happening," she muttered as she picked up the receiver. "Yes?"

"Hey, Bryson. Please tell me Karla is staying with you." The connection wasn't very good; Lars's voice kept cutting in and out. She'd actually heard only the first syllable of her name, and she'd had to fill in the *with*. If he'd said anything after that, she'd missed it.

She turned toward Karla. "Yes, Lars. Karla is with me. We're fine." She spoke slowly and distinctly, figuring Lars would likely have the same problematic reception on his end.

Karla smiled playfully. She was lying on her side, propped up on one elbow. The comforter barely covered her breasts. Bryson's stomach fluttered.

"Great, I—" Static cut off Lars's voice, then she caught the words "days, so got a little worried when she didn't answer."

"Bad reception. Karla's been here several days." Bryson put her hand over the mouthpiece. "Do you want me to tell him about your frostbite?"

"Not now. I'm over the worst of it. They'd just worry."

After several more seconds of static, so long she wondered if they'd been disconnected, Lars's voice cut through, "for two days."

"I lost you," she said. "Repeat that."

"The baby's doing great, and we just got word they're ready to discharge Maggie too because her BP's been good for two days."

"Great news. When?" She hoped she sounded more enthusiastic than she felt. Though relieved and happy that Maggie and Karson were well enough to leave the hospital, their homecoming also meant her time with Karla was about to end. She was heartsick and didn't try to hide her feelings. Karla read in her face that the news was a mixed blessing, for her own expression darkened.

The answer she most did not want to hear came through absurdly clear. "They're filling out the paperwork now. Can you come right away? We can meet you at the airport."

"Hang on, Lars." She glanced at her watch and calculated the amount of daylight remaining. If she left right away, and the floatplane was available, they'd get back to Bettles around sunset. "If Skeeter's plane is good to go, I can be there in three and a half, four hours. If it'll be much longer, I'll leave a message at the Bettles Air desk."

She hated the disappointment that clouded Karla's face as the news registered.

"Terrific, Bryson," Lars said. "See you soon."

"They're coming home, right? That's wonderful." Karla's effort to smile was only half-hearted.

"But I have to leave now," Bryson said as she approached the bed. "That part really sucks."

"I second that."

She sat on the edge of the bed and took Karla's hand. "Do you want to come along? Are you well enough to?"

Karla looked down at her feet. "I shouldn't be doing a lot of walking, and I'd be in real trouble if my feet refroze, but I should go."

"We can insulate them well, and you don't have to walk any more than you want to. But isn't it better to stay here and rest?"

"With Maggie's BP problems and the baby only days old, I should go along." Karla squeezed her hand. "Besides, I'm not ready to let you out of my sight." This time her smile was full and genuine.

"Sounds like you've made up your mind." Bryson gave Karla a quick kiss. "And for the record, I'm not anxious to say good-bye, either."

They changed into warm clothes, and Bryson handed Karla a pair of Moon boots to wear. The lightweight Italian footwear was the most comfortable choice possible because it was designed to fit several sizes, and was also rated to thirty-five degrees below zero.

"We better take your things," Bryson hefted Karla's duffel and threw the strap over her shoulder so it would hang off her back, "since you'll be staying with Lars and Maggie from now on."

Karla frowned. "I know they need me, and I'm anxious to spend time with my new niece—"

"But the timing really sucks."

"Yeah."

As soon as they hit the porch, Bryson scooped Karla into her arms in their now-familiar way, insisting that she be carried to the Cub.

"This really isn't necessary," Karla protested as she automatically wrapped her arms around Bryson's neck. "I can certainly walk that far."

"Indulge me." Bryson gave her a mock-stern look, then kissed her soundly, silencing further arguments. By the time they started down the trail to the plane, she'd once again turned Karla's insides to mush.

She leaned her head against Bryson's shoulder. "I've never been so spoiled in my life."

"Long overdue, then, I'd say."

When they reached the river, Bryson paused at the water's edge, worry and concern on her face.

"What's the matter?" Karla followed her gaze to the Cub, which was covered with snow and ice.

"Looks like this will be my last flight out of here for a while," Bryson said, as she carried Karla across the ice-encrusted shallows to the gravel bar. "My little runway's getting too iffy for wheels. I'll have to wait until the river freezes solid and I can use my skis."

The amount of ice along the bank and around the gravel bar had increased significantly while Karla had been staying with Bryson, and huge chunks of ice floated downstream with the current. "What're you saying?"

"I won't be able to get back here." Bryson deposited Karla into the passenger seat and belted her in. "I can get all of you home in Skeeter's plane, but then I'll have to stay in Bettles for a while. Happens every year at this time."

"For how long?"

"Hard to say. Might be a couple days, might be weeks. All depends on Mother Nature." Bryson didn't look any happier about it than she was.

"That's certainly not welcome news," she said, dejected.

"I know. Sit tight for a while, I've got to clean off the plane."

It took Bryson forty minutes to clear away the snow and ice, warm the engine, and go through her preflight checklist. All the while, Karla tried to fight off the growing knot of apprehension in her stomach. The skies were clear, but she'd been in Alaska long enough to know that could change in an instant.

"All set?" Bryson knocked the snow from her boots and climbed into the seat in front of her.

"Ready as I'll ever be."

Bryson glanced at her in the rearview mirror as she belted herself in and donned her headset. "We'll be fine. Think about something else. Think about tonight."

"Tonight? You mean sleeping alone at Maggie and Lars's and missing you like crazy? Gee, thanks."

Bryson didn't respond right away, she was too busy preparing for liftoff. She slowly taxied the Cub to the far edge of the gravel bar and turned around. The distance to the other icy end of the makeshift runway seemed impossibly short to Karla, but Bryson somehow got the plane airborne with only inches to spare.

"I guess I forgot to mention that it'll be dark by the time we get back to Bettles," Bryson said once they were at cruising altitude above the mountain peaks. "We'll all have to overnight at the Den and continue to the lake in the morning."

"Which means?"

Instead of answering her, Bryson clicked on her microphone. "A2024B Piper to BTT. Skeeter, you there?" She listened for a moment, then continued. "Headed your way and will be there in twenty. Maggie's been discharged. Can I use the Cessna to pick them up?" After another pause, she said, "Great. And can you do me another favor? Ask Grizz to hold two rooms for us for tonight?" She listened again. "Thanks, Skeeter. See you shortly."

"*Two* rooms?"

Bryson grinned at her in the rearview mirror. "Was it presumptuous to think you wouldn't mind staying with me tonight?"

"Let's just say you sure know how to keep my mind on something other than where I am right now."

❖

Skeeter's plane was fueled and ready by the time they reached Bettles, so they were quickly underway to Fairbanks, and for this leg Karla occupied the copilot's seat again. It was eminently preferable to the setup in the Cub, because she could focus her attention entirely on Bryson instead of the expanse of desolate wilderness outside her window.

"Think Maggie and Lars will mind if I insist on having you all to myself tonight?" Bryson asked. "I'm thinking maybe dinner in our room, a nice bubble bath for two—"

"And then hours and hours of nonstop wild sex," Karla added with a grin, enjoying the way her words brought a flush of pink to Bryson's cheeks. "Sounds perfect."

"I'm trying to fly, here," Bryson warned. "And you're definitely hindering my ability to concentrate."

"I'll be good," Karla promised. When Bryson turned to her with skeptical raised eyebrows, she added, in a much more seductive tone, "I'll be very, *very* good."

The cabin was warm enough that Bryson had her gloves off, and her knuckles whitened as she gripped the steering column. "Not helping," she said, shifting her weight uncomfortably in her seat. "Like I said, you definitely have a heck of a cruel streak inside that luscious exterior."

"Luscious, eh?"

Bryson glanced her way and let her gaze drift lazily down Karla's body, though most of it was hidden beneath her thick down coat. "Mmm hmm," she said, licking her lips. "I can't wait to see if you taste as yummy as you look."

The words warmed her much more efficiently than the heater in the floatplane. "Now who's being cruel?"

"Truce, then." Bryson laughed and returned her attention to flying. "For now. Once I get you alone tonight, all bets are off."

"We'll see who tortures whom. Just wait." Their flirting had left them both with excited grins that were impossible to erase. Karla couldn't remember feeling this profoundly giddy sense of anticipation before, not even with Abby. "Can't this plane go any faster?"

❖

"I can't believe how much she's grown in just a few days." Karla reached over the seat back to offer an outstretched finger to her niece, and Karson wrapped her tiny hand around it. The baby was well bundled up against the cold in fleecy pink pajamas, stocking cap, and a thick quilted infant blanket. Lars had been forced to leave Maggie's side for the first time the day before to buy the items, along with the newborn safety seat, because they'd left all their baby things at home.

"I think she wanted to leave the hospital as much as I did." Maggie held up a bright red rattle shaped like a key and dangled it in front of the baby's face. Karson stared up at it, her distinctive hazel and gold-flecked eyes round. "Can't wait to get you home and in that new crib your father made for you, little one."

The plane dropped a couple of feet when it hit a small pocket of turbulence, and Karla clutched at the seatback until it subsided, then turned to quickly refasten her seat belt.

"After I drop you all off tomorrow, I'll hike home to get the skiff," Bryson offered as she gained some altitude to smooth out their ride. They'd already relayed the story of Karla's frostbite adventure, and Bryson had updated Lars on the advanced state of the freeze-up in their area. "I have to pack a bag anyway, since I don't know how long I may be stuck in Bettles." She glanced at Karla as she said this, and her eyes were sad.

"Sure you don't mind?" Lars asked. "I can go with you. Mags will be okay with Karla for a few hours."

"Not necessary," Bryson insisted. "No reason for both of us to go. Let's just hope the weather holds so we can lift off at first light and get the skiff home and out of the water before I have to leave."

"Appreciate the help," Lars replied. "Be a bitch to get the boat out by myself, even with the winch. And by the time Maggie'd be able to help, it'd be icebound for sure."

"Couldn't be worse timing for our homecoming." Maggie frowned. "I'd hoped you could spend some time with us, Bryson."

Karla and Bryson looked at each other with the same isn't-that-the-truth expression.

"Keep me posted on when the ice is safe, and don't worry. I'll fly in first chance I get and stay as long as I can." She gave Karla a wink the others couldn't see.

Never in her wildest imagination did Karla think she would wish for a long solid stretch of bitter-cold temperatures. But if that's what it took to get Bryson back to the bush and in her arms, it was certainly fine with her.

CHAPTER TWENTY-TWO

The Den was noisy with patrons, and most of the gathered locals jumped up when they came in, anxious to see the Rasmussens' new arrival. Several people also immediately pled for an impromptu performance of the Bettles Band, since all its members were stranded there for the evening, anyway, and everyone was desperate for any form of entertainment.

"I'm game," Lars said. "It's still early, and who knows when we'll get back here."

"We're in," Grizz agreed. "Ellie's been putting in a lot of hours learning 'Someone to Watch Over Me' and 'April in Paris,' and is anxious to try them out. Bryson?"

Bryson wanted only to slip upstairs with Karla, to pick up where they'd left off and enjoy every moment of their limited time together. But it was hard to say no to the eager faces of her friends. She looked over at Karla, who seemed to sense her inner struggle, because she gave Bryson a shrug and resigned grin that said *Go ahead. I understand.*

"Okay by me," she reluctantly agreed. "But it's been a long day and we need to get an early start tomorrow, so let's make it just a set or two, huh?"

"That's the business," Grizz said. "I'll get things set up."

Bryson was about to pull Karla aside for a few words of apology when she felt a hand on her shoulder and turned to find Geneva looking up at her with her familiar come-on smile.

"Hey, there, stranger. Nice surprise." She wrapped her arms around Bryson's waist before Bryson could react. "Need a place to sleep tonight?"

The stark contrast between her feelings for Geneva and the woman who'd captured her every waking thought in recent weeks made Bryson suddenly aware of how deeply Karla had gotten under her skin. She was falling in love with her.

Karla was watching the two of them intently from the nearby table she and Maggie had claimed to watch the band perform. It didn't matter that Karla would be leaving Bettles in a matter of weeks, perhaps forever. Bryson used this opportunity to set the record straight on where her heart resided.

She extricated herself from Geneva's embrace and faced her with a serious expression. "Gen, you know I think the world of you, right?"

"Uh-oh." Geneva's pleased demeanor faded. "Something tells me I won't like what's coming next."

"You're a good friend, and I hope that'll never change. But you need to understand—now more than ever—that there's no chance of anything romantic between us, ever again." She let her focus drift from Geneva to Karla, knowing that Gen would follow her gaze. As she'd hoped, Karla was still riveted to their exchange.

"Oh. I see." Geneva's subdued tone made it clear she grasped that something was different. "Sounds serious."

"Doesn't seem to matter that she won't be here long," Bryson admitted. "She's become very important to me."

Geneva exhaled a soft sigh. "In that case..." She kissed Bryson on the cheek. "I wish you both all the best, Bry. I mean that. She's a lucky woman." And with that, she squeezed past Bryson to return to work without looking back.

Bryson started toward Karla and Maggie's table, but Lars intercepted her halfway. "We're ready. Ellie wants to start with 'Someone to Watch Over Me,' if that's okay with you."

"Be right there," she answered, continuing toward Karla. A handful of townspeople was gathered around their table, congratulating Maggie and oohing and aahing over the baby, so Bryson stooped beside Karla's chair. "Sorry about this," she said in a low voice. "Guess dinner in our room is out. Why don't you order, and I'll grab something when we take a break."

"I'll do that. Just don't wear yourself out," Karla whispered close to Bryson's ear. "I have plans for you later."

Bryson headed toward the stage with a smile so firmly planted on her lips she couldn't possibly erase it.

They played a set of jazz standards to wild applause from the audience, none more enthusiastic than the clapping at Karla and Maggie's table. Bryson wolfed down a quick bowl of stew at their break, but declined Grizz's offer of a cold brew to go with it. She noticed Karla was sticking to cola as well and wondered if she, too, didn't want any alcohol to dull their enjoyment of the hours to come.

"Short set this time, guys, okay?" she told the other band members when they returned to the stage. If she didn't get to touch Karla soon, she'd go out of her mind.

When they announced they were done for the night, the crowd roared for an encore, but by then they were all ready to quit. Grizz and Ellie had orders backed up, and Lars was anxious to join Maggie, who'd taken a crying Karson to their room to put her down for the night.

"You have quite a talented ensemble," Karla said as Bryson sank into the chair Maggie had vacated.

"We have fun, and fortunately there's not a lot of competition to judge us by. But it was tough for me to concentrate tonight."

"Oh? And why's that?" Karla feigned ignorance, but the impish twitch at the corners of her mouth told Bryson she knew very well where her mind had been all evening.

"Come on, tease," Bryson said, taking her by the hand to lead her upstairs. "I got Grizz to give us the best room in the house."

"Something special about it, is there?"

"You'll see."

The room was larger than the one Karla had stayed in before and was evidently designed for couples seeking a romantic getaway. Scented candles adorned the headboard of the king-sized bed, and the private bathroom came equipped with a pair of plush fleecy robes and a deep Jacuzzi built for two.

Karla took it all in, noting the special touches she suspected Bryson had arranged: the bubble bath beside the tub and the basket of goodies on the table by the window containing fruit, cheese and crackers, and imported chocolates. Beside it was a bucket of ice containing a bottle of white wine and a half-dozen sodas.

"You approve?" Bryson said from behind her.

Karla turned to thank her for her thoughtfulness, but before she could speak, she was enveloped in Bryson's embrace, her mouth captured in a searing kiss. Bryson's hands clutched her ass, drawing their bodies firmly together, and within seconds she didn't even pretend to speak.

Just as her knees began to buckle, Bryson scooped her up and carried her to the bed.

"Now, where were we when we were so rudely interrupted?" Bryson released her onto the edge of the mattress. Despite Bryson's light tone, her eyes were undeniably intense as she stood over Karla, her gaze fixed on the soft swell of breasts beneath her sweater.

"I believe we were both naked, for starters."

"Ah. Indeed we were. It's all coming back to me now." Bryson bent to remove Karla's boots and her own. Then she slowly began to undress, just out of arm's reach, obviously enjoying the effect of her prolonged striptease on her audience.

Karla found it difficult to draw a deep breath. With each garment removed, her heartbeat accelerated, the drumming in her ears obliterating all other sounds, until finally Bryson stood before her, fully exposed. "You have such an amazing body."

"Thank you. I'm glad you're enjoying the show, because it's absolutely killing me not to pin you to that bed right now until you beg for mercy."

"Keep talking like that, and we may have a competition to see who pins whom."

Bryson laughed and pulled Karla to her feet. "Your turn." Karla started to reach for her, but Bryson dodged her with a grin and hopped onto the bed. "The sooner you get undressed," she said, climbing between the sheets, "the sooner I can…uh…" She gaped when she saw how fast Karla was peeling off her clothes.

By the time she stripped, Bryson's expression had turned from mirthful to smoldering. "Come here," she beckoned, pulling aside the coverlet.

Karla moved into Bryson's outstretched arms, and Bryson's mouth claimed hers in a slow, sensual kiss as their bodies came together along their full length. As the kiss built in heat and intensity, Bryson rolled on top of her and thrust a firmly muscled thigh between her legs.

Arousal burned in Karla as they clung to each other, tongues stroking deep, their full passion flaring. A bonfire of need and yearning and surrender engulfed her. When she raked her nails down Bryson's back, Bryson broke the kiss and threw her head back in ecstasy as a sound—half groan and half growl—reverberated from the back of her throat. Karla clenched Bryson's lean, muscled ass, and her hips rose to maximize the pressure of their pelvis-to-pelvis contact. Bryson looked down at her, brown eyes darkened by desire and lips rosy and swollen from their kisses. The hunger in her expression sent a thrill through Karla, ratcheting her excitement even higher.

"How you make me feel…" she gasped, heaving for air. It wasn't the kisses alone that left her breathless. The rush of adrenaline was dizzying, too. "…never like this. Never."

Bryson slowly nodded, and a combination of joy and relief came over her face. She bore down upon Karla again, kissing her soundly and shifting her weight to the side so she could caress her with one hand. Despite the ferocity of their kiss, Bryson's touch was maddeningly light as her fingers trailed down Karla's shoulder to her upper arm, then down her hip and thigh, and back up to her chest. When they reached the outer curve of her breast, she moaned. Bryson gently bit her lower lip as she claimed the breast with the full contact of her palm, producing a sudden rush of sensation. Her nipple was instantly erect, and moisture surged between her legs.

Bryson must have felt it, too, because she thrust her thigh more firmly against Karla's center, rocking against her, creating a delicious friction that brought her dangerously close to climax. Another minute or two and she would have come, but Bryson stopped to move down her body, trailing wet kisses from her neck to her collarbone, then down her cleavage. Bryson's tongue traced the curve of one breast, and then her mouth closed over the nipple and sucked, hard. Karla's hips bucked upward as she raked circles into Bryson's back with her nails.

Another surge of wetness poured out of her as Bryson lavished her other breast with her mouth. The maelstrom of sensations brought her once again to the precipice; she bit her lip so hard she tasted blood.

Her enormous need for release was intolerable. She wanted to make this incredible buildup of excitement last, but she was incapable of self-control. She grabbed Bryson's hair and pushed her head lower as she opened her legs. "Please, Bryson. I'm so close."

When Bryson delivered her with measured and well-placed strokes of her tongue, she cried out and clenched at the sheets, then collapsed in a fog of overload. As she calmed and caught her breath, Bryson sweetly kissed her thighs and abdomen, working her way back up Karla's body to lie on her side beside her.

Karla rolled into her embrace and buried her face in the soft warm skin at the base of Bryson's throat. Her body thrummed with aftershocks. "Oh *my*," she whispered, gripping Bryson tight.

"You're amazing." Bryson kissed her forehead. "Sooo hot."

"What you do to me, Bryson. What you do to me." She couldn't begin to convey how utterly and completely she *felt* when Bryson touched her. Her body, head to toe, her senses, her mind, her imagination. All of her roared to life like she had been dozing too long. Full speed ahead, all the bits and pieces of her working in harmony to achieve the perfect orgasm.

"I can say the same." Bryson clenched her jaw. The effect of Karla's touch was unbelievably powerful. Though she held Karla with infinite tenderness, her body still shrieked with arousal. She was so far gone, falling hard and fast, first enamored by Karla's loveliness and vulnerability, then enchanted by her humor, open honesty, and strength. It had taken such courage for her to deal with all she'd been slammed with. No matter what the challenge, Karla faced it with quiet resolve.

Bryson so wanted to freeze this moment. Everything she'd dreamed she should feel—that spark, that special chemistry, that gut instinct that this was the one—she was finally experiencing. Why now? Why Karla? It seemed so unfair. Bryson memorized every detail. The softness of Karla's hair and skin, the aroma of her perfume, mixed with the scent of their arousal, the sound Karla made when she climaxed, and the heightened sensations of her own body.

Karla stirred from her lassitude, disengaging slightly from their embrace to place a long, wet kiss at the hollow of Bryson's neck, then another just below her ear. "My turn." Her voice was husky and full of promise.

She shifted to lie on top of Bryson and resumed her kisses, down her neck, chest, and stomach. As she did, she cupped Bryson's breasts, teasing the nipples to erection with strokes of her thumbs. Bryson's pulse quickened and her breathing accelerated, loud in her ears. The pressure building at the juncture of her thighs was incredible. When

Karla's mouth closed over one sensitive nipple and sucked, she ground her pelvis upward and tightened her grip in Karla's hair. "More."

Karla sucked harder and tweaked the sensitive nipple lightly between her teeth. Bryson groaned once, then again when Karla gave the other breast equal treatment.

"I can tell how close you are," Karla murmured as she moved lower. Bryson writhed beneath her, desperate for relief.

"Yes," she choked. "Ready beyond words."

She felt Karla's smile against her lower abdomen and heard her sharp intake of breath. "I love how you smell," Karla said, just before her mouth closed over Bryson's sex.

As Bryson went rigid in the first throes of orgasm, she clutched at the headboard to anchor herself. Teeth clenched, she rode the rush of release like a wave, building and building until the crest shattered her, sapping her strength.

They lay for another long while wrapped in each other's arms, exchanging sweet kisses and confiding specifics about their sexual fantasies and preferences. The provocative sharing led to several more hours of lovemaking: playful and flirty, then heated and raw, as they indulged each other in every way possible.

For once, Bryson was grateful for the long nights of winter. First light would mark the end of their blissful privacy and the beginning of what she feared would be an unbearable separation.

Chapter Twenty-three

December 14

"Feels like some sort of cosmic conspiracy is trying to keep us apart." Bryson absently picked at the label of her bottle, her second Black Fang that evening. She'd barely touched her plate of smoked-salmon tacos.

"We haven't had a warm spell like this one since '88," Grizz said as he poured two drafts. "Got to forty in Fairbanks in the middle of December. Same reason then, too. Some weird high-pressure system over Seattle."

"Global warming, that's what it is." Skeeter scowled from the barstool beside her.

Bryson continued as though she hadn't heard. "Hated missing Thanksgiving with them."

November had been the mildest in two decades in Alaska, and December was shaping up the same. They got a few frigid days here and there, but just about the time the ice on the lakes and rivers was getting thick enough to support a plane, temps would rise above freezing and everything would soften up again.

For the last month, she'd been stuck in Bettles and confined to airport runs, only able to contact the Rasmussen cabin through their satellite phone. Karla's time in Alaska was ticking away, and Mother Nature seemed to be cheating Bryson out of a rare chance at happiness.

"Keep your chin up." Grizz laid a massive callused hand on top of

Bryson's across the bar. "Forecast this morning says we've got a long spell of cold comin' in."

"Karla know how bad you're pining away for her?" Skeeter teased with a grin.

Bryson shrugged. "Pretty clear we're crazy about each other. But not like I've really said anything much. What's there to say? We both know this is only a brief thing. Talking about it'll just make it tougher to say good-bye when she goes."

"Or talking about it might give her good reason to come back often," Grizz said.

"She's already got that, with Maggie and Lars and the baby. I don't think it's a question of her not *wanting* to come back." Bryson took a sip of her lukewarm beer. "She's a nurse, so what does she get—two, three weeks vacation a year, tops? And it's not cheap to get here from Atlanta, I'm sure. Realistically, I'll probably be lucky if I get to see her a few days every couple of years."

"That's a damn shame."

"Tell me about it."

"What about you going down there to see her?" Grizz asked.

"Been thinking about that. Hell of a long way by Cub, and can't say as I'd relish trying to get anywhere near the air traffic at Hartsfield. But maybe I could do a trip or two a year. If she'd want me to, that is."

Geneva materialized beside her elbow with an empty tray. "White wine, a Lookout Stout, and a Jack Daniel's, neat," she relayed to Grizz before turning to Bryson. "Why wouldn't Karla want you to visit? From the look on her face the morning you all left, it's clear she likes you as much as you like her." There was no malice or jealousy in the remark. In fact, Geneva had surprised Bryson by supporting her during the weeks since she'd taken the Rasmussens home.

"She'll meet someone else before long. As she should. She's beautiful, bright, fun to be with. I'm sure she'll have a lot of opportunities to hook up in Atlanta." The seeming inevitability that Karla would move on depressed her. She conjured up a vision of Karla at a club, dancing close to some attractive stranger, and felt as though she'd been punched in the stomach. No way would she be able to feign happiness at seeing her with someone else, as Geneva apparently could.

"I think you're underestimating yourself, Bry. All I'm sayin'." Geneva set the drinks on her tray and returned to her customers.

The phone rang behind the bar and Grizz wiped his hands on a towel to answer it. "The Den." As he listened, a big smile spread across his face. "Same back atcha. Yeah, she's right here." He handed the phone to Bryson. "Her ears must've been burnin'."

"Karla?"

"Hi, Bryson. I'm missing you something fierce."

Her glum mood lifted significantly. "Lot of that going around. How's everybody doing?"

"Great. Maggie's incision's almost healed and she's able to do just about everything. BP's good. Karson's gained more weight and is starting to smile a lot. We're all getting a bad case of cabin fever, though."

"I'm sure you're not the only ones. The Den's been pretty empty except for folks within walking distance."

"It seems so unfair not to be able to see you when I've only got a couple of weeks left."

Bryson's heart fell. "I thought you were staying until after New Year's."

"Yeah. That's the bad news. I checked in at work, and my supervisor begged me to come back by the twenty-eighth to cover a maternity leave." Karla's voice was subdued. "And flights are cheaper then, too. So I'm booked to leave the day after Christmas."

That ticking clock got louder in Bryson's head. "Sorry to hear that." There was an awkward silence on the line. "On a happier note, a cold front is supposed to be headed our way."

"I'll keep my fingers crossed it gets here quick and hangs around a while," Karla said.

"No more than I will. See you as soon as I can get there."

❖

Karla hung up and turned to find Lars and Maggie watching her. They were curled up together on the couch, with Karson in her crib nearby snoozing off her last feeding.

"Any news from town?" Lars asked.

"Bryson says it's supposed to get colder. Not much else."

"Don't be discouraged," Maggie said. "I bet she'll be here before the week's out."

Lars got to his feet and stretched. "I need some fresh air. Gonna cut some firewood."

Maggie gave him a quizzical look but said nothing as he grabbed his coat and headed outside. There was enough firewood already split to last them at least a couple of months, but everyone had their own ways to deal with cabin fever. In truth, his leaving them alone *was* a ruse. Now that Maggie and Karson were both safely out of the woods, Karla had asked for some alone time to finally tell Maggie the truth about their mother's illness.

She took the seat on the couch that Lars had vacated and let her gaze linger on the makeshift Christmas tree in the corner. It was the first one ever erected in the Rasmussen cabin. Lars and Maggie loved the holiday, but they didn't believe in killing trees unnecessarily since the ones that grew here struggled so to survive the short growing season. So normally they went without one—instead stringing their lights and decorations on the windowpanes and ceiling. This year, however, because of Karla and Karson, they'd constructed a tree out of spruce boughs, wired to a frame that Lars had made. It was decorated with strung popcorn and cranberries, colored paper chains, and a variety of homemade ornaments.

"I put up a Christmas tree for Mom last year," she told Maggie. "Just a tabletop-sized, with a lot of little colored lights and some of her favorite ornaments. She'd pick one up whenever she traveled." Karla had held each memento in front of her mother's face, praying for a sign of recognition, without success.

She met Maggie's eyes, so much like their mother's that her heart ached. "The tree was more for my benefit than hers. I doubt she had any idea what it was, but I couldn't do much for her by then."

Maggie looked understandably confused. "What do you mean?"

"I told you she had a heart attack—that's what's listed on the death certificate. But it wasn't really what killed her. She had Alzheimer's."

"Alzheimer's?" Maggie's eyes widened for a split second as she absorbed the news. "Oh, how awful. That must have been very difficult for you."

"It's terrible to watch someone you love lose herself little by little.

The first hint I had that something was wrong was when she began to lose sense of time. We'd be at a red light and she'd insist it must be broken because it wasn't changing. Or she'd think a waitress had forgotten about us because our order didn't come in two minutes. Within a year she was having problems sometimes finding the right word for something. That's when I told her she needed to see a doctor. She resisted at first. I think she knew something wasn't right, but she was afraid to face it. To be honest, so was I."

Maggie didn't say anything, but she took her hand, and that small encouragement gave her courage to continue.

"Another year or so went by. She was living by herself, and I was so caught up with my own life I didn't see her enough to really get a handle on how bad she was getting. Then one day I got a call from a police department in Alabama. She'd gone out for groceries and somehow ended up three hundred miles away, knocking on a stranger's door in a panic, asking how to get home. That's when I forced her to seek help. She was diagnosed and started on Aricept to try to slow the progression of the disease. That's also about when she wrote that letter to me about you. Good thing, because within another couple of years she was losing her ability to read and write. Near the end, she barely spoke, and she couldn't make sense of anything—people, places, things. It was all a mystery to her; she was like an infant again." The image of her mother staring blankly at her, eyes devoid of any spark of recognition, haunted her.

Maggie squeezed her hand. "I can't imagine what you had to go through. I'm just sorry I wasn't there to help you through it."

"And I'm sorry that I have to be the one to tell you this. I wish to hell I didn't." Her stomach was tied up in knots. "Because there's a part of this you need to know. Something that will be very tough to deal with."

Maggie's expression changed from sisterly concern to apprehension, and she stiffened. "What is it? Tell me."

Karla took a deep breath. "The doctors were fairly certain, since she began exhibiting symptoms so young, that she had a rare form of Alzheimer's. It's called eFAD—early onset, Familial Alzheimer's Disease."

Maggie gasped. "Familial?"

"Yes. Scientists still aren't sure what causes Alzheimer's. They suspect genetics plays a role, but there's no proof of that, except with the familial type. It's the only kind that's been conclusively linked to a particular gene called a deterministic gene that's definitely hereditary. It affects multiple family members across generations. In other words, if a parent has it, then their children have a fifty-fifty chance of getting it, too."

Maggie's face went ashen. "Oh, my God. You mean…" Her gaze went immediately to the crib.

"Yes. You may have it. And so may Karson. I'm so sorry." Karla was accustomed to imparting such a grave prognosis to patients, but she had never hated the task more than at this moment.

Maggie's eyes filled with tears as she reached for the baby and held her close. She said nothing for a very long while. "There's…there's no chance this could be a mistake?"

"Yes, there's always a chance. The doctors weren't absolutely certain, but most people with Alzheimer's don't start showing symptoms until sixty-five or so, and Mom was diagnosed in her forties." Karla had a hard time facing Maggie with the final admission. "There are blood tests for the particular gene mutations prevalent with most cases of eFAD, but I opposed them. Both for Mom, and for me."

Maggie looked confused. "Why would you do that?"

"Because I don't want to know if I have it. I couldn't approach life the same way with that future looming over me, knowing I would end up like she did. And the tests aren't a hundred percent reliable." She felt like such a coward sometimes, but better that, she'd decided, than having to deal every day with the near-certain knowledge that she would lose her mind.

"But you're saying there *is* a test that I could take, and Karson, too?"

"Yes. There's one lab in Massachusetts that offers a commercial test. You have to have a doctor request it, though. And many won't until you've had genetic counseling, to make sure you're equipped to deal with the results. The tests are also expensive and not always covered by insurance, so you need to check on that as well."

"How long does it take to hear back from the lab?" Maggie asked.

"Two to three weeks, on average."

Karson began to cry. It was time for her feeding. As Maggie

breastfed her, the silence lengthening, a look of resolve came over her face. "I *have* to know," she said finally. "I have to know how long I have with her. I have to prepare for her future." She looked over at Karla. "I'm going to see a doctor in Fairbanks about it as soon as possible."

Karla looked down at her niece. "You're braver than I am, Maggie." Secretly, she'd hoped her sister would feel as she did—preferring to be kept in the dark and allow some reason for hope. Because if Maggie and the baby both showed the genetic predisposition for eFAD, then in all likelihood, she did too.

❖

"Still only three degrees, and I bet it got well below zero again last night," Lars reported with a grin as he shook the snow from his hat and coat. He'd headed down to the lake at first light, as he had every day for a month. "The ice is definitely thick enough for the plane now. You want to call her, or you want me to?"

Karla shot out of her chair, and Maggie and Lars both laughed. "She better be there and not off in Fairbanks getting groceries or something." The wait had been excruciating and she couldn't bear another minute of it, not when she left for home in only seven short days.

"The Den." Grizz's voice had become instantly recognizable after so many calls to Bettles.

"Hi, Grizz, it's Karla. Is Bryson there?"

"Bryson? Hmmm. Lemme see." His tone was definitely jovial, but her heart sank when he continued. "Sorry, she's not here. She took off about fifteen minutes ago."

"She's gone?" Her elation melted away. "When will she be back, do you know?"

"No time soon. Skeeter's taking her bookings for the next couple of days at least, maybe longer."

Couple of days? "Well, that bites. The lake is finally frozen. Where did she go? Is there a problem somewhere?" Bryson had sounded as anxious as she was to get together again. Karla couldn't imagine anything but a rescue mission or some other emergency taking her away for so long.

"No, no problem. Just said she had something important to do." He paused for a few torturous long beats, then chuckled. "If you want specifics you'll have to ask her yourself. I expect she'll be charging through your door in, oh, twenty minutes or so."

The burst of exhilaration made her woozy on her feet. "You'll pay for that, Grizz. Thanks!" She hung up the phone. "She's already on her way," she told Lars and Maggie. "And look at me. Crap." To the sounds of their laughter, she hurried to wash up and change out of the grungy sweats she'd been wearing for three days.

She was pulling on clean jeans when she picked up the sound of the approaching plane. The Cub buzzed the cabin, then veered off toward the lake. By the time she threw on her coat and boots and got outside, the noise had died. She met Bryson halfway up the trail and flew into her outstretched arms.

They hugged so tight that Karla had to fight for breath. Her heart was thumping like crazy. "God, I've missed you so much."

"No more than I've missed you." And then Bryson's mouth was covering hers in a searing kiss that reignited all the passion they'd shared their last night together.

Chapter Twenty-four

"You know," Maggie said in a low voice as she dipped another plate into the rinse water and handed it to Bryson to dry, "it couldn't be more obvious that you two have something very special going on. Karla couldn't stop talking about you these last few weeks, and I've never seen you so starry-eyed over someone."

Bryson turned to watch Karla, who was currently changing Karson's diaper. "Can't argue there. She's a wonderful woman. It'll kill me when she leaves."

"I think so much of both of you, you know that. Seems a damn shame that you found each other, only to be split apart. Have you talked about what happens after she goes home?"

"No. Not really. What's there to say? I'm hoping she'll come back when she's able. And I can maybe get down to see her once or twice a year, and try to get to Bettles more to webcam with her. But realistically, can anybody hope to sustain a relationship with that kind of limited contact? I expect she'll move on before long and that'll be that. So I'm just enjoying the time I have with her. I can't think about the future."

"I probably already know the answer to this, but you'd never consider relocating to Atlanta? Not that I'd want to see you go, of course."

Bryson tucked the stack of clean plates into the cupboard. "I've considered it. Long and hard. Sure, a big part of me would be willing to sacrifice just about anything to keep from losing her. But I'd be giving up everything else that's important to me if I moved away from Alaska. A big city isn't for me. I'd suffocate. And what would I do there?"

Leaving the wilderness, her mountains, and the cabin she had built with her own hands was unimaginable, as was giving up being a bush pilot. "I'm afraid one day I'd resent Karla for forcing me to make that choice."

Maggie dried her hands with a towel and wrapped one arm around Bryson's waist. "I wish I could do more for the two of you, but I'll have to settle for giving up my sister for a few days."

"What are you saying?"

"Lars and I can take care of things from here on. Carry her home, spoil her rotten, and cherish the time she has left. But bring her back for Christmas and give us a chance to say good-bye, okay?"

Bryson grinned and kissed Maggie on the cheek. "Have I told you lately how fabulous you are?"

"Not often enough. Now get her packed up and out of here. You don't have much daylight left."

Bryson gave her another quick peck, then hurried over to Karla, who was settling Karson back into her crib. She wrapped her arms around Karla's waist from behind and whispered into her ear, "Have you any idea what you do to me when you bend over like that?"

Karla inhaled sharply. "Mean. Mean. Mean," she grumbled. "Why are you getting me all stirred up when we don't have a chance for some private time to do anything about it?"

"Oh, but there is. Maggie suggested I take you home with me until Christmas. You up for that?"

Karla turned in her arms, grinning. "Really?"

"How fast can you pack?"

"Just watch me."

❖

They spent the bulk of the next few days in bed, with short forays out for meals and walks. On the morning of Christmas Eve, Karla was awakened by kisses and opened her eyes to find a breakfast tray loaded with her favorite foods. "Mmm. You're up early. How did you do all this without waking me?"

"I tried to be quiet." Bryson reached for a slice of toast. "But frankly, I've discovered you sleep like the dead if I thoroughly exhaust you the night before."

"Night before?" Karla laughed. "Morning, noon, and night before, you mean."

"Not that I'm getting tired of our routine, you understand, but are you up for a little adventure today? I've got something special planned. It'll involve going up in the Cub, but it's only a short flight."

She'd probably never fully embrace the idea of getting into Bryson's plane, but the prospect made her less anxious than it once did. She'd come to trust that Bryson's skill as a pilot was exceptional. "That's all you're going to tell me, isn't it?"

"Yup. It's a surprise."

"Okay, then. I'm all yours. So far, I have to say that your surprises have been more than satisfying." She glanced meaningfully toward the bedside table, where Bryson had stashed the strap-on that had gotten frequent use lately.

Bryson's cheeks flamed red. "Stop that. We'll never get out of here. Now eat up and get dressed. Put on the warmest things you have."

"Yes, ma'am. I so love it when you get all forceful like that."

At first light, Bryson flew them to Bettles. She steered Karla toward a small building tucked behind the post office. The sign outside read Arctic Independent Outfitters.

"Oh. This is where you and Lars work, right?"

Bryson nodded. "Come on, I'll show you around."

The door led to a small waiting area, with chairs and a television and a host of older magazines scattered about. At one end was a reception desk and a hallway leading to more rooms. An attractive woman Karla didn't recognize stood behind the desk, talking on the phone. She was five-ten or so and athletically built, with shoulder-length brown hair cut in a shag. Probably in her early forties. She hailed Bryson with a wave and cut short her conversation as soon as they approached.

"Hey, Bryson. Long time." When she rounded the desk and embraced Bryson, Karla felt a twinge of jealousy.

"Too long," Bryson replied, hugging the woman back with equal enthusiasm. "You ready to give up your day job and join the competition?"

The stranger laughed. "No, and no. But we should do dinner before classes resume. Have a lot of catching up to do."

"You're on. I'd like that."

Karla forced herself to smile as Bryson turned to make

introductions. Her heart sank at the realization she wasn't even gone yet, and Bryson was already making plans with an ex.

"Karla, this is a dear friend, Chaz Herrick. Chaz, Karla Edwards."

Chaz stuck out her hand and grinned at Karla. "Really happy to meet you, Karla. Bryson's told me a lot about you."

"Nice to meet you, too." Karla returned the handshake. She wanted to punch herself for feeling jealous and resentful of the fact that Bryson had never mentioned Chaz. After all, what did she expect? She had no claim on Bryson. She'd be leaving the day after tomorrow, and Bryson would go on with her life.

"Everything set?" Bryson asked Chaz.

"Yup. Just like you asked." Chaz winked at Bryson, who grinned. Karla felt another twinge of envy at their close camaraderie.

"I owe you. Come on, Karla. Let's get you suited up." Bryson took her elbow and led her toward one of the back rooms.

"Suited up? What's going on?"

"I'm not taking any chances on you getting frostbite again." Bryson showed her into a room filled with extreme-cold-weather gear—thermal parkas with fur-lined hoods, thick arctic gloves and face masks, and the white vapor-barrier "Mickey Mouse" boots designed for the U.S. military.

"Where are we going?" Karla asked as Bryson fitted her with an entire ensemble.

"You'll see."

Once they were both appropriately decked out, Bryson led them out the back entrance. Three dozen or more dogs, mostly huskies and malamutes, were chained beside small individual plywood dog houses. Another half-dozen dogs were hitched to a sled, standing off to one side.

Upon seeing the women, the dogs burst into a frenzy of excitement, straining at their chains and barking furiously.

"Oh, wow. We're going dogsledding?"

Bryson wrapped an arm around her. "Okay surprise?"

"The best. I can't wait."

"Come on, then." Bryson led her to the sled, which had a built-in seat in front, surrounded on either side by canvas to block the wind. Once Karla was comfortably settled in, with a thick lap blanket and her feet propped up on a cooler, Bryson climbed behind her to drive the sled.

As soon as Bryson put her weight on the rear footboards, the dogs went crazy, straining at their harnesses and barking to be underway. The sled bounced up and down a few inches, but stayed fast, thanks to a large metal claw-like hook that was deeply embedded in the packed snow.

"All set?" Bryson shouted over the cacophony from the dogs, as she placed one hand on the handlebar and reached down to grab the snow hook with the other.

"Let's go," Karla hollered back.

The sled took off along a well-packed snowmobile track heading north. The dogs were running flat-out, going twenty miles an hour, but it felt more like fifty. The only sounds were their pants for breath and the *shoosh* of the runners on the snow. In the distance was the Brooks Range. The days were the shortest of the year, the sun clearing the horizon for only a couple of hours before it disappeared again. When it could be seen, the world around them seemed always in twilight, with long, deep shadows stretching from every mountaintop and tree. Karla was almost afraid to speak, because she felt as though they were in some vast natural cathedral.

"Enjoying yourself?" Bryson asked after they'd gone a handful of miles.

She half turned to look up at Bryson, smiling and rosy-cheeked, the flaps of her fleece-lined bomber's cap flapping in the breeze. The perfect picture of the confident outdoorswoman, blissfully content in her wild, untamed environment. "This is incredible. Thank you for arranging it."

"My pleasure. We have Chaz to thank. She packed everything and got the dogs ready to go. Just sorry we couldn't spend some time with her. I think you'd like her a lot."

She doubted that. "I don't remember seeing her name on the Web site."

"She's helping out, she's not one of our regular guides. Chaz works for Orion Outfitters out of Winterwolf, leading kayak and backpack trips during the summer. The rest of the year she's a biology professor at the University of Alaska in Fairbanks. We became best buds when I went to school there. Chaz is a lot like me—endures the city but flees to the bush every chance she gets. Every Christmas break she and her partner Megan come up and spend a few weeks in Bettles leading sled-dog trips."

"Her partner? She's gay?"

"Yeah. They met when Megan was a client on one of Chaz's kayak trips. Megan was a vice president for World News Central in Chicago, but when they fell in love, she took a different job to move up here and be with Chaz."

"How long have they been together?"

"Three—no, almost four years, I think. They went to Canada to get married a few months ago. I stop in at their cabin north of Fairbanks when I'm in the area."

Karla went quiet, thinking about the similarities. This Megan had given up a great job and big-city lifestyle to move to Alaska for love, and apparently with no regrets if she and Chaz were still happily together. Could she do that? Change her whole way of life, leave all her friends and job behind and start over with Bryson and her new family here? Somehow, the challenge seemed less daunting than it should. Though her job in the ER was satisfying—she felt she was making an important contribution in people's lives—it also took a heavy toll. Too many of her patients were victims of urban violence: shootings, stabbings, rape, bar fights, carjackings. She saw the worst of what people could do to each other.

Alaska's beauty had soothed her troubled soul and helped her find the perspective she needed. The people here seemed to genuinely care about each other, so much they'd leave their doors unlocked to a stranger. Most important, though she'd only been here a matter of weeks, Bryson had completely captured her heart. She couldn't imagine being happier with anyone else.

But even if she could make such a drastic change, what did Bryson want? They hadn't discussed what would happen after she went back to Atlanta. Bryson seemed as caught up in their relationship as she was, yet she hadn't asked for more than these precious few days together and hadn't declared her love. Perhaps Bryson was this way with every woman she was involved with. Was she foolish to even be considering such a thing?

They were racing down a frozen river when Bryson laid a hand on her shoulder and pointed to a particularly spectacular group of rugged mountain tops. "Arrigetch Peaks. The entrance to the Gates of the Arctic National Park."

"Arrigetch?"

"It translates as 'fingers of the outstretched hand.' An Eskimo legend says their creator stuck his glove here, and the frozen fingers turned into granite to remind them of him. Cool, huh?"

"Stunning." The day was so clear she could see for miles in every direction. "How big is the park?"

"Thirteen thousand square miles," Bryson said. "Roughly the size of Switzerland."

"That boggles the mind. It makes me feel so small and insignificant."

"Kind of the opposite for me. Native people have lived here for fifteen thousand years or more, and not much has changed in all that time. I half expect to see woolly mammoths and saber-toothed tigers around the next bend. Being here makes me feel ageless, like I'm part of the whole history and evolution of the earth. Like I'm making time stand still."

Karla realized even more how much Bryson could never leave Alaska. It had formed who she was and was as necessary to her happiness and well-being as the clean air and crystal-clear water. If they were ever to be together, it would have to be here. Bryson wouldn't be Bryson anywhere else, certainly not in a concrete jungle that rarely saw snow.

They sped along in silence for another half hour, absorbing the ever-changing view, until they came to the first sign of civilization—a fabric-covered Quonset hut that had been erected next to the trail. Bryson slowed the dogs to a stop and set the snow hook. "Ready for some lunch?"

"Starving. What's this place?" Karla got out of the sled and stretched.

"It's one of the stopping points for our sled-dog trips into the Brooks Range. Got a little heater inside and some cots." Bryson took the cooler off the sled and led them into the hut. Chaz had packed them a small feast—chicken-salad sandwiches and coleslaw, a bottle of white wine, and brownies for dessert.

As they packed up to leave, Bryson looked at her watch.

"Are we heading back now?" Karla didn't want their adventure to end.

"Yes, we should. It'll be dark soon."

"Is it safe to be on the trail at night?"

"It's well-packed, so the dogs will follow it naturally. And I have a good headlamp. We'll be fine." Bryson secured the cooler to the sled. "It's all according to plan. There's one more sight I want you to take home with you, so you won't forget us too soon."

Karla closed the few feet separating them and hugged Bryson tight. "No chance of that. You've given me so many wonderful, unforgettable memories. The best ever."

Bryson kissed her, a slow sweet kiss that felt like good-bye. "I'll cherish every single moment we've spent together, Karla," she said, her voice breaking with emotion. "I really hope we'll keep in touch. I don't want to think about my life without you in it, somehow."

"I can't imagine how I'll just pick up where I left off, when I go home. The thought of not going to sleep wrapped up in your arms is awful."

"My cabin will seem very, very empty." Bryson let out a long, resigned sigh. "Well, we better get going."

Once Karla was tucked back into the sled, they took off again, headed back the way they came.

When darkness fell, it became clear why Bryson had kept them out so late. A brilliant display of northern lights streaked across the sky from horizon to horizon, undulating curtains of green and red and yellow. Karla had glimpsed the amazing sight from the Rasmussen cabin, but the surrounding mountains and frequent overcast skies had diminished their impact. On this clear, cloudless night, as they flew along the flat plain between the mountains and the village, the aurora borealis was an awesome spectacle. The most amazing natural phenomenon she'd ever witnessed. "There are no words for this."

"I never tire of it. It's always changing. Different patterns, different colors. You should see them on a night when there's a lot of shooting stars."

All too soon, they could see the lights of Bettles in the distance.

"I got us our same room at the Den tonight. We'll head to Lars and Maggie's in the morning."

Karla had told Bryson about Maggie's decision to have her and the baby tested for eFAD and had filled her in about her own fears about the results. Bryson had absorbed the news with a grim expression. "Do you think I'm being a coward…not wanting to know Maggie's test results?" she asked. Bryson's opinion of her had become very important.

"Not at all. You're incredibly brave, Karla. You took a lot of risks and faced a lot of your fears in coming here and finding Maggie. It's understandable you're reluctant to hear that kind of news. I'm not sure I'd want to know, either, if it were me."

Karla had never told Abby about the strong possibility she might have eFAD, because she'd been too afraid it would scare her off. Who would want to take a partner with such a wretched future? But Bryson struck her as the kind of woman who'd stick by someone she cared about, no matter the heartache ahead. "Does it put you off? Knowing I might have this?"

"It scares me," Bryson admitted. "Knowing you might not be yourself, might have to deal with what you watched your mother go through. But it doesn't make me any less inclined to want to spend every minute I can with you, as long as I can, if that's what you mean."

She was sure Bryson was speaking from her heart. But she also knew better than Bryson that the loved ones of Alzheimer's patients suffered the most, not those afflicted with the disease. Could she in good conscience place Bryson in that position?

The answer seemed clear. No. She couldn't do that to Bryson. She loved her too much. She would take the test, too. If she had the gene mutation, she'd spare Bryson the anguish of watching her lose herself. But if she didn't, she'd take it as a sign that they should be together. And she'd move heaven and earth to make that happen.

Chapter Twenty-five

Bryson awoke wrapped possessively around Karla, as though even in sleep she couldn't bear the thought of letting her go. She listened to the slow cadence of her breathing and unconsciously matched her own to it. *Don't go.* Though her life had sometimes been lonely, she had settled into a routine, had carved out a place where it was comfortable if not always complete. But being with Karla had changed all that. Now she needed more. Love doubled the joy of every experience, large and small. A good meal, a walk, an evening spent in front of the fire. Nothing would be the same again.

She wished they could be waking up in her cabin with presents under a tree and other adornments to make this a Christmas morning to remember. Grizz wasn't much on decorating; he'd strung colored lights around the window of their room, but it was the only sign of the holiday.

Karla stirred, shifting slightly so her face nestled against Bryson's neck.

"You awake?" Bryson whispered.

"Mmm. Sorta." Karla hugged her tighter. "Merry Christmas."

"Merry Christmas to you, too. Can't say I could imagine a more perfect gift than to wake up in your arms."

"Good. 'Cause I'm afraid I haven't had the opportunity to buy you anything."

"Your being here has been exactly what I wanted and needed." Bryson kissed Karla's forehead before pulling away to turn on the bedside light and retrieve a small package from her coat. "I did get you a little something. I hope you like it." She'd spent hours shopping in Fairbanks one day, trying to find the perfect gift.

Karla slowly unwrapped the colorful paper and opened the small box within. It contained a pair of jade earrings, rimmed with gold. "Oh, Bryson, they're lovely."

"Jade's the state gemstone. And the gold is from the Wild Lake Mine, not too far from Maggie and Lars's cabin."

"Oh, that's just too cool. Thank you so much." Karla hugged Bryson, then immediately put the earrings on. They crawled back under the covers.

"I'm glad you like them." Bryson hugged her close. "Now, where do you want to stay tonight? The sun's only up for a couple of hours, so if you want to spend all day with Maggie and Lars, we'll either need to bunk with them or come back here. I can take off from the lake at night, but I can't land at my cabin. If you choose my place, we'll only have about ninety minutes with them if we take off from here just before first light."

Karla groaned. "That sucks. I want to spend Christmas with them, but I'm very protective of the little time we have left together. I love this room, but at your place there's less chance we'll disturb the neighbors when you get all wound up and ready to come."

"Hey, you should talk. I'm surprised Grizz didn't come up here last night and ask us to keep it down."

"What can I say? You drive me crazy. I forget about anything and everything else." Karla kissed her neck while her hand slid purposefully down Bryson's stomach. "There is one benefit to these short days," she added, glancing at the clock. It was only seven-thirty. "We've got, what, four hours before the sun comes up and we can leave? Plenty of time for a proper good morning."

"More than plenty, sweetheart." The endearment slipped out easily, without any forethought.

"Sweetheart, huh?" Karla's tone went from playful to serious.

"Never called anyone that before," Bryson admitted, equally serious.

"Bryson…"

"Yes?"

"I thought of something else I can give you for Christmas."

"What's that?"

Karla's eyes were moist as she reached for Bryson's hand and placed it on her chest. "I give you my heart, Bryson. Near or far, no matter what the future holds, I want you to know that I love you."

She could feel the strong, rapid beating of Karla's heart beneath her palm, and her own pulse matched it. "I feel the same, Karla." Her voice was husky at the admission. "I'm so much in love with you the thought of you leaving is tearing me apart."

They moved into each other's arms and clung to each other, faces wet with tears. Bryson couldn't speak; the longing that enveloped her was suffocating.

They lingered in bed until just before first light, then headed to the Cub. Both agreed to put on a brave face when they arrived at the Rasmussen cabin. There was no need to let their despondency over the future dampen their Christmas with Lars, Maggie, and Karson.

❖

Maggie had prepared a Christmas brunch, and afterward, they turned to the happy task of exchanging presents. Most of the packages beneath the tree were for Karson. Maggie had sent Lars out shopping before she was released from the hospital, and he had gone overboard. But there was also a smattering of gifts for the rest.

Lars and Maggie gave Bryson a new sweater and set of carving knives, and she gave them a pair of powerful binoculars with a built-in digital camera. For Karla, Maggie had instructed Lars to seek out something uniquely Alaskan, and he'd chosen a splendid example of Inuit art—a polar bear carved from whalebone.

"It's amazing." Karla turned the piece over in her hands, examining the fine detail work. "Thanks so much." From her pocket, she withdrew a small bundle wrapped in tissue paper. "I'm sorry I don't have something for each of you. Didn't expect to be here over the holidays. But I have something for Maggie." She handed the gift to her sister. "It was our mother's. She rarely took it off."

Maggie unwrapped the delicate necklace and held it up for the rest to see. "It's beautiful, Karla. Are you sure you want to part with it?"

"It's been a great comfort me, I'll admit. But being here with all of you has helped me find my own inner strength." She glanced at Bryson and smiled before returning her attention to Maggie. "She'd want you to have it. And it matches your eyes." Karla helped her put it on.

"I'll cherish this." Maggie embraced her.

"And one more thing." Karla handed her another small tissue-wrapped gift. "Lars made the frame." It was one of the pictures she'd brought of their mother, taken in her teens, not long after she had Maggie.

Maggie stroked her thumb over the photo. "Thanks, sis."

"Not that Karson hasn't already raked it in this Christmas," Lars said, surveying the abundance of toys and clothes piled beside the baby's crib with a smile, "but there's one more gift we'd like for her from the two of you." He took Maggie's hand and they both looked at Bryson and Karla. "We'd like you to be her godparents."

"I'd be honored," Bryson immediately replied.

"I'd love that, too," Karla said. "But I'm not sure when I can get back here. When are you planning to have her baptized?"

"We'd like to do it fairly soon," Maggie said. "Probably in the next couple of months, and we realize it's apt to be tough for you to make it back that soon. But you can have a proxy stand in for you."

"Then I happily accept. And if there's any way I can be here, you know I will."

"Wonderful," Maggie said, embracing her.

"This calls for that bottle of champagne we've been saving." Lars retrieved the bubbly and they raised their glasses in a toast. "Here's hoping this Christmas is only the first of many we can spend together."

"Amen to that," Maggie added.

Bryson raised her hand and smiled. "That makes it unanimous. You have to be here, Karla."

"I'll do my best."

All too soon, it was time to say good-bye if they were to get to Bryson's before full dark. They all trooped down the trail to the Cub.

"I'm sorry we can't stay longer," Karla told Maggie as they hugged each other tight. "Thanks for understanding."

"Thank *you* for everything." Maggie started crying. "For finding me, for coming here, for helping with Karson. Please keep in touch as best as you can."

"I will. I promise. I'll miss you all so much." Karla's own tears began to fall. She kissed the baby good-bye and hugged Lars before climbing into the passenger seat behind Bryson.

"Be careful," Maggie yelled to Bryson over the roar of the propeller. "Precious cargo you have there."

Bryson waved. "Don't I know it. See you guys soon."

❖

Their lovemaking that night was bittersweet, punctuated with tears over their imminent parting. Bryson prayed that a storm would blow in and strand them there, but though a blizzard had socked in the southern part of the state, the forecast called for moderate snow and light winds in the interior. They got little sleep and were bleary-eyed when it came time for Karla to pack for the flight to Fairbanks.

The satellite phone rang just as they were heading out. "Bet that's Maggie, calling for a final good-bye," Bryson said as she reached for it. But the voice on the other end was Skeeter's.

"Bryson, we've got a bad situation." His voice was grave. "Three mountain climbers are in trouble up on Trapper's Peak. They tried to hike down this morning and one fell into a crevasse. A woman. They got her out, but she's got two broken legs and a broken arm, and who knows what else. From their GPS, they're at six thousand feet, on the edge of a glacier."

Skeeter didn't have to say more. He went quiet, awaiting her decision. Few bush pilots but her would risk such a flight, and the elevation was too high for the two private air-ambulance services that served Bettles in emergencies. The Anchorage Rescue Coordination Center might dispatch an Alaska Air National Guard chopper, but it would take hours to reach them. Trapper's Peak was in her backyard. "I'm on my way. Call you when I get in the air."

"Roger that. Be careful."

She briefed Karla on the situation as she packed a bag with extra supplies. "I don't have a choice, honey. I'm sorry. I can drop you in Bettles—it's on the way—but I'll have to take right off again. You can catch the Wright Air Flight later and still make it to Fairbanks in time, but I won't be able to see you off."

Karla's heart fell. "That's it? This is good-bye, then?"

Bryson hugged her tight. "Afraid it has to be. Come on, we have to leave."

"Is it dangerous, where you're going?" Karla asked once they were in the air.

"I've done a lot of glacial landings. But yes, there's always a risk. The winds that high can be tough, you can't tell the snow depth before you get down, and you have to worry about hidden crevasses. But I'll be fine."

"The woman who was injured—how serious is she?"

"Bad, I think. Multiple broken bones. Don't know what else."

Karla pictured the woman and her friends, high on the mountain, waiting for the welcome sight of the Cub. How many people had Bryson saved? "Are you taking a doctor up with you?"

"The nearest doctor's in Fairbanks. The clinic in Evansville just has a CHA."

"What's a CHA?"

"Community Health Aide. Not surprised you haven't heard of it, it's an Alaska thing. CHAs get basic medical training and staff rural areas. They're not equipped to deal with something like this. And the one in Evansville hates to fly."

The decision came more easily than she expected. "Then you'll need to take me with you."

Bryson half turned in her seat. "Are you serious?"

"Very. She'll stand a much better chance if I triage her on site before you move her."

"I'm not saying I disagree. Frankly, I'd feel a hell of a lot better about transporting her if you're there to treat and stabilize her. I can have an air-transport ambulance standing by in Bettles to get her the rest of the way to the hospital." Bryson paused while she steered the Cub through a narrow canyon. "But, Karla, I won't have room to take you both at the same time. You'll have to stay up on the mountain until I can come back to get you. And you'll miss your flight."

"There'll be others. And I'll just have to deal with waiting for you. Her life could depend on it."

"You're absolutely sure?"

"Yes."

Bryson turned the plane away from Bettles and headed northeast. She radioed Skeeter to update him and to tell him to get an air ambulance to Bettles ASAP. He'd already done that; one would be standing by when she arrived with the patient.

Twenty minutes later, they were circling the area. Two of the climbers appeared as tiny, waving specks of colored parkas in a sea of white. They'd erected a tent, and the injured woman was evidently inside. Bryson made several passes over the glacier, assessing the best approach. The winds here were capricious, shaking the little plane so fiercely at times that Karla fought to keep her breakfast down.

"Okay, get ready. Brace yourself," Bryson shouted over the prop as she lined up for an uphill approach some fifty yards from the climbers.

Karla gripped the back of Bryson's seat and watched in horror as they descended. She could make out no depth of field in the solid glare of white below. It was impossible to detect how close they were to the glacier's surface until the skis actually touched down.

The snow looked so soft and inviting that she was unprepared for the bone-jarringly bumpy ride that followed as Bryson fought to stop the plane before it reached an ominous-looking mound of white invisible from above. She held her breath and closed her eyes, cursing under her breath.

The Cub lurched to an abrupt halt, but they were safely down, with just enough room left to turn the plane around. "You okay?" Bryson asked as she unbuckled herself.

"I'll tell you when I get my stomach back."

Bryson retrieved her first-aid supplies while Karla slogged toward the tent. The snow was knee-deep, and she was glad she'd put on her long underwear. The two uninjured climbers met her halfway.

"Thank God," the first one, a blond man in his thirties, said. "I'm Eric. This is Al. My wife Jane's badly hurt. We don't know what to do. Please help her."

"I'm Karla. I'm a nurse. Does your wife have any medical conditions I should be aware of?" she asked as they walked to the tent.

"No, she's very healthy. Hardly been sick a day in her life."

The tent was a small dome model, designed for two or three people. The injured woman was lying on one sleeping bag, an unzipped second one covering her. She was conscious and groaned as Karla bent over her to assess her condition.

"Jane, my name is Karla. Try not to move around."

Bryson appeared in the entryway with a large First Responder

First Aid kit, equipped with a stethoscope and BP cuff, in addition to an impressive collection of gauze and tape and other essentials. "Anything I can do?"

"Not right now. You don't have a neck brace or backboard, do you?"

"I've got a foldable stretcher and soft collar."

"Great. Get them, and anything you can find to rig splints with." While Bryson did those tasks, Karla took her patient's vital signs, then used the paramedic scissors from the kit to cut away her clothes to assess her injuries. She talked to Jane as she worked, asking questions that helped focus her examination as she worked through the trauma triage protocol.

Jane's husband hovered just outside the tent, listening.

Bryson returned quickly with the supplies she'd requested. "How's she doing?"

"Vitals are good," she said, loud enough for the husband to hear. "Multiple fractures in both legs—all closed, and an open fracture above the elbow in her left arm. Possible broken ribs, and I can't be sure about any internal injuries. But under the circumstances, it could be much worse. No indication of head, neck, or back trauma. But I want her immobilized just to be safe. Is the plane ready to go?"

"I have to turn it around and pack down a short runway with snowshoes," Bryson replied. "Won't take long."

"Go ahead and do that while I splint her fractures. I'll need all four of us to get her on the stretcher and out to the plane, so come right back when you're done."

"You got it."

Within a half hour, Jane was secured in the back of the Cub, kept warm by one of the arctic sleeping bags. Bryson had to remove the passenger seat to make room for her. "It'll be dark soon. I'll have just enough light to pick up Karla, so you two will have to hike out."

"I want to be with my wife," Eric protested. "Can't you come back with a bigger plane?"

"I don't have time to argue," Bryson said. "Radio in when you get down the mountain and within sight of the river, and someone will pick you up there and take you to the hospital in Fairbanks. I suggest you get moving." She handed Karla her survival duffel. "There's a tent and sleeping bag and other supplies in there, including an emergency radio. Keep warm, and I'll be back as soon as I can."

"I'll be fine. Be careful."

As Bryson took off, the men hurried to stow their gear. "I can't thank you enough," Eric told Karla as they shouldered their packs. "It's damn lucky you could get here so quick."

Karla wondered how Bryson and the men would have managed without her. "You're welcome. Now get going. I'm okay."

The mountaineers were out of sight within minutes, leaving her alone on the mountain. The wind was starting to pick up, so she wrapped herself in Bryson's sleeping bag while she waited, praying the Cub could make it back before dark.

She could see for fifty miles or more, but detected no sign of another living thing, just snow and mountains and valleys. Formidable and frightening, yet startlingly beautiful. The sun skimmed along the horizon, painting an amber hue over the western sky and casting deep shadows from the cliff face behind her. She felt like the last person on earth.

Dusk began to fall, and just about the time she'd decided Bryson wasn't coming back, she heard the distant hum of the Cub's propeller. It was another ten minutes before she actually spotted the plane. By then it was too dark to make out much beyond the pair of white lights on the wings. She turned on the flashlight she'd found in the duffel and tried to signal her position.

Bryson came straight in this time, landing in the same spot as before. As Karla hurried to her, Bryson hopped out of the pilot's seat and turned the Cub around.

"You all right?" Bryson quickly refit the passenger seat into position and stored her duffel in the hold.

"Really happy to see you. I didn't relish spending the night up here alone."

They made it back into the air without further incident and were soon headed toward Bettles.

Karla leaned forward in her seat. "How's Jane?"

"Still stable when we got there. She went right onto the air ambulance. They should be at the hospital by now. She wanted me to thank you. You know, you made a huge difference today. I always really worry about these kinds of calls. Not the flying so much, but what injuries or problems I'll have to deal with. There's only so much I know to do."

"I'm glad I was able to help. We made a good team."

"That we did."

The lights of Bettles came into view, and Bryson radioed in their approach. "I got us our room at the Den," she told Karla as they touched down. "Sorry you missed your flight, but I have to admit I'm thrilled to get another night with you."

"Me, too, Bryson. You know, I almost hope that when I call to rebook, they tell me all flights out of here are full for the next six months."

The Cub rolled to a stop and Bryson came around the plane to help her out. But instead of heading toward the Den, she took Karla in her arms in a fierce embrace. She could feel Bryson trembling, but it was too dark to make out her features.

"You're shaking. What is it?"

"Karla, you…you could…" Bryson's voice broke, and Karla realized she was crying. "You could just not go back."

"What are you saying?"

"I want you to stay. To build a life here with me. I know it's asking a lot. We haven't known each other that long, and you'd be giving up so much. But I love you, with all my heart. I've waited my entire life for you and I just can't let you go. I'd do anything and everything possible to make you happy." Bryson's hand caressed her cheek. "Please. Think about it? I need you. *We* need you. Maggie. Lars. Karson. The whole village, and beyond. Your skills could save a lot of lives."

"I have thought about it, Bryson. I've thought about little else." Her pulse was racing. "Actually, I made a pact with myself, to have the Alzheimer's test…to see whether I could be with you without saddling you with the prospect of having to take care of me. To watch me go through what my mother went through. I planned to come back if I didn't have this awful future. I was going to surprise you."

"Don't you know none of that matters?" Bryson kissed her, long and hard, then hugged her close. "Life is full of risks and uncertainty, sweetheart. I know that better than anyone, doing what I do. I've learned it's best to seize whatever happiness you can, while you can. As long as I have you, I can face anything life may throw at us."

"I want so much to believe that, Bryson. I do. But—"

"Karla, I know you've been through so much that it has to be tough to trust what I'm saying. But I believe with every fiber of my being that we belong together. That your coming here wasn't just about finding Maggie, but also about finding me. That fate had a role in all of this, somehow. If you search your heart and find you feel the same, then shouldn't we follow what seems to be our destiny?"

Was it that simple? That destiny had brought her here? It certainly seemed so. Being here with Bryson felt *right.* Completely and absolutely *right*. Preordained. To fight that seemed unconscionable. "On one condition."

Bryson inhaled sharply as she tightened her arms around Karla. "Whatever it is, the answer is yes."

"I'm grounding you for at least a week, so we can make love in every way imaginable."

Bryson laughed. "Done." She lifted Karla and whirled her around, then kissed her. "Come on. I know some folks who'll be just about as happy as I am about this. You get one phone call and maybe some dinner, then it's straight to bed. And don't expect to get one wink of sleep tonight."

Karla's heart soared as they strolled toward the Den, arm in arm. "Yes, ma'am. Have I mentioned I love it when you're so forceful like this?"

About the Author

Kim Baldwin has been a writer for three decades, following up twenty years as an executive in network news with a second vocation penning lesbian fiction.She has published five other solo novels with Bold Strokes Books in addition to *Breaking the Ice*: the intrigue/romances *Flight Risk* and *Hunter's Pursuit* and the romances *Force of Nature*, *Whitewater Rendezvous*, and *Focus of Desire*. Four of her books have been finalists for Golden Crown Literary Society Awards. She has also published two books in the Elite Operatives Series in collaboration with Xenia Alexiou: *Lethal Affairs* (translated into Dutch as *Dubbel Doelwit*) and *Thief of Always*. The third book in the series, *Missing Lynx*, comes out in February 2010.

Kim has also contributed short stories to five BSB anthologies: The Lambda Literary Award–winning *Erotic Interludes 2: Stolen Moments*; *Erotic Interludes 3: Lessons in Love*; IPPY and GCLS Award–winning *Erotic Interludes 4: Extreme Passions*; *Erotic Interludes 5: Road Games*, a 2008 Independent Publishers Award Gold Medalist; and *Romantic Interludes 1: Discovery*. She is currently at work on her tenth novel. She lives in the north woods of Michigan, but takes to the road with her laptop and camera whenever possible. Her Web site is www.kimbaldwin.com and she can be reached at baldwinkim@gmail.com.

Books Available From Bold Strokes Books

Erosistible by Gill McKnight. When Win Martin arrives at a luxurious Greek hotel for a much-anticipated week of sun and sex with her new girlfriend, she is stunned to find her ex-girlfriend, Benny, is the proprietor. Aeros Ebook. (978-1-60282-134-7)

Looking Glass Lives by Felice Picano. Cousins Roger and Alistair become lifelong friends and discover their sexuality amidst the backdrop of twentieth-century gay culture. (978-1-60282-089-0)

Breaking the Ice by Kim Baldwin. Nothing is easy about life above the Arctic Circle—except, perhaps, falling in love. At least that's what pilot Bryson Faulkner hopes when she meets Karla Edwards. (978-1-60282-087-6)

It Should Be a Crime by Carsen Taite. Two women fulfill their mutual desire with a night of passion, neither expecting more until law professor Morgan Bradley and student Parker Casey meet again…in the classroom. (978-1-60282-086-9)

Rough Trade edited by Todd Gregory. Top male erotica writers pen their own hot, sexy versions of the term "rough trade," producing some of the hottest, nastiest, and most dangerous fiction ever published. (978-1-60282-092-0)

The High Priest and the Idol by Jane Fletcher. Jemeryl and Tevi's relationship is put to the test when the Guardian sends Jemeryl on a mission that puts her not only in harm's way, but back into the sights of a previous lover. (978-1-60282-085-2)

Point of Ignition by Erin Dutton. Amid a blaze that threatens to consume them both, firefighter Kate Chambers and property owner Alexi Clark redefine love and trust. (978-1-60282-084-5)

Secrets in the Stone by Radclyffe. Reclusive sculptor Rooke Tyler suddenly finds herself the object of two very different women's affections, and choosing between them will change her life forever. (978-1-60282-083-8)

Dark Garden by Jennifer Fulton. Vienna Blake and Mason Cavender are sworn enemies—who can't resist each other. Something has to give. (978-1-60282-036-4)

Late in the Season by Felice Picano. Set on Fire Island, this is the story of an unlikely pair of friends—a gay composer in his late thirties and an eighteen-year-old schoolgirl. (978-1-60282-082-1)

Punishment with Kisses by Diane Anderson-Minshall. Will Megan find the answers she seeks about her sister Ashley's murder or will her growing relationship with one of Ash's exes blind her to the real truth? (978-1-60282-081-4)

September Canvas by Gun Brooke. When Deanna Moore meets TV personality Faythe she is reluctantly attracted to her, but will Faythe side with the people spreading rumors about Deanna? (978-1-60282-080-7)

No Leavin' Love by Larkin Rose. Beautiful, successful Mercedes Miller thinks she can resume her affair with ranch foreman Sydney Campbell, but the rules have changed. (978-1-60282-079-1)

Between the Lines by Bobbi Marolt. When romance writer Gail Prescott meets actress Tannen Albright, she develops feelings that she usually only experiences through her characters. (978-1-60282-078-4)

Blue Skies by Ali Vali. Commander Berkley Levine leads an elite group of pilots on missions ordered by her ex-lover Captain Aidan Sullivan and everything is on the line—including love. (978-1-60282-077-7)

The Lure by Felice Picano. When Noel Cummings is recruited by the police to go undercover to find a killer, his life will never be the same. (978-1-60282-076-0)

Death of a Dying Man by J.M. Redmann. Mickey Knight, Private Eye and partner of Dr. Cordelia James, doesn't need a drop-dead gorgeous assistant—not until nature steps in. (978-1-60282-075-3)

Justice for All by Radclyffe. Dell Mitchell goes undercover to expose a human traffic ring and ends up in the middle of an even deadlier conspiracy. (978-1-60282-074-6)

Bold Strokes
BOOKS
WEBSTORE
PRINT AND EBOOKS
Romance
Mystery
Intrigue
MATINEE BOOKS
LIBERTY
EDITION
BOLD
STROKES
BOOKS
Adventure
victory
EDITIONS
AEROS
e
Erotica
Fantasy
Sci-Fi
http://www.boldstrokesbooks.com